HANDLE ME

THE ROYALS SAGA

Alexander & Clara

Command Me

Conquer Me

Crown Me

Smith & Belle

Crave Me

Covet Me

Capture Me

A Holiday Novella

Complete Me

Alexander & Clara

Cross Me

Claim Me

Consume Me

Smith & Belle

Breathe Me

Break Me

Anders & Lola

Handle Me

X: Command Me Retold

THE ROYALS SAGA: THIRTEEN

HANDLE ME

GENEVA LEE

ESTATE

HANDLE ME

Estate Publishing + Entertainment

Copyright © 2023 by Geneva Lee.

All rights reserved.

This book or any portion thereof may not be reproduced or used in any manner whatsoever without the express written permission of the publisher except for the use of brief quotations in a book review.

This is a work of fiction. Names, characters, businesses, places, events and incidents are either the products of the author's imagination or used in a fictitious manner. Any resemblance to actual persons, living or dead, or actual events is purely coincidental.

www.GenevaLee.com

First published,2023, first ed.

Cover design © SergValen/Adobestock.com.

*To sisters,
especially kid sisters*

CHAPTER ONE

ANDERS

As long as I've been racing, people have asked me why. Every driver gets asked that, and every time the person asking wanted some deep, philosophical answer. I was running from my past or racing towards my future or some other bullshit. The truth was not that profound.

There hadn't been much else to do, growing up. It had only taken one time behind the wheel—one dose of pure, unfiltered adrenaline—and I'd been hooked. There was nothing like the vibration of the engine when I shifted gears. I didn't care about the crowds or fame. I wasn't trying to prove anything. On the track, it was me, the car, and my own mortality. The only thing that ever competed with it in my book was sex. I'd never been able to decide which was better. At least, it used to be that way.

"You're taking that turn too wide. Tighten it up, Your Highness!" Wilkes shouted in my earpiece.

Translation: I needed to go faster.

"Sod off," I shot back. I shifted gears, going full throttle as

I headed into Copse. I wasn't a fan of my new nickname, but I had a better chance of convincing the guys the world was flat than getting them to stop calling me that. They just needed a reminder I was the one behind the wheel. Wilkes wanted fast. He'd get it. I entered Copse blind. Taking this corner was always a leap of faith. I had to trust myself and my car. I didn't hesitate. My wheels hugged the track as I took the turn, knocking it down into seventh before I felt the familiar lift. I shifted into eighth as I took the first left. I'd been told early in my career that you had to be suicidal or stupid not to be scared of this circuit. I had no clue which category I fell in, but these days I'd rather face it than what waited for me past Silverstone's gates.

Reporters—if the bastards could be called that. Women—that bit wasn't as bad. And a security detail.

At least on the track, I was free. Out there? My life was becoming a bloody circus act.

All because twenty-six years ago, some wanker I'd never met shagged my mom. Now that wanker was dead, all his dirty secrets were coming out, and I was the biggest scandal of all. The illegitimate son of a dead king with an older brother determined, for inexplicable reasons, to make me one of the family.

"Get your head out of your arse and drive!" Wilkes barked over the comms.

I snapped back into focus and accelerated into the final corner, only taking my foot off the pedal when I straightened my wheels. The team ran toward the astroturf as I slowed the Renault to a stop.

"Don't bother telling me," I said to my performance coach. I didn't want to know my lap time.

Wilkes told me anyway. "One minute and thirty-two fucking seconds."

He stalked off, leaving the rest of the crew to deal with my sorry ass. Another distracted day on the track, and I'd screwed my lap time harder than a sailor on leave. It wasn't just practice at this level. Every lap counted when it came to securing the sponsorships that kept the multi-million dollar team running. More days like this, and the only companies willing to sponsor me would be retirement villages. Wilkes flew onto the track, headset in hand, yelling so loudly he was turning purple.

That couldn't be good. Shit. At this rate, I wasn't even going to get a retirement home to sponsor me.

Then I realized he wasn't screaming at me. Tugging my helmet off, I pushed out of my seat and strained to get a look at what had my team boss frothing at the mouth. The crew surrounding the car made it impossible to see. I climbed out of the Renault and got a glimpse of what—or rather *who*—had him so worked up.

One look at the brunette and I couldn't blame Wilkes for losing control. She wasn't just a distraction; she was a walking wet dream. The wind whipped her glossy, dark hair around her face. Oversized black sunglasses shielded me from getting a better look at her. That hardly mattered. Her body demanded all my attention. Tight denim hugged her hips and tapered down to a pair of stilettos so tall, they looked dangerous. If she'd walked onto the track in those, she wasn't just confident; she was daring.

The black blazer buttoned at her waist dipped low to reveal enough cleavage that my balls ached. In the space of thirty seconds, I imagined every wicked thing I wanted to do to her.

A crew member hurried past, holding a tire, but I grabbed his shoulder to stop him. "What the hell is going on?"

"She just showed up and walked in like she owned the place," he told me. His gaze scanned the mystery woman appreciatively. "I mean, I kinda hope she does."

"You and me both," I muttered and pushed him toward the car. He could look, but he couldn't touch. Whoever she was, she was mine. I'd make sure of it.

"Anders!" Wilkes bellowed my name.

I ran a hand through my helmet-flattened hair as I jogged over. It stuck to my skin in the day's sticky heat, and I swiped at the sweat gathering on my forehead. Dialing in my most charming smile, I slowed as I reached them. She turned and pushed her sunglasses onto the top of her head, and I stopped short. I recognized that face, or I nearly did. She looked a lot like someone else I knew, which meant she wasn't a stranger. She was the fixer my newfound family had sent to clean up my image.

Charlotte Bishop.

The five-minute phone call we'd shared had consisted of her giving me orders for four minutes and fifty-nine seconds. I'd known she was bossy. I'd had no idea she was gorgeous.

"Mr. Stone," she called over. "I assume you forgot our appointment."

Appointment? I must have missed that part during her never-ending list of instructions on how to behave since the world found out I was the bastard son of the late King of England.

"We spoke on the phone," she prompted when I didn't say anything. "Well, I spoke on the phone. You hung up on me." Her nose wrinkled in annoyance as she recalled our first contact.

I couldn't keep a smirk off my face, however. "If I'd known what you look like, sweetheart, I would have been a gentleman."

Wilkes barked a laugh as though that thought was un-fucking-believable. Her head whipped around to stare at him.

"Ignore him," I advised her. "I do."

"And that's why your lap time was off by three seconds. Three!" He held up three fingers as if a visual might help me count. Wilkes shook his head with disgust and turned on her again. But this time, he didn't bite her head off. Hell, he almost sounded shy. "Miss Bishop, don't walk onto a racetrack when there's a car on it."

She offered him a sweet smile that didn't match the attitude radiating from her. "Noted. Thank you, Richard. And call me Lola."

I nearly choked when she said his first name. No one had called Wilkes *Richard* in years. I imagined his own mother didn't use his first name. But more surprising was the bashful way my grizzly bear of a coach hung his head and grinned back.

"It's okay. I just wouldn't want to see you get hurt." He looked over his shoulder at me and his expression soured. "We need to go over the readings. If you don't shave that extra time off, you're going to start losing sponsors."

"Damn, you think I don't know that?" I asked through gritted teeth. The last thing I needed was for Miss Bishop to know I was struggling behind the wheel. I was pretty sure that information would be reported straight back to my family. The only thing worse than having my older brother deliver what amounted to a hot babysitter to my door was getting a lecture from him. I barely knew Alexander, but that hadn't stopped him from sticking his nose in my business at every opportunity in the name of my new *family*.

I pushed past Wilkes and headed toward the club.

Lola caught up with me before I reached the locker room. "Look, I didn't come all the way from London to have you ignore me."

"Sweetheart." I turned on her.

Her eyes narrowed, revealing only a sliver of blue through her thick, black lashes. "Don't call me sweetheart."

"Okay, *boss*. Look, I didn't ask you to come here. Now if you don't mind, I need a shower." I didn't wait for her response. Pushing through the door, I stepped inside and began to peel off my tracksuit.

The door burst open behind me, and she stepped inside. It wasn't going to be easy to shake Lola Bishop. "Actually, I do mind. You seem to be suffering under the delusion that I want to be here, Mr. Stone."

"Anders," I corrected her. "And no, I'm not suffering under any delusions. It's pretty clear you're as pissed about this situation as I am."

"Well, *Anderson*." She stretched my name into its full form and batted those fucking eyelashes. I knew better than to trust the innocent face she pulled. "I'm only here to make sure you can keep your nose clean and your ass out of trouble. If you can do that, we're good."

Her words were as frosty as her demeanor. What would it take to melt the ice queen? "Is this because I hung up on you, Lola?" I asked. "If I'd known it would get your knickers all bunched up, I wouldn't have."

"I can assure you my knickers are not now—*and never were*—in a bunch."

"Is that so?" I snorted and locked my eyes with hers. "Tell me more about the state of your knickers."

"I'm not here to play games with you," she said coolly, but color bloomed on her cheeks. The first and only sign I'd rattled her. "I just want to talk."

"And I just want a shower."

She tilted her chin, her blue eyes sparkling defiantly as she assessed the situation. Then, she shrugged one petite shoulder. "What's stopping you?"

It was a challenge. I'd been racing long enough to know when a flag had been waved. So this was how the prim, no-nonsense Miss Bishop wanted to play it? I was game. I finished unzipping my tracksuit and shucked it off my shoulders. It fell to my waist, revealing my bare upper body. Today had been hot and all I wore under the suit was a coating of sweat. Her eyes lifted to the ceiling as she pretended not to notice.

"As I was saying," she continued on with the barest strain in her voice, "if you would cooperate with me, we could get this over with."

I kicked off my shoes before pulling my suit off entirely. Lola's eyes flickered down, widening into saucers at the sight of my boxer briefs. She gulped and looked back up.

"I'm cooperating. You wanted me to listen." I brushed past her to open my locker door. She shuddered slightly at the contact. "I'm listening."

"Anderson—"

"Anders," I corrected her again.

"Anders," she muttered, her jaw clenched. "Can we get your little show over with, so we can get to work? I need to be back in London this weekend."

"Absolutely."

Lola thought she'd issued an order, but I saw it as an invitation. With one swift move, I shed my boxers and threw them into my locker. She startled as they sailed past her diverted eyes and she glanced down. Her mouth fell open when she got a look at the entire package she'd been sent to handle. Her tongue slipped out to wet her lower lip, but she didn't speak. I'd managed to shock her silent. I waited a moment, enjoying the ego boost, before I continued, "You were saying?"

CHAPTER TWO

LOLA

Anderson Stone was naked.

My brain refused to process more than that simple fact. Although I was dimly aware I should stop staring, no matter how I tried, I couldn't.

Because it turned out Anders had every right to his arrogant attitude.

"I'm sorry," he said with a smirk that suggested he was anything but apologetic. "Is this making you uncomfortable?"

That was a challenge if I'd ever heard one. I squared my shoulders, lifted my head, and glared. "No. Why would it be of any consequence?"

A muscle ticced in his jaw at my subtle dig, but he shook it off. "Let's be clear about this. My brother is worried about my image, not me. I've got everything under control."

"Really?" I arched an eyebrow and began to count on my fingers. "Since you found out who your father really was, you've crashed your car during a race, got into a fistfight with your brother at a bar, and been on the cover of every tabloid in the world, looking like you just rolled out of bed."

"Out of bed, huh?" he repeated, intentionally bypassing my point altogether. "Is that what you imagined? Seeing me roll out of bed?"

"It wasn't a compliment," I said flatly, ordering my body not to think about the images he was planting in my head. Anders might have made me blush, and he might have caught me staring, but there was no way I was going to pad his ego any further. "And from the looks of it here, your lap times are suffering. You and I have very different ideas of what under control means."

His grin fell from his lips, and he stalked away. I followed, doing my best not to look at him and failing miserably. His broad shoulders continued into a lean, muscled back that narrowed into a tight ass so perfect I could probably bounce a penny off of it. God clearly had a sense of humor because Anders was as gorgeous as he was infuriating.

Get a grip, I commanded myself silently. This was ridiculous. He was not the first naked man I'd ever seen, so why was I acting like a teenage girl? "As I was saying," I continued loudly, "the family thinks I can help you navigate the press and prepare you for—"

"I don't give a shit about the press," he cut me off.

"Not giving a shit is not a strategy," I said tightly. "You need a strategy, or they will eat you alive."

"Why?" He whirled around to face me, bringing his body uncomfortably close to mine. My nipples tightened into painful beads that poked against the lacy restraints of my bra. Heat pooled in my core, curiosity mixing with my annoyance.

I already knew I hated him, but my body hadn't gotten the memo. It seemed much more interested in this bastard than I was.

It took me a second to realize he was waiting for an answer. I knew he wouldn't like a single reason I gave him, but I offered one anyway. "Because I know your brother, and the more trouble you cause, the more security he'll send to follow you around. You think a couple of bodyguards hanging around are bad? You think *I'm* bad? Imagine twice as many guards. Imagine him calling you every single day to tell you off. Imagine that he forces you to move back to London where he can keep an eye on you personally."

But Anders remained unfazed. "He wouldn't."

"Are you sure about that?"

"Believe me. He doesn't give two pence about me. He just wants to keep his family out of the tabloids."

"Newsflash," I said sourly. "You're part of his family, which means that reasoning applies to you, too."

"The family he *cares* about," he clarified in a cold voice.

So that was what had him so bent out of shape. "Well, by all means, hang yourself to prove you can, but I didn't come all the way to the middle of nowhere to soothe your wounded ego."

"Is that so, boss? What did you come here for?" He leaned toward me. I wasn't sure if he was trying to intimidate me or seduce me.

I wanted to back away and put some much-needed space between him and me. But every inch of my body resisted the sensibility of that plan. Awareness rippled through my body, raising goosebumps where our bodies nearly met. One step from either of us, and we would touch. I was so close to being in his arms that I could almost feel them around me. The harder I tried to resist my imagination, the more it took hold of me.

He was trying to back me against a wall. Metaphorically, at least. I wasn't sure what would happen if he physically did that. I hated that part of me wanted to find out.

"I came because I was asked to," I said softly. "My family needed my help."

"And you always do what your family asks you to do?" he pressed.

"No," I said. My answer caught him off-guard, and he blinked.

"No?"

"No," I repeated. "But when my family needs my help, I try to give it to them."

"I guess you're a better person than I am."

I took a deep breath, choosing to ignore how close he remained to me. "I've had more practice."

"While I've been wasting my life driving cars?" he guessed. A single crease appeared on his forehead. Did he know I could see past his macho act to the angry man who'd found out his whole life was a lie?

I couldn't blame him for being upset, but I absolutely could blame him for how he handled his feelings. But calling Anders out on his anger wouldn't get me far, and it definitely wouldn't get me any cooperation.

"Let's try this again," he muttered, gazing down at me with eyes the color of a stormy sea. "Why are you here?"

I locked my eyes with his, so he couldn't accuse me of

lying, because I meant every word I was about to say. "I came to help you."

"Why?" he demanded.

I forgot he was standing naked in front of me. I forgot our bodies were nearly touching. I forgot that moving any closer would place me in his arms. It didn't matter that my hormones were doing somersaults or that every instinct warned me to get away from Anders before he blew up his life. It didn't matter because, deep down, I knew exactly why I was here.

"Because I know," I murmured.

His head tilted, and a strand of light hair fell across his forehead. "What do you know, boss?"

"I know what it's like to be *the spare*." My lip curled around the word, betraying how much I hated it. "I know what it's like to always be in the shadows. I know what it's like to be the one with all the same expectations and none of the respect."

"Is that so?" he said humorlessly. "Well, it's new to me."

"My sister wasn't always the Queen," I reminded him. "My whole life changed when she fell in love with your brother. Not because of anything I did, but because of everything I wasn't. *Believe me*, I understand you better than you think."

He paused as if digesting my answer. After a moment, he stepped away from me and walked toward the showers without a word. But before he turned it on, he looked back. "I'm not jealous."

"Neither am I." I frowned at his interpretation of my words. That wasn't what I was saying at all. I didn't envy my sister Clara her title, or her crazy life. I just missed having a normal life that belonged to me. I was about to tell him that when he found the right button to press.

"Look, boss, if you want a tiara, I'll buy you one, but you can't fix yourself by fixing me."

Since the moment I'd met him, I'd kept my annoyance on a low simmer. Now it heated to a full boil. Words crowded on my tongue, each sharp response vying to be the first dart I threw in his direction. But before I could, he flipped on the faucet. It sprayed from the shower head and filled the empty space around us with the sound of rushing water. Anders stepped under it and tipped his head to wash his hair. Water streamed in rivulets down his golden skin, racing toward his groin.

He straightened from his shampoo and moved to wash the rest of himself. Anders closed a hand around his shaft and began to wash himself suggestively. I tore my eyes away from his poorly disguised attempt to provoke me.

"There's another option," he called over the water.

"And that is?" I refused to look at him. I wouldn't encourage his antics.

"You could join me," he offered, and I whipped around to stare at him. He couldn't be serious. But the only thing he wore was a smug grin laced with a sort of grim determination. "You know what you need, right?"

"This should be good," I muttered. First, he flirted with me, and now he would solve my problems? Anders wasn't just hot. He was a hot mess.

"A good fuck." He stroked himself for emphasis.

I blinked, uncertain what was more shocking: the lewd

way he continued to touch himself or the fact that he'd actually said that.

"I could shag all that well-bred, family-duty bullshit out of you. What do you say, boss?"

I swallowed back the white-hot rage I felt and arranged my face into a mask of disinterested contempt. Then I looked directly at the hand suggestively stroking his dick and grimaced. "No, thanks. I've got better things to do."

I didn't wait for him to respond. I knew it would hurt more, so I turned and walked out of the shower room. Anders wanted to play games. He thought he could screw with me until I finally gave up and left him alone. But he didn't know me. I didn't give up that easily, especially when it came to putting a man like him into his rightful place: under my thumb.

I went straight to his locker. He'd been so busy putting on a show that he'd never considered he'd left himself open for attack. I found his keys in his pocket along with his wallet. He had made his move. Now I would make mine.

Anders didn't want to cooperate? I didn't need him to participate.

I pushed through the locker room doors and headed straight for the exit.

The Rolls Royce that had driven me into Northhamptonshire waited by the curb. The door opened as soon as the driver saw me, and he jumped out to open my door.

"Miss Bishop," he greeted me as I slipped into the plush backseat. He got back into the driver's seat and turned to me. "Do you want me to take you to your cottage?"

The palace arranged everything for me before my arrival.

A place to live. A driver. I even thought I'd caught a security detail keeping an eye on me at the track. The only person they didn't prepare was Anders himself. My sister Clara had told me she liked him. I had no idea why. The guy was a total asshole.

"Actually..." I shook my head as I dug a driving permit from Anders' wallet. "I need you to take me somewhere else."

He didn't question me as I rattled off the address on the card. He pulled away about the same time Anders came running out of the building, wearing nothing but a worn pair of jeans.

"Should I stop?" the driver asked slowly.

"No," I said cheerfully. He nodded and turned out of the racing complex. Swiveling in my seat, I waved as Anders chased after the car in his bare feet. He flipped me off. I blew him a kiss.

Anders might not want my help, but I'd just delivered my first lesson.

Don't fuck with the boss.

CHAPTER THREE

ANDERS

"What the hell happened to you?" Wilkes asked when I stalked back inside. He scanned me from top to bottom, his eyebrows knitting together when he saw my bare feet.

"Nothing," I bit out. I wanted to scream 'Lola Bishop happened to me', but I wouldn't give him the satisfaction.

"Okay." He didn't sound convinced, but he didn't press me for more details.

A few guys from the crew threw looks in my direction. I glared back, but they only grinned. I couldn't blame them. If it was one of them in my situation, I'd find this brilliant. But it wasn't one of my guys. Hell had delivered a beautiful angel straight to my racetrack to torture me. I had no doubt the crew would be placing bets on which one of us would win this war at the pub later. Right now, I had to admit she'd won this round. I just needed to get home and plan my attack. There was no time to waste, not with a woman like her around. I got a few steps toward the locker room when I realized that without my keys or my wallet, I was shit out of luck.

I groaned and turned to call behind me. "Hey, Wilkes! Can I get a ride?"

"Sure," he said, stopping. "Do you need a shirt, too?"

"Give me two minutes." I ignored his question and headed into the locker room. Lola had left me my clothes. At least, everything but my socks. I rooted around for them before finally giving up. I pulled a clean T-shirt over my head and tried to tug my motorcycle boots on. Without socks, I was forced to jam them over my bare feet. I had to hand it to her. It was a clever fuck off. Taking all my clothes would have been juvenile, but my socks? That was just irritating enough to make me simmer.

"Took you long enough," Wilkes grumbled when I finally came out of the locker room. "Does it take you a long time to get pretty?"

"Ask your new best friend. You sounded like you were about to braid her hair earlier."

"There's no harm in being polite." He shrugged, but his head hung sheepishly.

"That's why you went from screaming at her to kissing her feet?" I'd never seen my coach fall all over himself like he had in her presence.

But Wilkes didn't seem as affected by Lola outside of her presence. "Don't be jealous, Your Highness. Do you need me to kiss your ass and make it feel better?"

"For fuck's sake, will you stop calling me that?" When they'd started using the nickname, it had felt like a way to make an awkward situation into a joke. Except I couldn't change who my father or my family was, so now it didn't feel like good-natured ribbing. It felt like being stabbed repeatedly with a sharp stick. It didn't hurt exactly, but I still wanted it to stop.

"I think it's catchy." Wilkes whistled a tone-deaf tune as we headed out to his G-wagon. "Where to? Need a pint?"

"She took my wallet." I slumped into the passenger seat. What the hell was I going to do about Lola?

"Did you provoke her?" Wilkes asked as he started the Mercedes.

"You could say that." I wasn't about to tell him what I'd said to her in the showers. Although he was only fifteen years older than me, I thought of Wilkes as something like a dad. I'd never known my father. My *real* father. My mother had given me the name of the husband she lost in the Gulf War and I'd worn it proudly, even though I'd always known the math didn't add up. He'd been dead before I was conceived, which meant I was another man's son, but I'd respected her wishes to honor Todd Stone with the title. In my eyes, he was a hero. I'd looked up to him every day of my life. When I finally discovered who had fathered me, it had been a punch in the gut. Not only because I lived a life so far from the privilege the rest of my biological family experienced, but also because, like Todd, my true father was dead. Maybe that was why I'd relied so heavily on Wilkes during my early days when I transitioned from motorcycles to Formula One. He seemed to feel the same way, or maybe he just thought someone had to keep me in line.

But I'd never been one to stay inside the lines. I'd made a career out of pushing myself as close to the edge as possible.

"I'll buy you a pint," he said with a sigh.

I suspected it would cost me another lecture, but I didn't mind. At least the last place I would find Lola Bishop was at the bottom of a beer glass.

A COUPLE OF HOURS LATER, I was four pints down. Most of the crew were congregated at the Dark Horse, taking up a half dozen tables between the lot of us. I'd been stuck listening to Wilkes disseminate advice on women for the better part of my time here. This was hilarious because not only had he never been married, I couldn't remember the last successful relationship he'd been in. After another pint, I told him that.

"I think that's my cue to take you home, Your Highness," he muttered.

I grimaced at the thought of going home. "I don't even have keys, remember?"

"Don't tell me you've forgotten how to climb through a window." Wilkes tilted his head knowingly. "I seem to recall catching you here many a night in the last ten years."

"Mum's house was a bit easier to break in and out of," I said. He had a point. My own house, the bachelor pad I'd bought with my racing winnings, came with the annoyances of nosy neighbors, who disapproved of a single bloke living in the family enclave. One wrong move, and I wouldn't need my keys at all. I'd be spending the night in the company of the local police inspector.

"Why would she take your keys?" Wilkes asked. "Or your wallet?"

"She probably went shopping." Lola struck me as the high-maintenance type. I'd gotten to know her sister fairly well over the last year, but Clara, despite being the Queen, was down-to-earth and kind. Lola acted like she was the one wearing the crown.

"Well, some of us need our beauty sleep. I should get going."

I shrugged. I could always sleep on a bench in the garden. The weather in early May could be unpredictable, but it wouldn't kill me. Wilkes settled the tab. I leaned by a wall, catching snippets of conversation from a nearby table.

"He's not the same since the accident. It's screwing with his head."

I really hoped they weren't talking about me. Yeah, I'd had a bad crash earlier this season, but I was back behind the wheel. My lap time would get better. The important thing was that I hadn't let the crash keep me away from the track. They might not believe it, but I would show them.

"That's not it." His friend shook his head. "He hasn't been the same since he found out. He's probably waiting to move into Buckingham."

Anger surged through me, and the world seemed to fade to black as I digested his words. This was exactly what I was afraid would happen. It was why I had told Alexander I didn't want anything to do with him or *his* family. I'd been naive to think it would be that easy to ignore my past. How could I when everyone was more interested in it than I was?

"You ready?" Wilkes asked as he met me by the door.

"Yeah." I shoved my hands in my jeans and followed him into the spring evening.

"Everything alright?"

"Define alright?" I shrugged. It was the best answer I could come up with. "I mean, my older brother sent a nanny to keep an eye on me, my lap time is shit, and apparently, I'm angling to move into Buckingham Palace."

Wilkes slowed his pace and then stopped altogether. "You are?"

"Just according to some idiots in the pub." I didn't bother to fill him in on the details. There wasn't much, if anything, Wilkes could do about it for me. The only thing I could do was prove them wrong.

"Look, that's why they sent her, right? To teach you how to be a...prince?" This time Wilkes wasn't teasing me. He was completely serious.

"A prince? They don't give bastards titles, remember?" He should know that. If Albert had legitimized me before his death, it might have been a possibility. Personally, I was glad that he hadn't.

"Doesn't change the facts," he said meaningfully. "Maybe she can help you. I see the crowds hanging around, trying to catch a glimpse of the Royal–"

"Bastard," I interjected.

"Family," he finished, ignoring my interruption. I couldn't blame him.

"They'd have better luck in London." Or wherever they were off to now.

"They don't want London," Wilkes said with a sigh. "They want the fairytale. You're the fairytale."

"I'm the bastard." Maybe I was feeling sorry for myself, but I hadn't asked for any of this. I had a life incompatible with duty or obligation. "I mean, aren't bastards shipped out to the country to lead quiet, anonymous lives?"

His laughter bellowed in the oversized cabin. "I think that's exactly what happened, except we have the tabloids and the Internet. You're goddamn lucky it took them this long to find out."

Luck had nothing to do with it. I'd been buried alive by a father who didn't want anyone to know I existed, and unearthed by a brother who wished he'd never picked up the shovel. "I don't know what they want with me," I finally said. "I'm not cut out to be one of them, and even if I was, I'm not legitimate."

"I don't think that matters much anymore, but if you want to know what they expect, maybe you could ask the messenger."

I stared at him, momentarily confused.

"Lo-la," he said, spelling it out for me.

Maybe it was the lager muddying up my brain or my subconscious wanting to forget about her, but I'd nearly forgotten she was involved. "I think she's the heart of my problems. Not the solution."

"If she's the heart of them, it's because she walked straight to that spot." He gave me the side-eye from behind the wheel. "Give her a chance."

Maybe he was right. Maybe I should give her a chance. But he was wrong about one thing. She hadn't chosen to help me. She'd been forced to, which was a fact she'd made abundantly clear. And even if she'd wanted to help me before, I doubted she would anymore. But that wasn't the real problem.

The real problem was that Lola Bishop was a goddess. Not the beautiful benevolent kind you wanted to worship, though. She was a dazzling but terrifying goddess. The kind that delivered storms to shipwreck soldiers, turned men into animals, or just rained vengeance in general. She demanded respect from her cold, lofty pedestal. And it was clear that a royal bastard like me would never reach her. Not really.

But Wilkes had a point. She knew exactly what the royal family wanted. I could get that much out of her if I didn't kill her—or fuck her—first.

"Maybe I will," I said reluctantly, "unless she keeps stealing my shit."

"Do you really think she stole it?"

"I think my empty pockets prove she did, mate," I muttered.

"No. Think about it. What would she want with those things?"

"To make my life a living hell? Why do women do anything?" I leaned against the passenger door's armrest. Maybe I'd had one too many tonight. The answer hadn't been at the bottom of those pint glasses, and now it was screwing with my head. Another poor life choice brought to me by my own stupid ass.

"If she wanted to do that, she would have taken your clothes," he pointed out.

"She took my bloody socks!"

"She stole your socks?" Wilkes snorted as though he found the petty act amusing. "All I'm saying is that she had to have a real reason to want your keys and wallet."

"What would that be?" I was too buzzed to put the pieces he was giving me together.

"Why do you need them?"

"To start my bike? Pay for a round? Get in my house?" As soon as the last option left my mouth, I groaned. "She took them to get into my house."

"Yeah, and you were too busy sulking to realize that."

"I wasn't sulking." I thought about it for a moment. "Okay, I was, but why would she want to go there? I mean, she's not expecting to stay with me, right?"

"I doubt that," he said gently.

I'd expended the last clarity I had to get here. Wilkes thought he knew what Lola was up to, but I didn't dare guess. I could only hope she hadn't set fire to my house to teach me a lesson. But when Wilkes pulled the Mercedes into my driveway, the house was still standing. It was quiet. The family neighborhood was in bed already. The only sign of life was a single light on in an upstairs window.

Not just any upstairs window, my bedroom window.

"You want me to come in with you?" Wilkes asked.

I shook my head. Whatever had motivated Lola to come here tonight wasn't going to end well. I doubted she'd come over and climbed into my bed to wait for me, but a guy could dream. "I'm good."

"Need help breaking in?"

"Nah." Something told me that I'd find my front door unlocked and waiting. "Cheers."

Climbing out of the SUV, I ambled toward the house. When I reached the door, I shoved my hand in my pocket, forgetting that my keys weren't there. Behind me, the headlights of Wilkes's car flashed over me as he pulled out of my driveway and headed back to his life. It was the moment of truth. Could I predict even one of Lola's actions? Reaching for the door, I found it unlocked. Maybe I could.

I walked through the empty house, not bothering to look around the ground floor. There was only a couch and television in the front room, neither of which had been disturbed. I'd never bothered to buy much furniture. I took the steps two at a time and stopped when I reached the top one. Rubbish bags were piled at the end of the hallway, outside my bedroom door.

"What the hell?" I muttered to myself as I walked over and yanked one open. It was full of my clothes. Whipping around, I discovered the entire contents of my closet lay in piles on the floor of my bedroom. There were piles on my bed. Everywhere.

Had she come...*to give me a bloody makeover?*

This had gone too far. Maybe I didn't look the part of a prince, but I wasn't about to change who I was to please her—or any of them. I bent down and picked up a bag. Everything was going back in its place, and I was going to put Lola in hers the next time I saw her. I hoisted the bag higher to give me room to grab another. Tonight, I would crash, and then I would sort out this mess. Walking inside the bedroom, I dumped the bags on the floor by the walk-in closet. I yanked off my boots, my brain alternating between raging at Lola's audacity and thinking of all the ways I wanted to torment her. Hooking a finger under my collar, I tugged off my T-shirt and tossed it in the corner. My jeans followed. That would probably really get a rise out of her. She'd gone to all the trouble of putting my life into neat piles. Maybe that was the ice queen's problem. She was used to being the one in control. She needed someone else to take charge for once.

It was a service I'd be pleased to offer her. Just as soon as I delivered a good spanking to her. My dick twitched at the thought of her ass. Then again, thinking like that might only cause more trouble. I'd seen many a friend fall victim to a magical muff. I wasn't about to make the same mistake.

I hit the lights and shuffled toward the bed in the dark. I climbed into it and went to shove the clothes she'd left on the other side off when I realized it wasn't my belongings piled there. Lola Bishop had put herself in her rightful place: *my bed.*

CHAPTER FOUR

LOLA

Anders found me in my dreams. It turned out that there I didn't mind that he was cocky as hell or pushing my buttons. One dream shifted into another, and he had a starring role in all of them. In one, he climbed out of his car, bent me over it, and took me around the track. Then we were in the shower. He didn't make suggestive comments or lewd gestures. He just picked me up, braced me against the wall, and showed me. In this one, he'd caught up with me, shirtless with bare feet after I'd stolen his keys, and decided to punish me. He pulled down my jeans, rubbing circles on my backside. Anders lifted his hand, and I tensed, waiting for him to spank me. Instead, it grew brighter around me. No! No! No! I rolled over and buried my face into the pillow, unwilling to exit the dream. My thighs clenched together as I fought to stay unconscious. It was slipping away, but I hung on until his palm cracked across my bare skin. He murmured something I couldn't make out as he rubbed my stinging flesh. I wiggled my hips toward him as I waited for the next round.

Instead, I made contact with something hard. Very hard. I was enjoying the spanking, but I wasn't about to say no to that. Not with it poking me through my jeans. How had those gotten pulled back up? Why did the dream keep changing at the best possible moments? I ground encouragingly against his lap. A strong arm wrapped around my waist and pulled me closer.

I pressed into him as hard as I could. A hand dipped between my legs and started to stroke the wound-up bundle of nerves. I moaned his name, and he rubbed harder, edging me closer.

"Please," I whimpered, covering his hand with mine and urging him to move harder and faster. But it wasn't enough. I fumbled around for the button of my jeans. Unfastening it, I slipped my hand into my knickers to find myself wet from all the dirty fantasies that had invaded my sleep. I slid a finger to my clit and began to knead it under the weight of Anders' hand.

"Fuuuuuck." I bit my lip as my body tightened. "Don't stop."

He increased his pace to match mine, his palm rocking against the hand in my pants. It was the hottest dream yet, and I gave in to it.

"Oh God, Anders!" I was so close. "Don't fucking stop."

Anders complied, taking over entirely. He worked his hand over mine until I shattered. But the hungry ache in my core lingered. No doubt the product of whatever dream was coming my way next. I flipped over and hooked an arm around his neck, dragging his mouth to mine. He didn't hesitate to deepen the kiss. After a few moments, he rolled me onto my back and shifted his erection to press against my still throbbing clit. But I wanted more than that. More than his hands or lips. I slid my palm down his back before reaching around to grab his—

He broke the kiss and pushed onto his elbows. I groaned in frustration, fighting to get control of the dream before it shifted to another fantasy.

"Careful, boss," Anders muttered groggily. "You're giving me ideas."

My eyes flew open, and I blinked at the bright sunlight invading the room. Two things were immediately apparent. The first was that I was in bed with Anderson Stone. The second was that this wasn't a dream.

Oh my god, was I sleep shagging? Was that a thing?

A grin hooked his mouth as he stared down at me, looking half asleep himself.

For one completely mental moment, I considered pretending I was still asleep and just going with it. The hungry pulse between my legs told me that my recent orgasm was as real as the arousal I still felt.

But I wasn't about to give in to weakness. I shoved him away and scrambled out of his bed. I nearly tripped over a pile of his clothes as I refastened my jeans and searched for a way out of this debacle.

Anders sat up and folded his arms behind his head, watching me with a smile that grew each second. He pointed his toes, stretching his legs and showcasing their impressive muscles. But it wasn't his legs that caught my attention. It was the tentpole straining against his boxer shorts. I shut my eyes, prayed he hadn't caught me staring, and turned away from the temptation.

"What are you doing?" I demanded. "You can't...just..."

"Just what?" he repeated slowly. "You said my name. Well, you moaned it. I just responded."

"I did not!" *I so did.* There was no way I was admitting to that, though. I searched the room for the heels I'd kicked off somewhere the previous evening.

"*Anders! Don't fucking stop!*" he mimicked me in a high voice.

"You are..." *What? Come up with something, Lola!* "You thought I just crawled into your bed and fell asleep waiting for you."

Anders leaped out of bed and stormed toward me. "That's exactly what you did!"

He wasn't wrong, and I wasn't about to tell him that.

"Yes," I said, turning on my iciest voice. "I felt so bad for walking out on your yesterday that I did just that after I reorganized your closet. Don't be a fucking idiot."

"I never said it made sense!"

He paced the length of the room, giving me glimpses of his annoyingly perfect body. Why were the beautiful ones always such arrogant asses?

"I mean, I was sleeping," I continued, trying to find an argument amongst my excuses.

"And you said my name," he reminded me. "*Repeatedly.*"

"So, wait, were you awake in bed with me?" I demanded. "Why were you in bed at all?"

"*Because it's my bed!*" he exploded. He paused, his fist balling up so tightly that his knuckles went white. I braced myself, expecting him to put it through the wall. Instead, he shook his hand loose and, with a strained calm, turned to me. "Why were you in my bed?"

"I got tired." That answer was easy because it was true. I'd spent the better part of the evening sorting through Anders' life and putting it into piles. It was clear he'd never bothered to do that before. "I laid down."

Frustration rolled off him in waves. He opened his mouth to speak, shut it again, and then repeated the first two steps a half dozen times.

I'd frazzled him, so I seized my opportunity. "I was asleep." I clung to that fact like a life preserver. "Obviously, I had no idea what was happening."

"You said my name," he grumbled again. But this time, something clicked, and a slow smile spread across his face. "Wait, if you were asleep—"

"I was," I interjected quickly.

"—and you said my name. Well, *moaned it, really.* Were you dreaming about me?"

Now would be an absolutely delightful time for the apocalypse to occur. But no sounding trumpets or horseman appeared to save me. "I don't remember my dreams. I could have been saying anything in my sleep."

"I think you're lying."

So, Anders wasn't going to be a gentleman and let me escape with only my dignity ruffled. He was going to tease me about this until I cracked. But he didn't know me yet. He had no idea how much pressure I could take. If he thought he could break me, he was in for a surprise.

"Let's get one thing straight." I crossed to where he stood

and glared up at him, wishing more than ever that I had my shoes on. "I have no clue what happened. I just woke up kissing you."

"Is that so?" He leaned down, bringing his face closer to mine. "You forgot that your hand was on my dick."

I refused to so much as blink, even though heat colored my cheeks. My body might have betrayed me, but there was no way I would confess that I remembered a single thing.

When I didn't speak, he lifted an eyebrow, looking both impressed and agitated. "Tell me the truth, boss. You were dreaming about fucking me. You woke me up begging for it. Would it have been so bad to actually give in to what your body obviously needs?"

"My body what?" I shrieked, my eyes widening until they watered. "You think I need a shag?"

"No." He shook his head. "You need a fuck. To be specific, you need to fuck me."

"Why would you think I need that?" I spit back even as a shiver raced up my spine at the suggestion. I'd almost done just that. I'd even considered pretending to still be asleep when I realized what had happened. I didn't know what was worse: claiming sleep as an alibi or Anders seeing right through the attempt.

"Do you want a list?" he said with a snort. He opened his hand and counted on his index finger. "You fell asleep in my bed."

"That doesn't mean anything," I shot back.

He ignored me and continued. "You woke me up grinding that plump, little ass against my morning glory."

"Now I know you're lying," I said with a shrug. "I wouldn't do that."

"You called my name, grabbed my hand, and pushed it against your pu—"

"You put your hand there first!" I realized my mistake instantly, but it was too late.

"Did I?" he asked. "I was hardly awake. I don't really remember."

I smashed my lips into a thin line, gathered up the shreds of my dignity, and made my choice. "I don't know."

"You don't know?" he repeated. "So, you don't know who touched who first?"

It was physically painful to shake my head. I hated ignoring the facts, but what choice did I have?

Anders leaned closer, and I caught my breath, waiting for him to kiss me. Instead, he brought his lips to my ear. "Now, who's lying, boss?"

CHAPTER FIVE

ANDERS

I couldn't decide if I wanted to kiss Lola or kick her out. She stared up at me with wide, brave eyes that refused to back down, and I knew the answer instantly.

Kiss her. I definitely wanted to kiss her. And then I wanted to carry her back to my bed and finish what she had started. But doing that fell clearly into the *rewarding bad behavior* category. I wasn't sure what pissed me off more: that she was trying to pin this whole situation on me or that she couldn't admit to the truth. She wanted me as much as I wanted her. Sure, it was entirely physical and probably fueled as much by our total contempt for each other as any attraction we felt. And yeah, what I wanted to do to her could only be described as a hate fuck.

But I saw the same naked desire staring back at me from those blue eyes. Lola wasn't satisfied with our stolen encounter. She wanted more. She wanted to climb back into bed and pretend that she was asleep while I delivered a few more orgasms. She wouldn't admit that, of course. She couldn't. That would make her look weak, and I was beginning to suspect that she hated vulnerability more than she hated me.

Still, I was certain of a few things.

1. Lola had started things in bed.
2. She was never going to admit it.
3. I'd never wanted a woman so much in my life.
4. (Or 3a) To clarify, there was no way I was giving her the satisfaction of acting on it.

"Look, let's just forget this," she said, surprising me. "If you say you were sleeping—"

"I was sleeping," I interjected. We could forget it if that's what she wanted. At least, we could try to forget it.

"So was I," she said hotly. "I guess you must just be more physically active in your sleep."

Lola Bishop had thrown the gauntlet, and I wasn't about to back down. I should have known she wouldn't just let us drop this, not if it meant admitting she might be even a tiny bit responsible. "I wasn't the one with my hand down my pants, boss."

"That...is...just so unfair!" she spluttered, stomping across the room.

The physical distance helped, but not much. "Yeah, well, I call it like I see it."

"It wasn't like you were innocent. I felt that." She pointed an accusing finger at my erection. My poor dick hadn't softened at all since we'd broken physical contact. In fact, it had gotten harder.

I grabbed it through my boxers. "I've got news for you. It's like this every morning, even when I don't have a horny, bossy snob begging for it in her sleep."

"I did not beg!"

"That's what you take offense to?" I couldn't help laughing. I shoved a hand through my hair, wishing I could grab her by her perfect ass and take her over my knee. "So you admit to the horny and bossy bit?"

"I'm the horny one?" she hedged. "That thing is like a heat-seeking missile!"

"Yeah." I tossed my hands in the air. She was just now getting this. I'd been saying it the whole time. "Look, when my brain is turned off, my dick is in charge and it translates the situation according to the only language it speaks: *fucking*."

Lola crossed her arms over her chest, her nostrils flaring, but rather than feigning disgust, she cleared her throat. "And you think that's different for women?"

I blinked. Had I heard her wrong? "What?"

"Do you think that women don't have dirty dreams?" she pressed, tilting her chin up as she spoke. "Just because we don't wake up with a bloody sausage roll sticking out of our pants, doesn't mean we don't get aroused while we sleep. So why don't we both just chalk this up to what it was: biological impulses outside our conscious control and nothing else?"

I'd wandered into a sodding biology seminar.

"That's it, then." I stalked over to my closet door to find something to wear. "This was just our bodies taking control?"

"Exactly," she said, sounding relieved that I seemed to be getting on board. "Obviously, it could happen to anyone."

"Only if two *anyones* wound up in bed together," I pointed out. She could spin this anyway she chose. It was what she did for a living, after all. But even if she had a point about our bodies taking over, she was the one who'd climbed into my bed.

"It won't happen again," she said, understanding exactly what I was driving at.

Lola was a piece of work. First, she'd tried to pass her embarrassment off. Now, she thought she could smooth things over, establish rules that should have been obvious in the first place, and ignore what had happened between us.

"Why don't you grab a shower?" she suggested, misreading my silence as agreement. "Then, we can discuss what to do with your wardrobe."

"I need to be on the track by one," I muttered. How could she just switch from being the writhing sex goddess in my bed to all business like that?

"I'll be done with you by noon."

I gave up on my closet when I discovered it had nothing left in it but a few button down shirts I wore for funerals and weddings. Instead, I leaned over and dug an old concert T-shirt out of a nearby pile.

"That's the donate pile!" She scurried over and reached for the contraband clothing.

I lifted it over my head, holding it out of her reach. "Let's get one thing straight. In my house, we never throw out a Rolling Stones shirt. Got it?"

She arched an eyebrow, but finally shrugged. "Keep it. But the rest needs to go."

I glanced around the room. I'd been a little too tipsy last

night to process how much of my life she'd tossed on the floor. "What the hell do you want me to wear?" I shot her a lopsided grin. "Or do you just want to keep me naked as much as possible?"

"Tempting." Her upper lip curled on the word. Her sarcasm might have been cutting if it wasn't so obvious how hard she was trying to muster it. "I have an appointment in town to see to new clothes."

"What? Look, I didn't sign up for a makeover."

"Well, it's your lucky day because you're getting one." I didn't trust her sweet smile. It came too easily.

"It's not like you're going to find anywhere to shop around here." I rescued a pair of my favorite jeans from a pile near the bathroom door.

"I know that," she said with a snort, moving to guard the pile before I saved anything else. "We're going for measurements."

I didn't like the sound of that. What was she up to? "Measurements for what?"

"Suits. Tuxedos. Proper trousers."

Three of my least favorite things. I told her that.

"Anders, you can't hide behind old clothes." She rolled her eyes dismissively. "You're a royal now, like it or not."

"Or not," I said through gritted teeth. "I'm not my brother. I'm not running this country."

"Thank God for that," she murmured.

Finally, something we could both agree on. "Give me one good reason I need all that shit."

Lola tilted her head, her teeth catching her lower lip and dragging it into her mouth for a moment as if she was thinking. I couldn't look away. She had me exactly where she wanted me. "Because you'll look sexy in suits."

So much for playing fair. It seemed nothing was out of the question when it came to Lola getting what she wanted, and I got the impression that whatever Lola wanted, she got. She could pretend that she didn't remember what happened in my bed or that she hadn't called my name as she came in my arms, but one thing was abundantly clear.

Lola might not admit it, but she wanted me.

"I'm gonna shower," I announced like it was my idea. "And then we'll head into the city."

"You sure you don't want to join me?" I already knew she did. I caught the way her eyes skirted down my body when she thought I wasn't looking. She might have ceased control. She might have gotten off in her dirty dreams. But she was stretched as taut as a tightrope.

"I'll pass," she said dryly. "I'm sure you have another loo around here."

"What about your clothes? Do we need to stop by your place and pick something up? I wouldn't want anyone at the track to get the wrong idea."

Her nostrils flared again, and I made a mental note to track this phenomenon. Something told me it was one of her tells. I just wasn't sure yet what it was saying. "I have my bags with me. No need to worry about my reputation."

I laughed. "It's not your reputation I'm worried about, boss."

The smile fell from her face. "I'll meet you downstairs."

I lingered in the doorway as she marched out of my bedroom. Before she reached the hall, I delivered one final blow to her carefully-composed reality. "And Lola?" I called her name and she pivoted toward me. "With all due respect to your biological impulses, when you're finally ready to ask for what you need, I'll be waiting."

"And what do I need, Mr. Stone?" she asked with narrowed eyes.

I answered with my heart, as sincere as any genuine moment I'd ever shared with her. "What you need is a good shag."

CHAPTER SIX

LOLA

I was going to piss my sister off...just as soon as I reached her. When she'd asked me to intervene and help Anders, she failed to mention that he was a giant ass. The fact that she was conveniently not answering her phone or returning any of my calls probably wasn't a coincidence. She'd known exactly what she was doing when she'd sent me here.

I redialed her, and it went straight to voicemail.

"Clara, you owe me big time for this. Like, I'm going to need a list of all your husband's houses, so I can pick one to recuperate in after I'm done dealing with this wanker." I sighed, knowing she had way more important concerns occupying her time. "Call me back."

I'd left my bag in the front entry, and I lugged it into one of the guest rooms on the first level. Why did he need a place this big? Half the rooms were empty. There was hardly any furniture. What was the point? The room I'd found myself in must have functioned as a guestroom because it was properly put together. Although, I struggled to believe Anders had done it himself.

Nightstands sat on either side of the double bed, each with a small brass lamp. I plopped my luggage onto the floral quilt that was both welcoming and out of place. The room was cozy and far more lived-in feeling than the rest of the house. I wandered into the attached bath and opened a drawer in the vanity. Inside was a toothbrush and some face cream. Another drawer revealed lipstick and bobby pins. I guessed Anders had a lot of women spend the night, but whoever used this room felt comfortable here. Had he made space for her, or had she done it herself? Given the spartan accommodations in the rest of his house, it was hard to imagine he cared either way. Still, whoever she was, she hadn't dared to put her belongings in his room.

I closed the drawers and turned my attention to the mirror. I'd looked worse. My hair was a mess, thanks to my falling asleep without putting it up properly. My lashes could use a good fluff, and the remnants of yesterday's makeup needed to come off. Not that I had much time to get myself in order. I refused to walk out of here looking like a mess, though. The last thing I needed was to send Anders any more mixed signals. How could I convince him that he needed to care about how he looked if I was a wreck? Digging my brush and toiletries out, I tamed my hair into a polished topknot. Then I committed the cardinal sin of cosmetics by touching up my makeup from yesterday instead of starting over. With any luck, I'd be mostly ready before he managed to be out of the shower.

Memories of him standing in the shower jumped to mind, but I shoved them aside. The last thing I needed to do was think about him in the shower. Or think about him naked. Or think about him at all, for that matter. So, I'd come here to help him. That didn't mean he needed to occupy my every waking thought, right?

But not thinking about Anders was easier said than done, especially after the accidental orgasm he'd given me this morning. That was just an embarrassing mistake. We had both been half asleep and acting purely on some primal instinct. It hadn't meant anything, and neither had my dreams. He had starred in my dreams because he'd swallowed up most of my day with his shenanigans. And the dreams had been sexual because he'd flirted—or maybe harassed was a better word—me right before I'd come to his house last night. All of it could be explained.

I shimmied out of yesterday's jeans and yanked off my thong, which was soaked thanks to the stolen moment I'd had with him. Just the memory sent a spike of arousal through my core. Without him here to remind me why it would have been a terrible idea—a service he provided effortlessly every time he opened his mouth—I wondered what would have happened if things had gone any further. We'd been a few layers of fabric away from crossing the line entirely. I'd been this close to knowing exactly what he could do with that massive equipment he kept putting on display. I had a feeling I wouldn't be disappointed. He knew how to use his hands.

"Stop!" I ordered myself. "You are not some horny schoolgirl. You are a confident, sexy woman who can do better than Anders."

"Agreed," a deep voice added, and I nearly jumped out of my skin.

"Do you knock?" I shrieked, grabbing the first thing poking out of my bag and pinning it over my bare lower half. Unfortunately, I'd grabbed a lacy chemise that obscured very little and only seemed to draw more attention to my half-dressed state.

"The door was open," Anders said, lounging against the wall. He didn't look away. He didn't pretend to be a gentleman. He let his eyes wander across me slowly. I felt them wander over every inch of bare skin. He studied me with the intensity of a man enjoying an exhibit in a gallery. "Besides that, I showed you mine."

"Which I never asked you to do," I hissed, wishing my top went past my navel.

"I just came to tell you I was ready." He glanced over at my bag. "You aren't staying here, are you?"

I rolled my eyes. My sister had arranged a royal residence nearby for my use. That was one of the perks of having a family in positions of authority. I was about to tell him that and remind him I'd be thrilled to never step foot in his home again when it hit me: Anders responded to pressure. He'd gotten ready in record time, even for a guy. If I exerted a little more force, I might turn him into a diamond. And the best way to apply that pressure, was consistently. I arranged my face into a cool composition, which was a feat considering how terribly exposed I felt. Playing it cool while knickerless wasn't for the faint of heart. "Is that a problem?"

"Nope." He shrugged. "Not for me."

"Or me," I said firmly. He could read whatever he wanted

into our encounter in bed, but that had been an accident—and a mistake I wouldn't make twice. "May I use this room?"

"I'm not using it."

For a man who seemed fluent in double entendre, he could be dense. That, or he wanted me to spell it out for him.

"I assumed that whoever left the lipstick might be back...." I trailed away, leaving the door open for him to follow through.

Anders considered this for a moment before he shook his head. "She won't care." He strode to the door and paused there. "I'm ready when you are. I need to be to the track at—"

"One," I finished for him. "I heard you the first time you said it."

"I've seen how women like you shop."

I restrained myself from responding to the 'women like you' comment. "Men are easier to shop for."

His lips curled into a crooked smile. "We are, huh?"

"Especially a man like you," I said sweetly.

"Why's that, boss?" His curiosity lingered, but sharpness glinted in his eyes.

"Because a man like you...." I repeated, letting my words linger until he was hanging on my every breath, hoping I might accidentally give another clue away. "...a man like you only takes two seconds to size up."

"Is that so?" he said in a rough tone. "I guess I always believed it when they said you should be yourself."

"I wasn't talking about your personality." I looked him over, stopping on the bulge barely hidden under his jeans. Was he always this...pronounced?

"Ouch." He pressed a hand to his chest like I'd wounded him. I sincerely doubted he cared what I thought about him.

He made me want to scream. Not a little annoyed shriek, either. I wanted to open my mouth and bellow from some primal, untapped reservoir until the frustration brewing inside me was finally released. But I wouldn't give him the satisfaction. Instead, I held the scrap of lingerie covering me with one hand and pointed to the door with my other. "Can I have a minute to get dressed? Then I'll call the car?"

"The car?" he asked blankly.

"My driver," I said impatiently. "He can drive us into Birmingham and—"

"You think I'm going to get in a car and let some stranger drive me to the store to—"

"I don't care," I erupted, losing my cool. "I know you're pissed that there are reporters following you and that your family isn't what you thought and that you think I'm going to burn all your blue jeans. But get over it! Life happens whether you have plans or not."

His mouth remained open from when I'd interrupted him. Anders blinked a few times as if he was processing my outburst. After a few seconds, he cleared his throat. "I think you've misunderstood me."

"Oh, I have?" I marched over to him and jabbed my index finger into his chest. "You've been pressing every one of my buttons since that first phone call. Maybe you can whip your dick out and get other women to fall all over themselves, but it takes a little more to impress me."

"What does it take, boss?"

"A man who doesn't care what other people think about him, for starters," I said.

"You think I care?" he roared.

"Oh, I know you care," I said. "And a man who knows exactly what he wants."

Anders took a step closer, pressing his hard chest against my pointed finger. "I think I've made it clear what I want."

I swallowed hard, trying to ignore the implication of his words. "And a man," I added weakly, "who doesn't play games."

"Is that your problem with me?" he asked in a soft voice. "Maybe it's not playing games that's the real problem."

"Then what is?" My heart raced inside my chest, making my head spin.

"You've only played with men who lose." A slow smile curved across his face. "I play differently."

I raised an eyebrow, not trusting myself to speak.

"I play to win, boss." He brushed a finger over the tip of my nose and added, "And I never lose."

Maybe that was true, but he'd never been up against me before. Anders thought he knew me, but he had no idea. I took a step back, putting some much-needed space between us. "Neither do I."

"This should be interesting," he murmured. "But about the shopping."

I started to argue with him, but he held up a hand to cut me off.

"I was just going to tell you not to call your driver. I prefer to be the one behind the wheel."

Of course he did. I resisted the urge to crawl under the bed and stood my ground. Would I ever stop embarrassing myself around him?

"Fine," I said in as haughty of a tone as I could muster, starting toward the door. "Let's go, then."

"Okay." But he stayed put, watching in amusement as I made my stand. "Are you coming with me?"

I groaned. "What? You don't want to drive me?"

If that was the case, maybe he could stop driving me crazy. I was about to tell him this when he tipped his head meaningfully toward my feet.

My bare feet.

I closed my eyes as horror washed over me. I already knew what he was going to say before he prowled by on his way out the door. "I just thought you might want to put on some pants first." He paused when he reached me and leaned closer. "Although, I'd be happy to take you for a ride without them."

Lifting my hand, I pointed a trembling finger to the door. "Out. Now."

"That's what I get for being a gentleman," he grumbled as he made his way from the room.

I slammed the door behind him and crumpled against it in embarrassment. Anders definitely wasn't a gentleman. Otherwise, he would have pointed out that I'd lost my thin covering at some point during our fight. Instead, he'd let me walk around with my lady garden hanging out. It was just another reason to dislike him, another flaw to add to my growing list of his character flaws.

Things had gotten out of hand since I'd arrived, but that was going to change now. Anders could resist his family and his responsibilities all he wanted. Because I'd figured out his blind spot.

Me.

CHAPTER SEVEN

ANDERS

I'd nearly gotten over the sight of Lola's perfect ass on display. Unfortunately, my dick had not. I adjusted it in my pants, cursing her under my breath. Now she wasn't just going to be hanging around, she was going to be living with me? My poor balls were going to be so blue they might fall off. I needed to do something about her, and I needed to do it fast.

There was only one way to get her out of my life and my thoughts. I had to play along with her ridiculous demands. I'd play dress up and behave for now. But it was time to have a talk with my brother. Was it his idea to send the world's most fuckable woman to teach me how to be a gentleman? He must really hate me, if so.

I stomped into the garage, remembering that my motorcycle was still at the track thanks to Lola's thievery. Still, the garage was my happy place. As soon as I was with my cars I felt calmer. That lasted until Lola stepped in behind me. She'd put on a pair of black leather pants, but I wasn't sure they were going to be any help keeping my mind off her ass. They hugged it too tightly. Her top was looser. It was made of some type of silky fabric that fell over her curves, drawing attention to the swell of her breasts. She'd left a few buttons undone, showing a hint of white lace that sent ideas racing through my brain.

How was I supposed to behave when she looked like that? Especially after I'd gotten a glimpse of her face post-orgasm? My pants grew a little tighter and I reached for the nearest passenger door, opening it for her, and strategically hiding my erection.

Lola looked at the car and shook her head. "Don't you have anything safer?"

"Safer?" I repeated, staring at her.

"I'm not a big fan of cars," she admitted.

That statement should have killed my erection. Could I really look past such a deep character flaw? What kind of person didn't like cars? "This isn't a car," I explained to her. "This is a Ferrari, and it's perfectly safe when I'm behind the wheel."

"In that case." She rolled her eyes and dropped into the seat. I lingered for a second until she was situated and reaching for the buckle.

Lola might not like cars, but she looked good in the bucket seat. Its red leather perfectly matched her lipstick, which was not helping me squash my dirty thoughts. I shut the door gently and circled to the other side.

"So you don't like cars," I prompted as I slipped into the driver's side. I hit the button for the garage door before turning on the car. The Ferrari roared to life and Lola startled. Her buckle was the only thing that kept her from jumping out of her seat. That was the thing about 711 horsepower engines, they tended to make the seats vibrate. "What do you think of it now?"

She glared at me, wiggling back. "I was just surprised."

I imagined yanking off her pants and placing her on the seat with nothing between her and the engine's powerful vibrations. One time around the track, and I was sure I could make her come. I swallowed and gripped the steering wheel tighter. Thoughts like that weren't going to keep me out of trouble.

"Where are we going?" I asked in a strained voice, hoping she didn't notice.

"We have an appointment in Birmingham."

"Birmingham? That's an hour from here. I have to be—"

"I thought you drove fast," she cut me off.

"I do, but if you're planning to make me go shopping, there's not enough time." I glanced at the dash and saw it was already ten.

"I'll worry about the shopping. You just get us there as quickly as you can."

"I thought you wanted me to drive safely," I pointed out.

"You said it was safe if you were driving," she said, her words dripping with challenge. "Prove it. Take me for a ride."

If Lola wasn't careful, I was going to wind up doing just that. Not that there was time right now. If we needed to get to Birmingham and back before I was due at the track, I needed to focus. I couldn't waste time imagining all the delicious ways I could show her exactly what I could do in this car.

I pulled out of the garage, determined to segue into a less

arousing topic than the car's horsepower or showing Lola what she was missing. "What do you drive, then?"

"Drive?" She blinked at me as I turned onto the street.

"Your car," I prompted.

"I don't have a car." She laughed as though the idea was ludicrous. "I live in London."

"Lots of people have cars and live in London." I waited for her to refute my observation, but she only shrugged. "Or can you not afford one?"

"Afford one?" she echoed.

"Yeah," I said, trying to sound casual. "I mean, I know you aren't technically a royal." Lola's connection to the royal family was by marriage only.

"Don't you read tabloids?" she asked.

"Not if I can help it," I muttered. I'd never had much interest in celebrities or royalty, even after I'd found myself entangled with my new famous family. "It's just a bunch of gossip and lies."

"Some of it is true," she said lightly, but her gaze traveled over me like she was seeing me for the first time. "You haven't even read the stories about yourself."

"Fuck no," I barked, laughing. "I can't imagine the things they say about me."

"But you want to be famous," she said slowly.

I glanced over at her, one hand on the wheel. "Why would you think that?"

"Eyes on the road," she demanded, fidgeting nervously in her seat. Maybe she wasn't as composed as she let on. "I just assumed that's why you raced."

"For fame?" I blew a stream of air through my lips. Of

course that's what she would think about me. "I don't race for fame."

"Money?" she suggested.

"It doesn't hurt." I shot her a grin, earning me a wide-eyed look of panic. "Relax, boss, I could drive this with a blindfold."

"I'll take your word for it," she murmured. "Just don't crash the car." Lola clenched her hands together in her lap, her knuckles blanching white.

"I race because I love it," I answered her softly, hoping to distract her from being a backseat driver. "Out there, it's just me and the road."

"And a bunch of other racers." Nothing impressed her.

"Yeah, on race days. But I'm not really competing against any of them."

She shifted in her seat, turning her body to face mine. "Then why race?"

"I can't explain it," I admitted. "It's just a feeling—like I belong behind the wheel."

Lola fell silent, and I wondered if I'd said something wrong. "That must be nice," she said after a few seconds.

The sadness in her tone surprised me. Until this moment, I wouldn't have thought it was possible to ruffle Lola Bishop. But, now, somehow I had done just that.

"Maybe you should get a car," I suggested. "Or do I need to read some tabloids to find out why you don't drive."

"It's not necessary to own a car in London. Besides that, I don't know how to drive."

I nearly stopped the car on the spot. "What do you mean you don't know how?"

"Calm down," she said. "I never learned. We moved to London when I was kid, and there was never any reason for me to drive. I went to university in the city. I had access to the Tube. What's the point?"

"The point is that you can do this." I shifted into a higher gear as we hit a stretch of lonely highway. I pressed my foot against the gas pedal and the Ferrari shot forward.

"Fuck!" Lola shrieked. Her hand flew out and gripped my arm tightly, but I didn't let up on the gas.

"You wanted me to get us there quickly."

"And alive," she reminded me.

I downshifted, dropping the speed a bit until she relaxed. We had plenty of time to get there. It wasn't worth it to scare the shit out of her. And the longer we took on the drive to Birmingham, the less time we would have to shop. In my book that was a win-win.

"If you buy a car, I'll teach you how to drive it."

"Is that so?" She released a trembling sigh. "I think I'll pass."

"Cars really scare you, huh?" Earlier this morning, I would have thought she was fearless. She certainly acted that way.

"My sister almost died in a car accident, remember? Or did you miss those headlines, too?"

Fuck. Why hadn't I remembered that? The accident had made more than the tabloids. It had been on the front page of every paper in the world and all over the Internet. "I'm sorry," I said sincerely, "but the offer stands. If you ever want to learn how to drive…"

"I'll let you know." She relaxed a bit into her seat. "How much does this car cost?"

"This?" I searched my brain, trying to remember. "About two-hundred-and-fifty... thousand pounds."

"Okay," she said, not batting an eyelash.

"You could get something cheaper for your first car," I suggested. I had no idea why I found myself so invested in getting Lola behind the wheel. Maybe it was her obvious love of control, but I couldn't imagine she'd dislike driving.

"I was just curious."

So, I wasn't going to get her to talk about cars. That left me searching for other safe topics of conversation. The truth was that I knew almost nothing about her. I'd been too angry when she'd first butted into my life to look her up. When I'd found out she was Clara's sister, I'd expected her to be more like Clara. But while they were two of the most beautiful women I'd ever seen, Lola was Clara's opposite in every way. "What do you do?" I asked. "I mean, for a living when not "helping" family?"

"I'm helping a friend launch a fashion subscription," she explained.

I shot her a blank look, and she sighed.

"People pay us money to borrow expensive clothes instead of buying them."

"People pay for that?"

"Yes, Mr. Jeans and a T-shirt, they do," she said in a huff.

"Sorry. I didn't mean to offend you, I was just surprised."

"Sometimes it's like you live under a rock." She drummed her fingernails on the center console thoughtfully. "You don't read tabloids, no subscription boxes—you have heard of the internet, right?"

"That I've heard of." I glanced up to check my mirrors, noticing a black Range Rover had joined us on the highway. My chest constricted even as I tried to shake it off. It didn't mean anything to see another car on the road.

"But I don't have a *traditional* job," she continued. "I'm still looking for where I fit."

"That sounds like a luxury." The Range Rover switched lanes, gaining on us. I slowed down, hoping it would pass, but it didn't.

"Well, I am worth twenty million pounds," she said matter-of-factly. "That buys me some time to decide."

I was still watching the SUV as her words hit me. I nearly drove off the road. The tire vibrated as it hit the shoulder and I jerked the wheel, pulling us back into our lane. "*Twenty million pounds?*"

Lola clutched my arm, a panicked squeal escaping her perfect map.

"I've got you," I said casually, even though her touch left me feeling anything but.

She peeled her hands away, shaking her head like she was clearing it, and her give-no-fuck attitude returned. "Trust fund." Her voice trembled slightly beneath her imperious mask. "Clara has one, too, but I don't think she really needs it anymore."

I had so many questions for her that I couldn't decide where to start.

"Oh! Birmingham." She pointed to a highway sign.

I'd never been so grateful to get off the road. But as I merged onto the exit, the Range Rover followed. "Shit."

"What's up?" Lola asked, looking around the interior cabin.

There was no use hiding it from her. My questions would have to wait. "That car is following us."

CHAPTER EIGHT

LOLA

I strained against my seatbelt trying to get a look at the car Anders was talking about. Part of me wanted to laugh at him. But the truth was that I was royalty's sister-in-law and he was royalty, even if the tabloids liked to attach the word bastard following that fact. I'd had a front-row seat to the paparazzi following my sister around London. But this felt different. Maybe it was because Anders was closer to being a playboy than prince charming.

"Which car?" I asked, peering out the window. Why did I find this exciting? Racing down the M6 while some random car followed us shouldn't make my pulse speed up? But here I was, caught up in the moment.

"The Range Rover. It's always a damn Range Rover," he muttered. He jerked the Ferrari into the next lane and slowed down.

"What are you doing?" I asked. "They're going to catch up with us!"

"That's the point, boss." As soon as the black car was parallel to us in the next lane, Anders rolled down my window. The Range Rover kept its tinted windows raised, making it impossible to see inside. Anders lifted his hand and saluted them.

"Anders!" I batted his hand down, knocking it into my lap.

"Hey, I was working on my public relations," he grumbled. He brushed the back of his hand down my thigh before he returned it to the steering wheel.

I caught my breath, trying to keep a shiver at bay. His bare-knuckle had barely grazed my leather pants, but it had been enough to capture my body's full attention.

Anders said something under his breath, and I shook myself to focus. "What?"

"Nothing," he said in a gruff tone.

I pinned a no-nonsense gaze on him. He could try to avoid talking to me. He could try to hide behind whatever inexplicable physical attraction we both felt toward each other. He could try a lot of things. But if he thought I would just lose interest after I asked a question, he was going to learn quickly that wouldn't work.

"Is this just normal?" he asked, smacking his steering wheel. "Having bodyguards and publicists and no life of my own?"

I took a deep breath and listened to him rant. Regardless of how obnoxious he acted, he'd earned the right to vent about the sudden lack of privacy.

"I guess," I answered truthfully. "Have you talked to Alexander about it?"

He barked a harsh laugh. "I'll bring it up the next time we have afternoon tea."

"Yes, laugh at the idea of talking about your issues," I said flatly. "Because bottling them up is really working out for you."

"It was," he said. Bitterness etched his features making him look much older than he was for a moment.

I actually felt for him. None of this could be easy. But being angry and rude wasn't going to change any of it. Why couldn't he see that? Why was he so determined to make his brother his enemy? Alexander could be overbearing. I really didn't know how my sister put up with it, but he seemed to have good intentions. At least from where I stood: on the outside looking in. "Look," I said, mustering as much force as I could behind my words, "I'm not saying you have to be best friends, but maybe you should ask him to clue you in on any security details."

Anders shot an annoyed look at me before turning his attention back to the highway. A muscle ticked in his jaw as he drove us into the city proper. His eyes lifted to the mirror and he sighed.

"Still following us?" I asked in a soft voice.

He didn't answer.

I dug my phone out of my bag and checked to see if Clara had returned my call. My sister had her hands full with a toddler and a baby on the way, so it wasn't a surprise that she hadn't called me back. Still, considering I was here doing her a favor, it would be nice. I slid open my contacts list and hit her name. It went straight to voicemail.

"Who are you calling?" Anders asked.

I started to say no one but thought better of it. If I wanted Anders to open up to me, I would have to start opening up to him. "My sister. I wanted to check in with her."

"She's probably with my brother." Anders pulled up to the valet stand in front of Barnaby's.

I could tell exactly what he thought about that. A man in livery walked to my side of the car and opened the door to help me out. Anders didn't wait for him to come around. He got out and turned, dropping an elbow on the car's low roof. "Where do I park this?"

The parking attendant blinked in confusion and looked at me. I shrugged. I didn't understand cars, and I certainly didn't understand why Anders treated it like it was his actual baby.

"Sir, I would be happy to—"

"Please point me in the right direction," Anders cut him off. "You're not getting behind her wheel."

The attendant's eyes goggled as he looked from the car to him to me.

"He means the car," I explained as I crossed my arms. "Just let him park it, Anders."

"Nope. Either I park it or I wait out here for you to finish your shopping," he said.

"We're shopping for you!" I couldn't keep the fury out of my voice. Why did he have to make everything so hard all the time?

"I guess you'll have to help me convince this nice fellow to let me—a professional driver—park my own goddamn car in a garage. Hell, I'll even tip him."

That's what this was about. He wanted me to work my

feminine wiles on the older gentleman until he bent the rules.

Except I'd never been very good at charming strangers. Plus, there was an easier way. Taking my wallet out of my purse, I drew out two fifty-pound notes. "Let him park the car and I'll tip you a hundred quid."

The hesitation vanished and the attendant pointed down the street. "Turn at the signal. You'll see a private garage just past. Park it anywhere on the street level."

"Thanks." Anders looked to me. "I'll be back in a few minutes."

But I was busy staring at the signal which had to be over a kilometer away. "You aren't really going to walk all the way back here. Our appointment will nearly be over."

"I could use the jog," he said, lifting his mobile phone. "Plus, I have a call to make."

I didn't dare ask who he was calling, I only hoped that if he was about to reach out to his brother that he didn't immediately start cursing him out.

"Fine." There was no point in fighting. I was starting to understand that Anders was more like a jackass than I'd first realized. If he decided to dig in his heels, we weren't going anywhere.

I watched him drive away with a sinking feeling that I couldn't quite explain.

"Miss," the valet said politely as he opened the door to the store.

"Thank you." I managed a smile as I started inside. I was nearly through the door when I remembered his tip.

He waved it away. "I can't take money without doing work."

"I need one man to listen to me today," I told him as I reached over and tucked the notes into his breast pocket. "So just take this."

"If it pleases you," he said, sounding uneasy.

"It does." I didn't stay for the next round of apologetic refusals. I had grown up in London. My memories of America all came colored with the tint of a childhood I didn't quite remember. I'd even developed an accent over the years. But every once in a while, I was reminded that I was not a full-blooded Brit. This was one of those times. Just more proof that I didn't quite fit in anywhere.

I smiled as I disappeared into the glossy storefront, relieved to have a few minutes by myself, fully clothed, and in no danger of Anders finding me in a compromising position.

Barnaby's had enough pedigree to see me through getting Anders out of his ratty old clothes and into ones that suited his newfound importance. But the company was in the process of a massive rebrand aimed at attracting a younger clientele. The store which had once catered to men on their way to the House of Lords was now becoming a hotspot for fashion-forward young celebrities like footballers and actors. I'd managed to secure them two new feathers for their cap. Anders wasn't just royalty, he was also a rising star on the racing circuit. With any luck, he would find he actually liked some of the clothing here.

My alone time was short-lived. I was only a few steps into the store when a stylish Chinese man approached. It was obvious from his blue tartan suit and Gucci loafers that he was the stylist I'd arranged to work with today.

"Miss Bishop?" he asked.

For a second, I honestly thought he wasn't sure and I found myself delighted at the novelty of being asked who I was.

The delight was short-lived, though.

"I'm only joking," he said quickly. "Of course, I know who you are, Miss Bi—"

"Lola," I interrupted him. Tasteless jokes aside, I needed him on my side before Anders returned. Two against one was way better odds.

"Lola," he said, as if trying it on. He smiled like it fit. "I'm Ralph. And where is...?"

"Parking the car," I explained.

Ralph's face fell into a puzzled expression.

"Don't ask," I said.

"I won't," he agreed. "Should we wait or can I show you to your private showing room?"

"I'll wait." I wasn't about to give Anders a single excuse to bail on me. I would be right here by the door in plain sight. Who knows what would happen if he came inside to find me gone? Would he even come looking for me? Or would he just go right back to his car and drive away like I'd done to him last night?

Last night.

"Oh bollocks," I said under my breath.

"What was that?" Ralph asked, craning his head.

"Nothing! Let's just stay here until he gets back."

Ralph filled every second we waited with a rundown of

every designer they carried in stock as well as ones they could order in if we had difficulty finding what we needed. I was beginning to wonder if he would ever run out of small talk—and if Anders was coming back.

"Maybe..." I reached for my mobile and began to dial Anders's number just as he stepped through the door.

"Well, isn't he a delicious Viking of a man?" Ralph said softly.

"Don't let him hear you say that," I warned him. "His head can't handle much more inflation of the ego."

"Noted." But Ralph's eyes sparkled as Anders headed directly toward us.

"Where are the racks?" Anders asked, looking around the room.

"This is the showroom," Ralph explained. "Let me show you to your private dressing chamber."

"But I haven't picked out anything to try on yet," he said, pushing a wayward strand of hair from his eyes.

"I saw to it already," I jumped in before Ralph said something that sent Anders running for cover.

"You picked out my clothes. You really are bossy," he said through gritted teeth. But it wasn't annoyance straining his tone, it was something else. Whatever it was lit a fire inside me.

"They pulled the clothes, but I will choose what you buy," I said sweetly, shrugging. Let him think I was bossy. Maybe it would be easier to help him fall in line. "What did your brother say?"

"Nothing. As usual. I told him to have Clara call you," he added.

It was an oddly thoughtful gesture, especially since he must know I was calling her to complain about him. "Thanks."

The showroom Barnaby's had set up for us had three racks of clothing waiting near the dressing room's door. Two olive-green velvet chairs sat opposite a three-way mirror, and on a coffee table, there were a number of magazines and a bottle of champagne on ice. Around the ceiling a faint glow of neon pink light illuminated the dark, velvet-flocked wallpaper. A number of glass display shelves boasted footwear from Prada to Nike and everything in between.

"You'll find this season's best pieces along with a number of pieces from the fall collections," Ralph told us and we stepped inside.

Anders fell silent as Ralph showed off everything the room had to offer, down to a fridge and snack bar stocked for us in case we got peckish.

"Is there anything else we can do for you?" Ralph asked.

"I've got it from here," I told him, adding a whispered, "for now."

I waited until he left before I turned to Anders, who was already raiding the bar for crisps.

"You're not really going to eat those?" I asked even as he took the first one out and popped it into his mouth.

"I'm hungry," he said with a devilish grin.

"You're going to get oil all over the clothes."

"In that case..." He drew his hand out of the bag and took his time sucking the salt from the tops of each of his fingers.

I hadn't noticed how wide his mouth was before. Now I

couldn't think of anything else but how it would feel to have those lips claiming me as his.

I swallowed, determined to stay on target. "I'll get you something to eat later."

"What did you have in mind?" His gaze wandered from my face down until it stopped hungrily between my legs.

"Chicken!" I blurted out the first answer that came to mind. It was hard for me to keep a clear head when he was planting ideas inside it.

"Not exactly what I was hoping for." He licked his lower lip slowly. "Maybe you can hook me up with dessert?"

My eyebrows shot up so fast, I swore they could have flown off my face. Anders was determined to unseat me in every way possible.

He followed me as I made my way across the dressing room. I stopped in front of the racks of designer clothing they had pulled for him to try on and started dutifully flipping through the hangers.

Anderson stepped behind me and reached to do the same, putting his rock-hard body into achingly close contact with my backside.

"I'm just in the mood for something sweet," he murmured as I drew a blue blazer off its hanger.

I didn't dare to look back at him. "And what makes you think that's me?"

"Call it a hunch," he said. "There's only one way to find out."

My eyes shuttered for a moment as I willed myself to overcome his tempting offer. I was not going to give in to Anders or his indecent suggestions, and I certainly wasn't going to let him see that I'd even considered it. Opening my eyes, I spun and shoved the blazer into his arms. I plucked matching pants from the rack and thrust those at him, too.

"Try those on," I ordered.

Anders reached behind his head and hooked his collar with a finger.

"In there!" I pushed him toward the dressing room door.

"Sure you don't want to help me, boss?" he asked as I shooed him inside. He immediately began to take off his clothes.

I slammed the door shut, wishing for a few more glimpses of his perfect body. I could resist him. I could keep him at a distance, but would it be so bad to appreciate the view. I went straight across the room and poured myself a glass of champagne. I might as well just drink out of the bottle. I was on my second glass while perusing a copy of *Trend* magazine when Anders appeared wearing the suit I'd picked out.

A second became a minute as I took in living proof that men in suits were just sexier. Its deep sapphire color set off his eyes. The suit itself was cut in a modern style that was tailored to fit closely to his body, and he'd kept it casual by leaving the white Oxford he wore under the jacket unbuttoned at the top. The jacket showed off his biceps and broad shoulders. Anders turned in a circle and I caught sight of his tight ass in the trousers. He looked good enough to lick and for a minute, I forgot my determination to keep things professional between us.

"What do you think, boss?" he asked with a wink as he adjusted a cufflink.

"You should only wear this." It slipped out of my mouth

before I realized what I was saying. I scrambled to correct the mistake. "It's better than T-shirts and jeans."

"I don't need a suit," he said, shaking his head. "I've got one and that new tuxedo you sent me last week. I can't wear this to the track."

"Is that so?" I challenged him. "Giovanni Rossi wears Dolce & Gabbana to press conferences. Michel Germaine wears Dior regularly."

"Who cares?" he asked, but there was conflict in his eyes. I'd done my research. I could list at least five more racecar drivers who appreciated men's fashion enough to appear in various style columns. Anders had to have noticed, too.

But I knew exactly how to convince him he needed this suit in particular. "You can wear it tonight."

"Where?" he asked. "I don't have plans."

"You do now," I said smiling sweetly.

His eyes narrowed into steely flint streaks.

"You have a date," I explained.

"With whom?" he asked slowly.

I licked my lips, gathering up my courage and hoping I looked detached. "With me."

CHAPTER NINE

ANDERS

"Where is your head?" Wilkes demanded as I climbed out of the Renault and tried to shake off my piss-poor lap time.

Thank God Lola had asked me to drop her at my house before I went to the track. I couldn't imagine what she'd think if she'd seen that performance. Then again, she didn't drive, so maybe she would still be impressed.

"Earth to Prince Anderson!" Wilkes snapped his fingers to get my attention.

I shook my head, trying to physically jolt her out of my thoughts. "Sorry. I'm preoccupied with something."

"*Something* wouldn't happen to be a particularly fit publicist who stole your socks, would it?" he asked. "Because I didn't see her on the track today, so what's she doing in your head?"

I tossed my helmet to one of the crew who shot me a sympathetic smile. Everyone on the team had been on the receiving end of a Wilkes lecture. I had a feeling that by the time I managed to free myself from Lola's iron grip, I'd hold some type of record for most lectures given by a coach in history.

"I didn't get much sleep last night," I told him. It wasn't so much a lie as it was a fib. I'd passed out, which hardly counted as sleeping, and I'd been woken up early by Lola grinding her perfectly round rear against my—

Wilkes punched my shoulder. "Again? It's like talking to a wall."

"Sorry. It won't happen again. Let's take it around the track one more time."

"No fucking way." He laughed at the suggestion. Wilkes paused to look at a computer screen, sighed, and let his head fall before muttering, "Not good."

"Seriously. I've got this," I said.

He straightened, casting a doubtful look at me, before jerking his thumb toward the offices. "Inside."

The only thing worse than Wilkes laying into you on the track was him asking to speak to you privately. A public lecture usually consisted of screaming and a few insults, but behind closed doors, he hit you with what really hurt.

Disappointment.

I followed him inside and shut the door behind me. It wasn't the first time I'd been in here. I knew the drill.

"Son, you gotta get your head out of your ass," he muttered. He sank down into a bucket seat from an old decommissioned F1 car that had been converted into an office chair.

"I know," I started. "I'm getting rid of her as soon as—"

"You can't get rid of this," he cut me off. "I know you didn't ask to find out who your dad was, and I know you didn't ask for it to be Albert. But you know now. Everyone knows. Getting rid of her isn't the solution."

"She's fucking with my head." I dropped into the seat across from him. "That's it. I've got this under control. And sod *my family*. I'll tell them to go to hell. Say the word."

"You're going to tell the King to go to hell?" He laughed softly. "Good luck with that."

"You forget that he's my brother," I said bitterly.

"Maybe..." He hesitated for a moment. Conflict wrinkled his forehead as he tried to think of what to say.

"This is my life," I told him. "This. The track. The team."

"Maybe it was, but things have changed. Look at what happened a few months ago. You nearly got killed out there."

"That crash wasn't my fault!" I jumped to my feet. "Rossi lost control. I could have wound up in the wall. I made the best choice I could."

"You cut it too close, pushed it too far. You were trying to prove something," he argued.

"We're all trying to prove something!" I was blind with fury at his betrayal. All I needed was to have one more person in my life turn on me. "You've forgotten what it's like to be out there."

It was a step too far. Like most former drivers, Wilkes hadn't walked away from the wheel willingly. He'd survived his own crash, but he'd never been able to keep his focus after. It was one of the reasons that he was great at what he did now. Usually.

"This isn't the *yips*," he said. "You've lost your *flow*. It's not safe for you out there."

I didn't even realize I'd taken a swing until plaster crumbled to the floor. I pulled my hand out of the wall. Dust had caked along a few bloody spots on my knuckles. I'm sure Lola would be curious about that.

Lola. Why the fuck had I immediately thought of her? Was she the problem? Or just an easy excuse? I didn't know anymore. But even now when I was having my dreams kicked to the curb, I was thinking about her. That couldn't be a good sign in terms of my focus.

Wilkes didn't say anything as I brushed plaster off my hand and sat back down.

"If I don't belong here and I don't belong there, then where the fuck do I belong?" I asked him.

He lifted his shoulders, smiling sadly at me. "That's all anyone is trying to figure out."

"I'm not ready to quit," I told him.

"Yeah, I suspected that." He nodded like he understood. Maybe he did. He'd watched his own career end.

Fuck, that wasn't what was happening was it? One crash couldn't set me back this far. I wouldn't let it. Not with the whole world watching me now—watching and waiting for me to fail.

"So, what do I do?"

"Hell, if I know," he said.

"Great. That's very reassuring," I grumbled. "Look, I don't want anyone to know what's going on. Can we keep this quiet?"

"That shouldn't be too hard. Between the crash and your

family, it won't be hard to convince people that you're being groomed into royalty."

"No," I groaned. "You aren't actually suggesting that I go along with this stupid plan of theirs, are you?"

"Finding out you're a prince is a pretty good excuse to take a holiday from work," he reminded me.

"So, I'm just supposed to let her play dress up and have tea parties or whatever the hell they do all day?"

"I think you're confusing the royal family with nursery school."

"Am I?" I asked doubtfully.

Wilkes shook his head, a crooked grin hanging on his face. He might be right. It might be a good plan, but that didn't mean I had to like it—and he knew it. "You want to grab a few pints and get the rest of this out?"

"I can't. I have a date," I said through gritted teeth.

"A date?"

"Don't sound so surprised!" I chucked an empty water bottle at him. "I'm charming."

"Prince charming?"

I found myself wishing I had another water bottle to throw at him.

"Sorry," he said quickly, but the glint in his eyes said he was anything but. "I'll take care of dealing with the team and talking to the federation. You've got better things to do anyway." He shifted a few things around on his desk until he found a stack of business cards. He passed one to me. "Here."

"What's this?" I stared at the bouquet of roses printed on the card.

"You have a date. You should try to impress her."

"I don't think it's that kind of date," I admitted to him. "I get the impression Lola is planning to deliver a lesson, not romance."

"That's no excuse," he said. "You'd be a total wanker not to go for her."

"If that's how you feel"—I tossed the card onto his desk—"maybe you should take her out."

"That's not the winning attitude I expect from you. Where's your sense of competition?"

"Taking a vacation like you all wanted," I said bitterly.

"Are you telling me that you aren't even slightly interested in Lola Bishop?"

I pressed my lips into a thin line, trying to keep my face entirely blank.

"Exactly." He snorted. "Do yourself a favor and try."

"And how do I do that?"

"Make sure you smell good and buy her some flowers, idiot." He tossed the card back to me. "Make it the best date ever."

I swallowed, feeling a slight lump in my throat as I stood to leave. Wilkes couldn't make me quit, but he'd lost his faith in me. I felt worse than I had when I woke up from my crash. The only thing I could do was prove him wrong. I paused at the door, turning the florist's card over in my hands. "What am I supposed to do if I'm not driving?"

"Drive that pretty distraction crazy for a while?"

I had to hand it to him. That was a pretty solid place to start. And if Lola was going to keep distracting me, I might as well let her distract me from my unplanned hiatus from the circuit. She seemed to be the only thing easy to think about these days. Might as well lean into the distraction. I tipped my head in silent thanks as I opened the door. Checking my watch, I discovered I had just enough time to take his advice.

I had to make this the best first date ever.

CHAPTER TEN

LOLA

"Keep calm," I ordered myself. "This isn't a real date."

So why was I acting like it was? I'd been staring at two outfits for the better part of an hour. The point of this evening wasn't to work myself into a frenzy preparing for a romantic evening. It was to force Anders out of his comfort zone. He needed to learn how to act like a gentleman before he stuck his foot in his mouth at Buckingham or in front of the press. Since the world had discovered his connection to the royals, there'd been no end of paparazzi following him. Tonight would be no different.

And that was the problem.

I needed to guide him through how to act when surrounded by photographers, and how to behave at a fancy dinner—even when flustered. Helping him pick out new clothes was only the first step. I had to teach him how to be a prince.

I hadn't really thought this through. The tabloids were going to make crazy assumptions if anyone spotted us together. We'd been fortunate when we went shopping. Maybe we'd manage to stay out of the spotlight tonight. But how long could our luck hold? I had a terrible feeling that if I wasn't careful I'd be linked to Anders romantically, which was the last thing either of us wanted.

My phone rang, delivering me from my endless overanalysis of the outfits. I was only mildly disappointed to see it was my mother and not my business partner. My partner would have been helpful in an outfit crisis. Our entire business was based on fashion, after all. My mother was likely to dig her heels in and focus on the news I needed to deliver to her.

"I'm sorry that I missed you," she said breezily when she answered. "I was with my trainer."

My mom had been concerned with her figure before our sister accidentally fell in love with the prince of England. Since then, she'd committed no less than three hours a day to working out. It was exhausting just to think about it.

"I wanted to tell you something." I abandoned the outfits and went into the loo to finish getting ready.

"Is everything alright?" she asked quickly.

"It's fine. It's not that big of a deal." I'd learned a long time ago to manage her expectations to prevent a scene. It was a useful skill to have, but it didn't work as well over the phone—or when I was distracted over my non-date.

"Okay," she said, sounding unconvinced. "I was just worried. I've been trying to reach Clara for a few days. I thought maybe..."

"I'm sure Clara is fine," I said in a soothing tone. My older sister was probably avoiding her. Madeline Bishop could get a bit overwhelming, and Clara was nine months pregnant. "She's probably busy with doctor's appointments."

"Maybe you should call her."

"I will," I promised. "Look, you know how I went to Silverstone?"

"Yes," she said slowly.

"Clara asked me to help Anders deal with some of the PR fallout from the..."

"Scandal?" she repeated, instantly concerned.

It was as apt a term as anything else. "Yes. Anyway, he's been followed by a lot of paparazzi, and they're probably going to catch pictures of us together."

"How together?" she asked suspiciously.

This was exactly why I needed to prepare her in advance. She was as likely to jump to conclusions as the tabloids were. "I'm here strictly professionally. No matter what they put on the front page."

"The last time I heard not to trust the tabloids, your sister *was* secretly dating Alexander."

I cradled my phone to my ear as I haphazardly dangled one leg over the edge of the bathtub. I turned the water on to a trickle. "I can promise you that I am not dating Anders."

"What's that noise? You're too busy to have a conversation with me? You have to do other things at the same time?"

I rolled my eyes at her shameless guilt trip. "I'm getting ready to go out to dinner."

"Are you in the shower?" she asked as I sloppily applied shaving soap to one leg.

"Nope, I'm just shaving my legs."

"So, it's a real date," she said.

"No." I groaned, wondering if she'd heard a word that I said. "I'm going to dinner with Anders *professionally*."

"The only professional who shaves their legs before a business date is a call girl," she informed me.

"Mom, please." I shook my head. "This is exactly what I'm trying to avoid from the public, I don't need it from you when you know it's fake. I don't want you to think I'm involved with Anders."

"Then, why are you shaving your legs?" she pressed.

"Because I'm going to wear a skirt."

"You're a modern woman. You don't have to shave your legs to wear a skirt," she said.

I nearly dropped the phone in the bathtub. I'd grown up with very clear expectations on how to present myself. Expectations that were relics of a different time and place. My mother felt strongly about gender roles. She'd supported my education and business mostly because she saw it as a way for me to find a husband. Being a modern woman in her eyes was news to me. "It doesn't mean anything."

"You could wear tights," she suggested.

"With this outfit, I'd still need to shave," I said with a sigh.

"Not necessarily—"

"Mom, I only called so you didn't see me on a tabloid cover with Anders later this week and jump to conclusions."

"Well, that is thoughtful of you to save me from the same fate twice," she said with a sniff that suggested she still had yet to forgive Clara for finding out about my sister's relationship that way. "What are you wearing?"

My shoulders sagged at the question. I'd nearly forgotten

my dilemma. I wasn't sure she was the person to help me, but if Belle wasn't going to return my calls, what choice did I have?

"It's a bit cool up here. I was thinking either the Saint Laurent mini sheath, or that lacy Alexander McQueen we picked up a few weeks ago." As nosy as my mother could be, she did know my closet. She'd been there when I bought half of the items.

"The Saint Laurent," she said without pausing.

"Why was that so easy for you?" I grumbled.

"Well, a sheath is always a professional choice. At least, more professional than a lace dress," she pointed out.

I wiped the remnants of soap from my legs before stumbling back into look at the dresses on the bed. She was right. "Of course you're right," I said, frowning that it hadn't occurred to me. "I don't know why I didn't think of it that way."

"Lace does imply romance," she continued, "so if you want to avoid speculation..."

"The sheath," I agreed. "I wasn't thinking."

"Of course," she said in a proud tone. "Then again, maybe..."

"Maybe what?" I asked as I picked up the Alexander McQueen to hang up in the wardrobe.

"Are you sure nothing is going on between you two?" she asked.

I took a deep breath to refrain from hanging up on her or screaming into the phone. "Nothing. Zero. Nada."

"It's just that you picked out the Alexander McQueen..."

"I only brought a few items. It was new." Maybe we were

going about this all wrong. Clearly, she needed to go work for the tabloids spinning stories from flimsy threads like wearing a lace dress out to dinner or choosing to shave one's legs.

"You two would make a beautiful couple," she started.

I think the fuck not. I kept this thought to myself and said, "Look, I need to run. I'll call you later this week."

"Call your sister and tell her to call me," she shouted into the phone before I could hang up.

That was basically my position in life: carrier pigeon between my family members. It was like they were all incapable of talking directly to each other. Instead, they preferred to go through the medium of me. I tossed my mobile on the bed before carrying the lace dress to the closet, realizing I wanted to wear it. I hadn't gone out with a guy in a long time. I'd been far too focused on my fledgling subscription company. But she was right. The ivory dress skewed a little too bridal for someone trying to keep things professional.

The red dress required very little to make it stand out. Despite its close fit, its skirt flared slightly, and that, combined with its long sleeves, kept it from looking too sexy despite its color. I'd brought even less by the way of shoes—only fifteen or so pairs. Thankfully, I had a strappy pair of Louboutin sandal-style heels. I pulled my hair down from its messy bun and fluffed it, pleased to discover it had curled while up. A few spritzes of texturizing spray and it hung in thick waves around my shoulders. After a quick glance in the mirror, I decided to stop there. Any more, and I was in danger of looking like *I* thought this was a real date. As it was, I wouldn't be embarrassed to be photographed with Anders. It would be enough to keep him eating out of my hand, but nothing about how I looked would encourage him past harmless flirting. I hoped. This morning's unintentional orgasm could undermine plans. I couldn't let it.

Even if the memory of it kept creeping into my mind at the most inconvenient times.

Of course, the suit that had been rush-delivered from the tailors at Barnaby's was equally likely to stimulate my own mixed feelings—or rather, mixed hormones. Tonight would be good for us. We both needed to learn how to be together without fighting or flirting.

I dropped a few things into a Chanel clutch, took a breath, and opened the bedroom door. I hadn't given Anders a set time. I suspected we didn't need a reservation at even the fanciest restaurant around. Anders was a celebrity whether he liked it or not. That meant doors opened to him, as did tables. I opened my phone and began to text him that I was ready when a low voice interrupted me.

"Hey, boss."

"Shit!" I startled, dropping my phone.

"Sorry, I didn't mean to scare you." He stepped into the darkened corridor and my mouth fell open. I'd seen him in the suit earlier, but this was different. His blond hair was swept back and his face cleanly shaven.

It seemed that even guys shaved for fake dates. I made a mental note to tell my mother Anders was also a shitty feminist.

I looked him over, telling myself it was part of the job. I was teaching him how to be a gentleman, right? But as my eyes traveled down, I gasped when I saw what he was holding.

CHAPTER ELEVEN

ANDERS

This wasn't a date. Not a real one. So why was I standing here, holding a dozen pink roses? I'd had no idea what was taking her so long. I'd gone by the florist, gotten home, shaved, showered, and put on the new suit I'd found lying on my bed, and she was still in there. What did women do in the loo that took forever? And then it had hit me. She was avoiding me. Lola had been cured of whatever insanity had prompted her to insist on a date—even a fake one—this evening. I'd made up my mind to toss them in the bin before Lola saw when the door to the spare room opened.

Or maybe she had just been busy transforming herself into every dirty dream I'd ever had, because as soon as I saw her I could only process two words.

Fuck me.

The dress she was wearing was probably illegal in half the villages in Britain. It barely covered the perfect ass I'd been daydreaming about all day. Maybe it was the way her dark hair billowed past her shoulders that made her look softer. But this wasn't the no-nonsense, sexy as sin business woman who had walked onto my track yesterday.

She was so preoccupied with tossing things into a small black bag that she didn't even realize I was here. I swallowed and decided to take Wilkes' advice. This might not be a date, but I could drive her a little crazy.

Especially if she was going to show up looking like *that*.

"Hey boss," I said softly.

"Shit!" She jumped and dropped her phone in the process.

"Sorry, I didn't mean to scare you." I took a step closer to help her but thought better of it.

A gentleman would bend down and pick up her phone. But I wasn't a gentleman—or so she'd been telling me—and I wanted to see how short her skirt really was. She stared at me for a moment, phone forgotten on the floor, and I realized I must look like an idiot standing here holding flowers for a woman who'd made it clear she had no interest in me.

Lola shook her head a little. Then she bent gracefully at the knees and swiped her mobile from the floor. That was disappointing.

"Have you been waiting long?" she asked, immediately putting on her bossy, businesslike tone. "You could have knocked."

On second thought, maybe it was good she hadn't bent over and revealed her rear end. I might not have been able to stop myself from spanking her. My palm twitched at the thought of bending perfect Miss Bishop over my knee and showing her that she underestimated me.

"These are for you." I thrust the flowers at her.

She took them, chewing on her bottom lip. For a second, I could have sworn I glimpsed a smile. "Anders, you didn't have to do this. Tonight isn't really—"

"I know," I cut her off. "But you seem to be laboring under the misunderstanding that I'm a hopeless caveman in need of rescue. I thought I would prove that I can be a gentleman *when I want to be.*"

We stared at each other for a minute, each waiting for the other to make their next move. Finally, she tucked her black bag under her arm and smiled.

"Do you have a vase?" she asked, smelling the blooms.

"Um..." I had not thought of that. "I don't usually bring flowers home."

"Fair enough." She skirted past me toward the kitchen. "Let's see what we can find."

I followed behind her, enjoying the view as she swayed her hips. Did she realize she was doing it or was it a simple holdover from some prehistoric time when females shook their rears as a mating call? I wasn't sure, but I definitely felt the urge to throw her over my shoulder and answer.

"You probably won't find much," I warned her as she began opening cabinets, looking for an appropriate vessel for the bouquet.

"Don't you eat?" she asked.

"At the pub or my mum's."

She snorted as if this explained something. "I guess you usually take flowers to your dates at their houses." She gave up and closed the cabinet. "We can leave them in the sink."

"I don't usually take women flowers," I said.

"Never? I thought you were proving me wrong."

"I don't have much time to date. I'm on the road a lot," I reminded her.

"Oh, I thought..."

"What?" I asked, leaning back as she reached for the faucet and began filling the sink with water.

"There was some lipstick and stuff in the loo. I thought they were from an old girlfriend."

"Do you think I bring a woman home and tell her to sleep in another room?" I couldn't help but laugh. Maybe I needed to show Lola exactly what I did to the women I brought home. The trouble was that she'd brought herself here. Not the other way around.

"I don't know," she said defensively.

"Boss, when I bring a woman home, I take her straight to bed until morning." Let her think what she wanted about that.

"I just thought maybe you liked to sleep alone." She lifted one petite shoulder.

"Sleep is for times when there isn't a beautiful woman in bed with you." My response earned me a small gasp. It reminded me of how she'd sounded when she came this morning.

"Well, someone left their shit in your bathroom," she said stiffly after a long pause.

It took me a second to realize what *shit* she was talking about. "My mum stayed here after my accident to help me get back on my feet. It's probably her stuff."

"That makes sense." Lola didn't turn to look at me. She just arranged the roses in the sink quietly. "You two are pretty close, huh?"

"Yeah," I grunted. It felt weird to talk about my mother with her. Yet more proof that this wasn't a real date. I'd never discuss my mum on a first date. In fact, I couldn't remember a time when I'd ever brought her up with a woman.

This was the problem with having Lola here acting like lady of the goddamn manor. She was prying into my business. She'd already gotten rid of half of my shit. Hell, she'd woken up in my bed this morning! I was about to let her know that some lines needed to stay firmly in place if this was going to stay a no-touching relationship when she sighed.

"That's nice."

"Sorry, what?"

"You and your mother. Mine can be a bit much," she explained, tossing a grin over her shoulder. "Pray you never meet her."

"She can't be that bad." Now we were talking about her mother? Yeah, this was clearly not a date. Or it was the worst first date ever.

"She told me only call girls shave their legs before business dates," she informed me with a dry laugh.

"Was it that kind of business?" I asked before I could help myself.

Lola turned and flicked water at me. "She called today while I was getting ready. I couldn't get her off the phone."

Two things occurred to me simultaneously. Her phone call with her mum was the reason she'd taken so long to get ready. Not because she was trying to impress me. But the other seemed to completely negate the first thing. "You shaved your legs for our date?"

"Ugh!" She groaned and turned back to her sink of flowers. "Now you sound like her!"

"Hey, I appreciate the gesture, boss." I couldn't help smirking. I agreed with her mother. Not about the call girl part, but about what it meant that Lola had felt the need to groom herself in a way that suggested she anticipated being touched.

Date or not, I'd be more than happy to help her with that.

And then there was the itty-bitty skirt she was wearing. It practically begged me to walk over, grab her hips, and—

"Anders!" Her sharp voice interrupted the fantasy I was about to have of hoisting her onto the counter.

"Sorry. It was a long day," I said.

"I just asked if you were ready," she repeated. In the twilight filling the kitchen, her eyes were large, luminous orbs that studied me with curiosity.

I took one long, lingering look at her, wishing I'd just picked her up and done what I was thinking. "Boss, I'm always ready."

CHAPTER TWELVE

LOLA

The flowers meant nothing. So what if they were my favorite. He didn't know that. He couldn't. Anders was simply trying to prove something—or trying to get me into bed. I really couldn't be sure which.

And why the hell had I told him about shaving my legs?

Things just seemed to slip out when I was around him, and if I wasn't careful, the next thing to slip was going to be my knickers *right to the floor*. I managed to keep up a casual stream of conversation on the short ride into Towcester, but I ran dry as Anders pulled up to the restaurant.

When I'd searched for the finest dining nearby, I'd chosen the restaurant with the most awards and the most haute cuisine on the menu. It was part of my plan to polish my diamond in the rough. I should have done a little more research for my project.

Because the restaurant was in a hotel.

So much for controlling the signals I sent him. I'd already told him I'd shaved my legs, and now I'd directed him to a hotel. I was beginning to feel like an actual call girl.

Anders didn't say anything as he pulled up to the valet stand, but he adjusted the mirror, peering into it.

"You look fine," I told him.

"I look better than fine," he said with a gruff tone, shaking his head. "Actually, we've got company."

"Security?" I was going to have to call Clara again and ask her to speak with Alexander. If Anders' brother didn't call off his security teams, I wasn't going to get anywhere with him. Anders would be too busy obsessing over the constant intrusions.

"I don't think....fuck."

"What?" I unbuckled and twisted in my seat, but the low-slung sports car didn't have much by way of a back window.

"It's not security." There was a grim determination in his voice. A muscle ticced in his jaw, and finally, he opened the car door and got out. This time, he didn't demand to park his car. He passed his keys to the valet, glancing at whoever he'd spotted behind us.

If it wasn't security, then who was it? The parking attendant opened my door. That's when the shouts began.

Paparazzi.

We'd been lucky so far, and even though I'd expected them to catch up with us eventually, I hadn't expected they would be here when we arrived *at* a hotel. I'd thought someone inside would tip them off, and we would face them on our way *out* of the restaurant. So much for cleaning up Anders' image and prepping him for life as royalty. Now I just looked like his side piece.

"Welcome to the Whidbury, miss." He offered me his hand. I took it, bracing myself for the photos that would be in the morning tabloids. The revelation of a secret prince had been the juiciest story of the year, especially since Alexander had made it clear he recognized Anders as a member of his family and not just some bastard his father had tried to hide. That meant he was always front-page news. I kept my knees together as I shifted in my seat and took the attendant's hand.

He guided me carefully up, and I focused on keeping myself from flashing any of the cameras. But when I was on my feet, I realized the attendant had been replaced. Anders angled his strong body between me and the press as if he was trying to shield me. A lump formed in my throat. He didn't have to do that. In fact, he probably shouldn't do it at all. It was only going to make them more rabid. But I couldn't quite bring myself to say anything to him. Instead, I found myself grateful as he placed a hand on my upper arm and led me quickly inside.

"I didn't expect that," I admitted to him as soon as we were inside the lounge.

"Me neither."

In the warm, safe light of the hotel lobby, I realized I needed to get this evening back on track. I cleared my throat as we approached the hostess stand for Monday's, the restaurant I'd picked. "I'm sorry. It wasn't my intention to make it look like we're an item."

"Do you think I give a shit what they think?" He leveled a fierce glare at me.

"I don't know," I said, deciding to be honest with him.

"Regardless, it isn't helping your media image to be seen with me."

His eyebrows lifted, and his mouth quirked into a questioning smile. He turned and leaned closer, lowering his voice. "How is it hurting my image to be seen with a gorgeous woman?"

"Uh..." My mouth went dry as alarm bells sounded in my head. We weren't just off track now. We were standing in a hotel, racing toward the wall, and I wasn't sure we could stop ourselves before we hit it.

"Mr. Stone," the maître d' interrupted us before we crashed. "Your table is waiting."

"Thank you." Anders didn't look up. He lingered, his face hovering dangerously close to mine. "Are you hungry?"

I swallowed and nodded.

He finally straightened and crooked his arm. "Let's eat."

I slipped my arm through his and tried to ignore how hard my heart was pounding. I wrapped my hand around his forearm instinctively, only to send my pulse racing when I felt the thick banded muscles under my fingertips.

The maître d' led us through the main dining room, past a fireplace and a smattering of tables covered in white linen. It was midweek, so there weren't very many diners, but we caught the attention of a few as we passed. A woman in a garish feathered fascinator gasped and elbowed her husband. He looked up, rolled his eyes, and went back to his soup. Meanwhile, she was trying to get out her camera. A waiter rushed over to the table and began asking questions—and effectively prevented her from getting a photo.

"Hmmm."

"What?" Anders murmured.

"They seem to know how to handle celebrities around here. I wouldn't have thought..."

"Look, we might not be royalty or footballers, but racecar drivers inspire their own crazy fans," he said. "Monday's caters to some of the most famous men in my field when they're in town. I thought that was why you chose this place."

I wished I could claim it was. It would definitely be a good excuse for why I'd dragged him into a hotel. "I picked the place with the nicest menu."

"That makes sense, too."

Our table was nestled in the back of the restaurant, tucked into a private corner where we wouldn't be overheard. Judging from the relatively small space, we weren't going to get anywhere more private unless we wanted to eat in the kitchen.

"Mademoiselle?" The maître d' moved to pull out my chair, but Anders cleared his throat loudly. "Pardon." He stepped to the side and allowed Anders to do it as a server appeared carrying menus.

I settled into the blue upholstered chair and accepted a small menu printed on thick, crème linen paper. Anders took the seat next to mine and looked at the waiter. "Champagne, please."

"Would you like to see our menu, Sir, or—"

"A bottle of Dom will do," Anders said.

I bit my lip, trying to hide my surprise as the server bustled off to get the champagne.

"I can see the smirk you're trying to hide, boss." He said,

not looking at me, as he studied his menu. "I thought we could use a drink."

I couldn't disagree with that. It was just his choice that surprised me. "I didn't expect you to order champagne. It surprised me."

"I'm full of surprises." He spoke in a voice so low and rough that it scraped against my already fraying nerves and sent a jolt of desire surging through me.

I turned all of my attention to the selections on the menu but found it impossible to concentrate. I couldn't even make sense of what was on offer. I was beginning to wonder if I was wrong. Maybe I was on a date with him. Yes, I had boundaries, but Anders seemed to easily find new ways to get past them—and I kept encouraging him.

When the champagne arrived in a silver bucket a few minutes later, I was no closer to knowing what to order but more than ready for a drink. I accepted a crystal flute gratefully and took a sip. There was something comforting about Dom Pérignon. Maybe because I usually drank it at celebrations, I couldn't help but feel happy as thousands of tiny bubbles tickled across my tongue.

"Have you chosen what you would like to eat this evening?" the server asked. "Or do you have questions about the menu?"

Anders searched my face for an answer.

"Why don't you order?" I suggested to him. I couldn't bring myself to admit that the menu might as well be in Latin for as far as I'd gotten looking at it.

Anders nodded. "We'll start with the oysters."

"Excellent. And for the main course, or would you like to wait to order?"

"Actually, I have a question." Anders's eyes flickered to me. "I didn't see any chicken on the menu."

I choked on my champagne and barely managed to keep myself from spitting it across the table. I placed my glass on the table, glaring at him.

"Unfortunately, the chef isn't offering any chicken dishes at the moment."

"That's too bad." Anders continued staring at me. "I've been thinking about chicken all day. You could say I was craving it."

Oh my fuck.

"You know a plant-based diet might be good for you," I said softly, half hoping the restaurant might deliver him a bunch of tofu just to shut him up.

"The veal is excellent," the waiter suggested helpfully, completely oblivious to the tension growing at the table.

"Veal it is." Anders' eyes never left mine. "I'll have to satisfy myself later. Maybe for dessert."

The waiter said something else that sounded confused, or maybe it was just the hormones clouding my brain. As soon as we were alone, I realized I only had two choices.

CHAPTER THIRTEEN

ANDERS

I was an arse, and we both knew it. But I couldn't help it. I'd seen Lola's face when we'd pulled up to the hotel. She hadn't done her homework. I'd caught the boss unprepared. Her flustered reaction, complete with flushed cheeks, had sent my brain into overdrive, thinking about all the other bits of her I'd like to see turn that shade. For someone who obviously needed to be in control, she kept accidentally putting the reins in my hands.

The waiter left, and Lola continued to glare at me across the linen-covered table.

"Spit it out, boss," I said, reaching for my glass of champagne.

"I actually thought you were being chivalrous." She lifted one shoulder as she spoke. The move was so dismissive that I wondered if she was actually trying to provoke me into spanking her.

"Look," I said, leveling with her. "I know where you come

from everyone has a scepter up their ass, but around here, people know how to take a joke."

"Londoners can take a joke," she said coolly, "when it's funny."

"Ouch." I winced at the burn. "I thought it was funny."

"That's your first problem. You were thinking again."

She thought she could get under my skin. Was that her plan? To annoy me until I was distracted from the tension between us? Lola could play ice queen all she wanted, but I knew she felt the same attraction I did. If she didn't, she wouldn't blush every time something suggestive happened.

And I hadn't forgotten that it was my name she'd been moaning in bed this morning.

"So, no chicken," I said meaningfully.

"No chicken," she repeated firmly. "I'm sure you'll enjoy the veal. But seriously, maybe you should consider going vegan."

I suspected she wasn't talking about my diet. She just wanted to be clear that she was off the menu. I played with my fork, purposefully keeping my eyes turned away from her. "It's not just my craving I wanted to satisfy, you know."

Lola breathed in sharply. I glanced up at her, and she quickly took a sip of champagne in an attempt to cover the reaction.

"Tell you what," I offered. "I promise to be on my best behavior for dinner if you'll keep your mind open about dessert."

She studied me for a moment, her eyes narrowing slightly. It was clear she was trying to decide how to play this situation. If only she knew that any way she played it, she'd play right into my hands. I'd gotten a taste of Lola this morning. Now I wanted the full course.

Silence stretched between us, but finally, she took a deep breath. "Okay."

I managed to keep my surprise to a minimum. I'd expected her to fight me on it a little more. But maybe that was just it. Maybe she didn't want to fight it. Maybe she wanted to give in.

Maybe she wanted to *submit*.

My balls ached at the thought of the bossy Lola Bishop, with her slender wrists tied and her perfect ass in the air, waiting for me to decide her fate.

"But first, you have to answer some questions," she added, interrupting my fantasy.

"Shoot." I lounged back in my seat and waited.

"Why don't you want to be a royal?" she asked.

That wasn't what I'd expected her to ask. I stared at her, trying to formulate an answer that didn't contain more curse words than not.

"Should I start with something easier?" she asked as if reading my mind. "What's your favorite color?"

"Pink," I said.

"Pink?" she repeated.

"In my experience, my favorite thing in the world is pink. Well," I said, thinking about it, "sometimes brown or reddish, even purple."

Lola clenched her jaw and then let out a heavy groan. "Is sex all you think about?"

I answered without thinking. "Only around you, boss."

"This was a bad idea." She reached for her napkin and tossed it on the table.

"Wait!" I said before she gave up and I lost out on any chance of getting dessert. "I'm sorry. I will stick to nonsexual answers as long as you stick to nonsexual questions."

"How is..." She closed her eyes, but she did grab her napkin and settle back into her seat. "What's your favorite food? Wait, forget I asked that."

She was learning. I might as well give her the answer to what she really wanted to know. "I grew up here," I told her. "I wanted to be a driver as long as I can remember—and not just a driver. I wanted to be the best. But when I found out the truth, I was pissed. Because I knew that if anyone found out, that was all that would matter—being Albert's son. And when the story leaked? That's exactly what happened."

Lola remained quiet as I spoke, but then she nodded. "That's why you're mad I'm here. You feel like they're trying to force you to be someone you don't want to be."

"I guess," I said noncommittally. She was right, but for some reason, I couldn't quite admit that to her.

"So, what would your life be like if none of this had happened?" she asked.

Before I could answer, the waiter appeared with a silver tray of oysters on the half-shell. Lola picked one up as soon as he was gone and downed it. She dropped the shell back on the ice and waited for me to answer.

"Well, I was supposed to get this big break when they asked me to do the Monarch Games," I said, picking up an oyster. "It was going to put me on the map as far as Formula 1 was concerned."

"And you weren't, before?" She dabbed her mouth with a napkin before quickly adding, "I don't really know much about racing."

"That doesn't surprise me," I said with a light laugh.

"What does that mean?" Her cheeks went red.

"You don't drive," I pointed out. "It's pretty rare to meet someone who cares about racing but doesn't get behind the wheel."

"Is that a prerequisite?" she asked. "What if I just wanted to watch you race?"

"Tough shit," I grumbled. "That won't be happening."

Lola tilted her head, looking like a curious kitten. "What does that mean?"

There was no point in keeping it from her. She'd figure out something was wrong when I didn't go to the track. "I'm taking a bit of a break. Wilkes is worried about my times."

"If he's worried about your times, shouldn't you practice more?"

"Probably in most sports," I admitted. "But in racing, it means your flow is off."

"Flow?" she repeated.

How the fuck was I supposed to explain flow to someone who had never driven? All I could do was try. "It's like you're one with the car. You don't even think about taking a turn or braking or giving it more gas. You don't have to because you're the machine."

"Wow." She blinked a couple of times. "That sounds intense."

"It is, but it isn't. I guess it's hard to explain."

"I think I get it," she said slowly. "So, what now? You just take a break for a few days?"

I chuckled.

"Longer?"

"Who knows?" I shrugged, letting myself face the fear I'd had since the moment Wilkes had called me out this afternoon. "Some drivers never get it back."

"Was it the accident?" She sounded so genuinely concerned I didn't mind talking about it.

"I don't know. I can't really figure out what's what anymore."

She nodded. "A few years ago, when everyone found out who my sister was dating, I felt this insane pressure to be as interesting or relevant or important."

"Why?" I asked.

"I guess because I was always the driven one. My mother would say Lola is going places, and Clara is going to save the world. When she met Alexander, it felt like I was just stuck. I was just Clara Bishop's kid sister. Suddenly, I was in magazines, and everyone wanted to know who I was dating or what I wearing, but only because of her. Not because of any of the things that I had worked for. It's one of the reasons I got into business with Belle. I just wanted something where I could fade into the background. After all those years of trying to be somebody, I didn't get to pick out who the world decided I was."

Something cracked open in my chest as she spoke, and what spilled out shook me. It was like she was in my head. Suddenly, I saw behind the bossy persona and perfect appearance. Lola was trying just as hard to live up to all their expectations, knowing none of them would notice unless she failed. She was just like me. She wanted exactly what I wanted. "Lola," I said in a low voice, "I see you."

She smiled, biting her lip in confusion.

"I see you," I repeated. "Not what you are for them, but who you want to be—and, stealing my socks aside, I like what I see."

She was quiet for a minute as if waiting for me to make a joke about going to bed together. I just waited, staring into her eyes, hoping she would believe me. I knew how much she needed that because I did, too. "You mean that, don't you?"

"Every fucking word," I muttered.

She opened her mouth, but before she could speak, the waiter appeared. Why did servers always sense the worst possible time to interrupt someone? Were they trained to do that? Neither of us looked up at him.

"How were the oysters?" he asked, oblivious to the tension straining the air between us.

"Perfect," Lola murmured. She picked her napkin up and laid it on the table meaningfully. "Unfortunately, we have to go."

"Your main course should be out any moment," he said apologetically.

"Why don't you and some of the others enjoy it?" I suggested, tossing a couple hundred quid on the table. "We have to go."

He stared at the money and cleared his throat anxiously. Wringing his hands, he asked, "Was there a problem with the oysters?"

"No." Lola smiled at me like he wasn't even standing there. "We decided to skip to dessert."

CHAPTER FOURTEEN

LOLA

As far as I could tell, I'd either lost my mind or given up. But something about what Anders said made sense to me. It also had sent the desire I'd tried to keep under control into overdrive. I didn't really care that it was a terrible idea. I didn't care this was going to complicate things. I just wanted to be seen.

Completely.

For who I was.

I wanted to be wanted.

I was pretty sure a therapist could do a real number on both of us, but I was past the point of caring. Anders went to give the valet our ticket, but before he reached the doors, a man in a poor-fitting suit caught him. I moved closer and spotted a shiny, gold badge on his jacket.

"Mr. Stone. Reginald Taylor." He stuck out a hand, and Anders took it apprehensively. "We had expected you to spend more time in the dining room."

"Look, it's nothing against your food," Anders said,

shooting me a smirk over his shoulder. "We just wanted some privacy..."

"Well, that is the problem," the manager said, sounding apologetic. "It seems there are some members of the press outside. We're working on clearing them out, but I'm afraid if you leave now..."

"I see." Anders clenched his jaw. "I think we'd both prefer to make a quiet exit. Is there another?"

"They are at every entrance." The manager looked utterly flummoxed until he glanced over and saw me. I saw understanding light up his face.

King's brother.

Queen's sister.

It was a recipe for scandal. Every tabloid in the country would want this story.

I couldn't blame them. I'd known the attention was coming. But somehow, it had been easier to consider how to handle the press when nothing was going on between us. Now? I was headed to bed with him. It was easier to deny something that wasn't true.

"Why don't I stay here, and you leave?" I suggested suddenly.

Anders shot me a look filled with so much disappointment I felt like I'd kicked his puppy.

"I'm not leaving you here, boss," he said firmly. "We'll wait it out."

As if to immediately test this plan, a group stopped in the lobby and began whispering. One pulled out her phone, and the manager hastily stepped in front of me before she could get a decent photograph.

If we stayed, we'd be dealing with that the whole time. It might be as bad as being out there with the paid leeches. I opened my mouth to argue when the manager spoke up. "Actually, why don't you both stay here? We can arrange the Whidbury suite and have your dinner sent up. As soon as this situation is under control, we'll be happy to see you out of here without all the attention."

Anders raised his brows, giving me the chance to object.

"That would be lovely," I said before I could chicken out.

"Excellent. We've already arranged the room, and we will send up a trolley in a few minutes." He passed Anders a keycard stamped with the Eaton hotels logo on it. "It's on the top floor. You'll need this key to access it."

"Thanks." Anders flipped it over in his hand. "But why don't you have them send the food up in an hour. My boss here had some urgent business to see to. She'll need to attend to it immediately."

"Of course." He nodded, managing to not look in the least bit scandalized. Like the waiter, he was either very good at pretending that no funny business was going on, or maybe they didn't know what people did in their hotel. I really couldn't decide. "There is a private lift at the end of the corridor. Your key card will grant you access."

Anders nodded his appreciation, and the manager bustled off to deal with the situation outside.

"After you." Anders swept his arm out, and I walked past him, taking care to not show a hint of impropriety as we made our way down the hall to the bronze lift. Since it was reserved for what I imagined was the hotel's finest suite, its doors slid open immediately. We stepped inside, and Anders used the card he'd been given to send us to the top floor. He stayed to one side of the lift's compartment, and I kept to the other, both of us carefully avoiding each other.

Until the doors closed.

I turned to Anders, but before I could say anything, he caught my face in his hands and crushed his mouth against mine. Our first kiss had been stolen. The result of a fever dream come true. This was different.

Anders took this kiss, and I surrendered to him willingly.

My lips parted as he seized control of my mouth. He swept a tongue over mine, teasing and tasting as we explored each other. It continued until the lift announced its arrival.

I started to pull away, but he dragged me back, stumbling out of the lift blindly. We crashed into a wall. Anders slipped his hands under my short skirt and hiked it to my hips, pressing his body against mine as we continued to explore. A small cough interrupted us, and we jolted apart. It seemed that the lift was private, but the floor wasn't.

An older couple was standing in the corridor, doing their best to avert their eyes. "May we use the lift? We have a dinner reservation."

"Sorry." Anders stepped to the side and moved in front of me, allowing me time to smooth down my skirt. "Whidbury suite?"

"Down the hall," the wife said, her eyes sparkling.

"Cheers." Anders grabbed my hand.

"Have a lovely evening," I offered feebly as he began dragging me away.

"You, too," the old man said with a knowing nod.

"Oh my god," I whispered, feeling my cheeks begin to burn. So much for discretion.

"Why do I feel like they just gave us permission to go in here and do all the debauched things we want?" Anders asked as we reached the suite's door.

I couldn't help giggling. But the temporary interruption had given me time to clear my head a little. He opened the door and started to pull me inside.

"Wait," I said, holding up my free hand. "I think we should establish a few ground rules."

His shoulders slumped, but he nodded. "Shoot, boss."

I hadn't expected him to put me on the spot, so I blurted out the first thing I could think of. "No public displays of affection," I said, quickly adding, "or we'll wind up with paparazzi everywhere."

"Deal." He nodded. "Anything else?" He tugged at my hand a little.

"Rule number two." I held up two fingers in case he needed a visual reference. "This happens after-hours only. I'm supposed to be here to help you."

"I suspect I'm going to find getting you naked very helpful," he said with a smirk.

I ignored him and held up three fingers. "Three. We tell no one. No one can know."

"Fine." He sounded less pleased about that one.

"And last but not least," I said and took a deep breath before plunging forward, "this is just sex."

"Is that it?" he asked with a groan.

"Do you agree?" I held out my pinky finger.

He stared at me.

"Don't you have pinky promises here?" I asked, wondering if my American side was slipping through.

"Not after the age of ten," he said with a laugh, but he looped his finger around mine and shook. "Now can we..."

I stared at the door cracked open behind him. Once we walked through it, there would be no turning back. After a second, I nodded.

Anders yanked me through it and slammed it shut. But this time, he didn't kiss me. Instead, he pushed me against the wall and dropped to his knees.

"I've been thinking about this all day," he said in a low voice that sent me from simmering to on fire. He kept his gaze locked on me as he pushed my dress to my hips to reveal my lacy knickers. Anders hooked his thumbs around the waistband and drew them past my trembling knees to my ankles.

"One at a time," he coaxed, and I glared down at him. He responded with a deep laugh that turned me molten. He held out a hand. "Don't fall. These shoes look dangerous."

"You don't like them?" I took his hand, and he helped me out of my underwear.

"The shoes?" He shook his head and ran his tongue over his lower lip. "No, I like them. That's why I'm leaving them on. Now be a good girl, and take off your dress."

My mouth went dry. He wanted me completely naked in nothing but a pair of Louboutins and him on his knees in front of me. I swallowed and remained still. "I thought I was the boss."

"Rule number 5," Anders said, holding up his hand. "When you're naked, I'm the boss."

Oh my...

But I couldn't let him make that rule that easily. "Fine, but I'm calling you Your Highness."

"You can call me whatever you want as long as you do what I tell you." His tone brooked no further arguments. "Now spread your legs and give me a taste of your dessert."

He kept his gaze locked with mine as I did what he asked. Slowly I shifted my weight until I'd settled fully against the wall with my legs spread wide before him. Anders leaned in, bringing his nose close to my aching sex, and took a deep breath. "Smells just as sweet as I imagined."

It wasn't a surprise after all our flirtations that he'd fantasized about doing this, but somehow being here on the cusp of letting down my guard made the moment unbelievably hot. He lingered there for a moment, driving me crazy, before he slid both of his arms up to bracket my ass.

When he still didn't do anything, I finally snapped, "Something wrong, Your Highness?"

He grinned up at me, and then like I'd flipped a switch, he shifted forward and lifted me off my feet. In one smooth motion, he hooked my knees over his shoulders and stood.

"What the—" But before I could finish the sentiment, he buried his face into me.

Anders held me against the wall and began to lick and suck, working his tongue deeper. I forgot my complaint and crossed my legs around his back for support. This was the craziest thing I'd ever done, and as my orgasm built inside me, I started to look forward to whatever insane trick Anders had up his sleeve next. His mouth clamped down on the sensitive point between my legs, and I began to buck against him. My body fought the overwhelming sensation, but he didn't relent.

He simply continued until I cried out. My muscles locked, and he released it only to circle the engorged button with the tip of his tongue. I fell to pieces, but he held me firmly against the wall, urging every last tremble of pleasure from me until I fell forward. I grabbed hold of his head, nearly knocking us over, and he chuckled as he swayed on his feet.

After a minute, he loosened his hold on me, and I slipped down into his arms. Anders carried me to the bed. I popped open one eye and watched as he began to strip off the suit. I'd seen him naked before, but this time I didn't have to just look. I rolled onto my stomach and reached for his belt buckle.

"You think you can touch that, boss?" he asked, looking down at me with a hunger that took my breath away.

So he wanted to play a game. I didn't mind if it meant brain-melting orgasms. "Please, Your Highness."

Anders swore under his breath and then dropped onto the bed, rolling me over and under him. "Good," he praised me, brushing a kiss over my lips. I tasted myself on him and blushed. "Hey, boss, just so you know, *best dessert ever.*"

CHAPTER FIFTEEN

ANDERS

"Please, Your Highness." The words slipped wantonly from her mouth and landed directly in my crotch. There was no hint of the haughty woman who worked so hard to keep me at arm's length. I should have known that all I had to do was get on my knees to show her exactly who was boss.

Rolling her onto her back, I covered my body with hers. Lola's legs fanned open ready for my next course.

"Good," I said softly, leaning down to kiss her. I could still taste her sweet release on my tongue. I'd meant it when I said it was the best dessert I'd ever had.

Her hands slid under my unbuttoned shirt and pushed it over my shoulders. She moaned as she trailed her manicured fingers down my abs. Her hips shifted under me, searching for contact. It didn't matter that she'd just come. She wanted more.

Lola Bishop wasn't just naked under me. She had turned into a simpering, desperate creature. If I'd thought she couldn't get hotter, I was wrong. There weren't enough hours in the day to fuck her all the ways I imagined. I was willing to try, though. Suddenly, a break from racing didn't sound so terrible. Her fingers found my belt buckle again, but I reached down and swatted her hand away. It wasn't that I didn't want to feel her delicate fingers wrapped around my cock. I wanted her to remember who was in charge.

"You seem to be forgetting rule 5," I murmured, sitting back on my heels and reaching to unbuckle it myself. Lola bit her lip as I unzipped my trousers and freed my cock. Her eyes widened as I began to stroke it. "I'm the one in control."

She raised one eyebrow, her eyes narrowing slightly. Maybe she needed me to explain it better.

"Do you want this?" I asked, continuing to work my length.

"Yes," she whispered.

"Then you'll have to be a very good girl and follow the rules." I couldn't help smirking as her mouth fell open. "You were so polite a minute ago. You even said please. What did you want?"

"You."

"Come here and show me." I continued to pump myself with my fist.

Lola shifted on the mattress and crawled toward me. She stayed on her hands and knees, looking up at me with wide, pretty eyes. "*Please.*"

"Good." I reached over with my free hand and ran the back of it down her face. She shuddered with pleasure, and I grabbed a fist full of her hair. Tipping her face up to look into my eyes, I gave her what she wanted. "Suck my cock, boss."

I released her head, and she immediately lowered her mouth over my crown. I slid my hand down my shaft to the root, holding it in place as she slowly took me inch by inch into her hot, wet mouth.

"That feels so fucking good," I said through gritted teeth as she swallowed me deeper. She was still on her hands and knees, but her hair had fallen over her face. Reaching over, I shoved it out of the way, gathering it into a pile. The end result was that I not only had a great view but a handle. I pulled her hair gently, urging her up and down a little faster. Lola's lashes fluttered as she looked up at me with her mouth around my cock.

It was too much. "If you keep doing that, I'm going to come, and I'm not ready yet."

I had much better plans than that. I yanked her away. She protested until I coaxed her onto her knees and smashed my mouth against hers. Pulling back, I kept hold of her hair and looked her in the eyes. "I'm going to fuck you now until you come."

That was about the moment I realized I didn't have any protection. I paused, wondering just how good the customer service was at the Whidbury. Finally, I sighed. My balls hurt, and I was *this close* to finally burying myself inside Lola. "Bad news, boss. I don't have anything with me."

There was a pause, and her eyes fell. At first, I thought it was from disappointment, but then she lifted her gaze back to me and sheepishly admitted, "I have some in my bag."

"Go get them," I ordered her. She slipped eagerly from the bed, but when she stood up, I stopped her. "Go get them on your knees."

Lola glanced over her shoulder, looking a bit startled by this demand. I kept my face cool and removed, daring her to test me. "Anders...."

"On your knees," I repeated firmly. "I want to see how fast you'll crawl so that you can have my cock." Her eyes shuttered momentarily, and I knew that she wanted to submit as much as I wanted to dominate. But she continued to stand there as if she was thinking things through. I'd have to make myself clearer. "You can walk over here, but if you do, I'll fuck you until you get on your knees and beg to come."

She gasped and stared at me.

"Your choice. I just thought we could skip to the part where I reward you for being so obedient," I said with a shrug. Getting off the bed, I shoved my trousers to the ground. Maybe she needed a visual reminder of what she wanted. Her eyes flickered down my naked body, and then ever so slowly, she lowered herself one knee at a time to the floor. Lola paused on her knees, closing her eyes before she leaned and placed her palms on the floor. She shifted forward slowly but surely.

"You look so beautiful with your bare ass on display," I encouraged her, moving to keep her in my sight as she crawled toward the adjoining sitting room to find her bag.

She rose no higher than her knees to reach for the bag that had been tossed aside as we entered. She dug around in it for a minute and then shifted back to her hands and knees, a foil packet between her teeth, and she started back toward me.

"I saw how wet you are." I beckoned her faster with my index finger. Lola picked up her face. "You're so ready to be fucked, aren't you?" As she got closer, I circled around her and squatted down. She paused, condom still in her teeth, and let me move closer. "I asked you a question."

Lola bobbed her head.

"Good girl." I brushed a finger down her wet seam and then pushed it inside her. A strangled groan of pleasure escaped her, and the condom fell from her mouth. I picked it up, shaking my head. "You can't make it all the way back to the bed, can you?"

"No," she said so softly that I wasn't sure if I'd heard her.

"Do you need me to fuck you here?" I pushed another finger into her soaking entrance.

"Yes," she panted.

"Yes?" I prompted, holding still.

She wriggled her hips. "Yes, Your Highness."

"That's right." I slipped my fingers in and out, tearing the foil packet with my teeth. Lola shot me a frustrated look when I withdrew my hand to put on the condom. She was going to have to learn a little patience. I lifted my soaked fingers to my mouth and sucked them clean. "I wanted more."

Her throat slid as she watched me. I put the condom on and got on my knees.

Her head fell forward as I brushed the tip of my cock along her swollen seam. Then slowly, I pushed my shaft inside, taking the time to enjoy how she tightened around each inch of me she took. Lola moaned and began to circle her hips, but I grabbed hold of them and stilled her. I'd been a walking case of blue balls since she'd arrived. I wouldn't be able to last as long as I usually did.

"I like seeing you like this," I murmured, pushing in a little deeper. "Begging for it. This is what you needed, wasn't it?"

She cried out, the sound half-strangled, half pure ecstasy. I chuckled under my breath. "I'll take that as a yes."

I remained in control of her hips. She was so wet that she took me easily, but I had no desire to rush through this. Lola felt like she tasted: decadent. Her muscles squeezed against me, and I knew she was desperate for release, but I wanted to feel every sensation the first time she came on my cock. Slipping an arm around her waist, I guided us up until she was on my lap.

"Oh my God," she said, gasping as the new position allowed me to seat myself entirely inside her.

"Just me," I teased her, wrapping one arm around her abdomen so that I could guide her up and down.

"I need to come," she said breathlessly, picking up the pace on her own.

I let her take over, and she began to bounce up and down. "You need to come," I repeated.

"Yes," she cried, beginning to shake.

"Do you want my permission?" I whispered, pressing a kiss to her ear.

Lola choked on a strangled cry, barely managing to nod. I'd have to work on that with her. For now, I wanted nothing more than to follow her release.

"You may come," I said quietly. "But you have to tell me what you need me to do."

Her body arched violently away from me, but I held her

tightly, meeting her rhythm with my own. "Fuck me, Anders. Please fuck me."

I was more than happy to oblige, arching my hips to thrust into her deeper. She began to shake, and I allowed myself to join her. I poured inside her longer than I had in years. Lola screamed one last time and went limp in my arms save for a few trembling aftershocks. I held her against me, waiting for her body to completely relax. I wanted her to enjoy this, even if I was already winding myself up for another round.

"That was…" she started but fell silent.

"Incredible?" I offered.

Lola twisted her head around to look at me. "I think there are better words for it than that."

"Such as?" I prompted, unable to keep a cocky grin off my face. I agreed with her, but considering how tightly Lola usually held to her rules, I hadn't expected her to be so willing to admit it.

"Can I get back to you after next time?" She licked her lower lip.

"Again?" I was already starting to get hard.

She nodded but then stopped. "Actually, bathroom first."

I carefully disentangled her from me and stood to offer her my hand.

"Maybe this time you can crawl over and find a condom," she said saucily as she sauntered toward the attached bath.

"Rule number 5," I reminded her, earning a giggle.

"Fine, Your Highness." She snatched her bag on the way into the loo and shut the door behind her.

I threw myself in the bed and waited. Floor sex was excellent, but now I wanted to shag her in a bed. I started to tell her this when she came out of the door a few minutes later.

"I think it's time...." I fell silent as she lifted a panic-stricken face, and I saw what was in her hands. Rule number 6 would have to be no cell phones, but judging from the look on her face, we could establish that later. "What's wrong?"

She looked right at me, and it was clear that playtime was over. "We need to go to London."

CHAPTER SIXTEEN

LOLA

The only mercy the night showed me was that the paparazzi were gone when we left the Whidbury. Had I just shagged Anders? Yep. Was the debauchery interrupted by mother calling? Also yes.

There was nothing like doing the walk of shame straight to a family crisis. Anders stayed quiet as we headed toward London. He hadn't said much when I'd announced that my sister was in the hospital. He hadn't argued when I'd told him we needed to stop and pack a bag in case we got stuck in the city. I strongly doubted that he'd suddenly decided to start toeing the line.

I had a feeling he was a ticking bomb.

The one perk was that, thanks to his driving, we were making record time.

We passed a sign announcing that we were only 20 kilometers from our destination, and I sighed with relief.

"Is everything okay?" Anders asked in a quiet voice.

"I don't know," I admitted as I tapped the armrest. "She

didn't say much. Just that Clara was in the hospital already. She sounded worried. Apparently, Alexander isn't letting anyone in to see Clara."

"Alexander is too overprotective," Anders grumbled.

Of course he saw it that way. "I think he has pretty good reasons for acting like that. And Clara wasn't due for weeks. If she gives birth, there might be complications." My voice cracked as I admitted to my own fears. I wasn't super aunt or anything, but the thought that something might be wrong with my little niece or nephew tied my stomach in knots.

Anders didn't say anything for a minute. "She'll be okay. She's tough."

I nodded, unable to consider any other scenarios. If anything happened to her...

I couldn't escape my thoughts until the heat of Anders' palm landed on my thigh.

"You look like you could use a distraction," he suggested, slipping his hand higher. He shot me a wicked grin.

"What I need..." I lost track of what I was saying when it continued up. His fingers shoved past the lace of my knickers, and I slumped in my seat. This wasn't the place or time for this. "We shouldn't. You're driving."

"Trust me, I'm a professional."

That was a good point, and he was right. I couldn't think about anything else with his hands on me. Our night had been cut short. Something told me that Anders would have easily kept going for hours if it wasn't for the interruption.

"Open your legs for me, boss," he coaxed, and I did as he requested.

He continued to explore as his hand spread me open,

allowing him to press a fingertip to my clit. I shifted again to give him better access.

"There you go," he murmured. I moaned at the encouraging command in his voice. But before I could sink into the pleasure more, my phone rang.

"Shit." I sat up, pushing his hand away, and groaned when I saw the caller ID.

"Don't answer," Anders said, but I'd already hit accept.

"We're on our way," I said tightly.

"Good. Maybe you can talk some sense into your brother-in-law..."

I laid my head against the window as my mother launched into a tirade. By the time I finally got her off the phone, we'd reached the outskirts of the city. As soon as I dropped my mobile back into my handbag, Anders reached over. I swatted his hand away.

"Rule number 2," I said, feeling tired. "We're back in London."

"It's still after-hours," he argued.

"Fine," I snapped. There was no way I was going to let anyone know what had happened between us. Not when we'd both agreed it was just sex. It would only complicate things more than giving in to each other already had. Clearly, an amendment needed to be made to our prior agreement. "Rule number 6."

He frowned. "There's getting to be too many rules."

"One more," I said firmly. "London is off-limits."

"Boss, we're already inside London limits."

"Not geographical limits." I rolled my eyes, knowing I'd taken his bait. "Sexual limits."

"Wait," he said, turning the steering wheel in the direction of the hospital. "Are you saying that I can't touch you in London?"

"Exactly." Instantly, I felt relieved. It would be hard enough to keep out of the papers in Silverstone. But London might prove impossible, especially with another royal baby on the way. "We can't risk it."

Anders stopped the car.

"What are you doing?" I asked.

"Turning around. You appear to have lost your mind somewhere between here and back home."

"I need to get to that hospital before my mother blows and takes the whole place with her," I said hotly.

"Has it ever occurred to you that you don't have to fix everyone else's problems, boss?"

"That's not what I'm doing, but if you don't want to take me to check on Clara, then I can take a cab." I reached for my safety belt.

"Don't you dare," he warned me.

"Or what?"

"Or the next time I get you alone, I will fuck you until you forget all your stupid rules."

I swallowed but refused to give any ground. "I guess you won't be getting me alone anytime soon."

"We'll see about that. Maybe I'll just fuck you until it knocks your priorities into place," he said through gritted teeth, pulling back onto the road.

"There is nothing wrong with my priorities."

"Sure." Anders kept his eyes on the road. He gripped the

steering wheel so tightly that his knuckles had gone white. "Whatever you want to tell yourself."

"Screw you," I hissed.

His quiet laugh sent goosebumps shivering across my body. "Boss, you already did."

It was a good thing we were on our way to the hospital because he was going to need one. Neither of us said another word until we reached St. Mary's.

"Around back," I told him. "There's a private entrance."

"Of course there is," he muttered, but he followed my instructions.

I fumed as he spoke with the security guard and then parked the car. But when he turned off the engine, I rounded on him. "Look, this is what's going to happen. You're going down to the shop and buying flowers for your new niece or nephew. Then you're going to come upstairs and be polite to your brother and the rest of the family. And so help me God, you will tell Clara she looks pretty even if she looks like she just came out of a war zone. Is that clear?"

A muscle twitched in his jaw, and then, without warning, he grabbed me and crushed his mouth to mine in a savage kiss. Surprise overcame any resistance, and I found myself being pulled back to the suite at the Whidbury. Anders forced my mouth open, claiming my tongue until I'd forgotten where we were or what I'd been saying.

The second he drew away, it all came rushing back, and I glared at him, raising my fingers to my swollen lips. "You just broke rule number 6—"

"Starts when we get out of this car," he growled. "Now if—"

I opened my door and slid out before he could finish his sentence. He could amend the rules all he wanted, but I wasn't going to wait around to see how far he was going to push my limits. It was bad enough that paparazzi were camped only a few hundred meters from here. He didn't have to try to get us caught.

Anders followed me out, catching up with me quickly. My breath hitched as he got closer, half expecting him to pull something else. Would he push me against a wall? Would he hike my skirt up and remind me that only a few hours ago, I'd been riding his cock? But he simply fell into step beside me.

We didn't say a word as we got into the lift. I pushed the button for the lobby, and we rode in silence until the doors opened.

Anders stepped out and then turned a cold look at me. "Coming?"

"Flowers," I said without meeting his gaze and hit the button for the private floor where Clara planned to give birth. But before the lift doors slid closed, Anders stopped them with his palm.

"Make sure you stop on whatever floor does surgeries, so you can get them to remove that stick up your arse, boss."

My mouth fell open as he stepped away, smirking, and let the doors close.

By the time I reached my floor, I was absolutely sure of two things.

The first was that Anderson Stone was the best sex I'd ever had, and none of my other lovers even came close. The second was that I absolutely hated him.

The lift opened to reveal a waiting room full of worried faces. I rushed toward my mother for an update.

Madeline Bishop could be a tad dramatic, so when she looked up at me and her face fell, my heart stopped. Next to her, my father rubbed her shoulders consolingly.

"What's wrong?" I whispered. There were too many people here for this to be normal. Something was up. In the corner, I spotted Smith Price, my business partner's husband, talking quietly with one of the family's head security officers, Brexton Miles. They both wore grim expressions and what looked like tactical gear. Something wasn't just up. Something was *wrong*. I whipped around to press my mother for details, but she was studying me with a sour expression.

"Did you come from your date?" she asked.

"What?" I shook my head, trying to understand how she could be worried about that during a moment like this.

"You look like you were out late," she continued, her eyes lingering on my hair and swollen lips.

She knew, I realized with a sinking feeling.

But I wasn't about to admit to any of it. I squared my shoulders and focused on what was really important right now. "How is Clara?"

"In labor," she said with a casual toss of her head.

"I thought she was having another c-section. Is it too early? Have you seen her?" I peppered her with questions.

"I don't know," she responded with a sniff. "Alexander won't tell us anything. We heard she was at the hospital from BBC One."

"Where is Alexander?" I glanced around. The waiting room was full of people and balloons and presents, but my brother-in-law was nowhere to be seen. Clara must still be in labor.

"He's in and out," she said.

Regardless of what my mother thought, I agreed with Alexander. His place was by my sister's side, not out here soothing his mother-in-law's fragile ego. I was about to tell her that when the swinging doors that led to the delivery room opened, and he strode out.

Alexander had an appropriate authority to his presence, even now. His black shirt and pants hugged his muscular frame. I turned and glanced back over at Brex and Smith. Were they all wearing the same clothes? What, had they been playing some type of football? Alexander's eyes fell on me, and he relaxed a little as if he was relieved to see me. We weren't exactly close, but he knew I could be counted on to keep the Bishop side of his family in check.

"Everything okay?" I asked quietly as I joined him.

"It will be," he murmured, his eyes haunted. I wondered if he was answering me or trying to convince himself.

I was about to press more when the lift opened to reveal Anders holding the bouquet I'd sent him to procure. Alexander caught sight of him, and something flashed across his face. It was gone so quickly that no one else probably noticed. But I recognized that look.

It seemed Alexander hated his brother as much as I did.

CHAPTER SEVENTEEN

ANDERS

"No one sees her." Alexander was staying firm on this rule.

"Then, we'll wait." Lola's mother was every bit as stubborn as she was. She refused to leave the waiting room despite my brother's proclamation.

"So will we," Lola said calmly.

I refrained from tossing the flowers into a bin. Instead, I dropped into a chair and waited. It wasn't like I had somewhere to go. Lola took a seat on the opposite side of the waiting area. Her business partner, who'd I met in passing a few times, joined her and began to whisper. I assumed they were talking shop until Lola glanced over at me and then quickly turned away before I could look.

No one spoke to me. Why had I allowed Lola to convince me I should be here? At least she was one of them.

But it was clear no one was seeing Clara for a while.

"Get comfortable and keep it down. She needs to rest," Alexander said in a grim voice before vanishing behind the swinging doors. I had no idea if my sudden appearance was at the root of his rudeness or if he was always an asshole. As soon as he was gone, the group began to dissipate, but no one seemed ready to leave. A few of his closest security team seemed to be sweeping the halls, coming in and out of the maternity ward like they were taking shifts. Eventually, Belle yawned, patted her own swollen stomach, and pointed to the door.

"I'm going to nap and come right back," she whispered to me.

"Don't rush. We're here," I said.

Her eyes looked a little frantic as she nodded. Maybe she was starting to fear her own birth. As soon as her husband took her home, Madeline started in on the only other distraction in the room:

Us.

"What were you two up to?" Madeline asked, eying both Lola and me with hawk-like eyes.

"Dinner," Lola said, showing no sign that we'd skipped dinner and headed straight for dessert.

A frown tugged on my lips, but I wouldn't let either of them see me react. If Lola could act like nothing had happened, I could, too.

"It was a little late to still be out. It's nearly dawn." Her mother wasn't going to give up that easily.

"We've been here for hours," Lola reminded her calmly. "We had business to discuss."

"Are you sure it wasn't a date?"

"No," we both answered at the same time. At least we were still clear on that point.

"Maddy." Lola's father cleaned his glasses with a sigh. "Don't pester them."

"I'm just trying to understand why he's still here if they aren't seeing one another. Maybe Anders would like to go home. He's not exactly part of the family," Madeline said softly. She was talking to Lola now.

Lola's eyes flashed to me, her mouth falling open. But before she could scramble to explain away her mother's casual reminder that I was Albert's unwanted bastard, I rose from my chair and buttoned my jacket.

"No, I'm not," I said stiffly. "I should get back to Silverstone."

Lola shook her head, but it was Alexander's voice that stopped me.

"May I speak with you first?" he asked, coming back into the lobby. "Somewhere private."

I resisted the urge to say no, but only because, unlike how I felt about everyone else in this room, I liked Clara. She was the nice one in the bunch as far as I was concerned, and today should be about her, not her mother or her husband.

"Fine," I muttered.

He tipped his head toward the private hall.

I followed him past the swinging doors. Madeline glared at both of us, obviously angry that I was getting closer to her daughter than she was allowed to. Next to her, Lola began murmuring to her in a low voice. She really was the one who had to deal with all the difficult personalities in the family. That's why they'd sent Lola to handle me. Of course, being lumped into the same category as Madeline only made me resent being here more.

"I'd like you to stay in London."

I stared at Alexander. That was the last thing I'd expected him to say.

"I need to speak to you about some matters," he continued, his tone clipped and formal. "Family matters. And it would be better if you had additional security."

"Why?" I asked. He might think it was normal to act like we were discussing a business transaction, but it was weird. Maybe that's just the way it was amongst royalty. They were the ultimate family business. Another reason I'd never be one of them.

"There's been some developments." He shook his head as if he was trying to shake loose what he wanted to say from what he chose not to. "We need to discuss them, but I need to get back to Clara."

"Clara's the most important thing right now," I said firmly.

Lightning flashed in his blue eyes. Their color was the only physical characteristic we seemed to share. We did have one thing in common emotionally: I'd had a thing for his wife. It was one of many reasons I wasn't exactly on his good side.

"Yes, my wife is the most important thing to me." He chose his words carefully, but I got the message.

"Good." I meant it. My own feelings had been nothing more than a crush. Anyone who met Clara couldn't help but like her. But while I might be well past that attraction now, I would continue to hold my half-brother accountable for treating her well. I hadn't always found his behavior toward her acceptable. "How long do I need to stay in town?"

"In a rush to get back?"

My eyes narrowed. There was no way that Alexander knew I was on a break from racing unless he had people spying on me. Then again, he probably did. "Just curious. I have to tell the hotel something."

"About that," he said, "I'd like you to take one of the family apartments at Kensington Palace. With the baby here, there's going to be paparazzi, everywhere. It will be safer."

"For you or for me?" I muttered. Of course he wanted to keep me where I'd be forced to toe the company line.

"For you." There was a painful edge to his voice.

"Fine." It's not like I cared where I crashed, and I'd rather not spend London hotel prices to sit around and wait to be summoned.

"Anders." He paused, his expression becoming unreadable. "Thank you for coming."

"Um, you're welcome?" I wasn't sure if he actually meant it. It was clear that he didn't like me, and the feeling was entirely mutual. But before I could figure it out, he waved to a passing security guard.

"Have you met Brex?" he asked me.

"In passing."

"He's in charge of my London team at the moment. He'll get you settled into Kensington and make sure everyone knows who you are."

"That's not necessary." Thanks to the fucking reporters, everyone already knew that.

"It's better if the staff is prepped," Alexander said, ignoring me. "Brex will also oversee your security from here on out."

Something about the way he said 'on out' settled sourly in

my stomach. Before I could press for details—and make sure he meant while I was in London—a doctor appeared and called to him.

"Excuse me," he said, rushing away as Brex finally reached us. "Make sure he has what he needs."

"You got it, poor boy," Brex called.

"Poor boy?" I repeated.

"I'll tell you later." Brex smiled as we reintroduced ourselves. The tall black man had been with Clara at various points while she'd hosted the annual charity games thrown by the royal family. I'd been too preoccupied then to get to know him. Now, he seemed just as preoccupied as I had been. His brown eyes swept the hall constantly. "I can have a car take you to Kensington."

I glanced back toward the double doors where Lola was waiting with her family to see her sister. "I'll wait, if you don't mind."

"Suit yourself." Brex was already back to guard duty. I wasn't sure he ever really relaxed.

I found my way back to the lounge. As soon as I was through the doors, Madeline accosted me.

"Did you see her? How does she look? How's the baby?"

"I didn't see her," I said flatly.

"What? Why did he ask you to go back there?"

"He needed help with a lid. It was stuck."

Madeline's nostrils flared at the joke, and she stuck a long, manicured finger into my chest. "If you—"

"Come on," Lola interrupted her, taking her mother by the arm. "Why don't we go find something to eat?"

"I'm not hungry," she pouted.

"I am," Lola said, "so come with me."

Madeline glanced between us suspiciously. "I thought you two were at dinner. It's not even breakfast time yet."

"We got the call before we finished eating," I said, stealing a look at Lola. "Plus, it was one of those fancy places where they serve you pea shoots and call it a salad."

I dared her to contradict me again. But my excuse had worked.

"Then maybe you two should go get a bite." Madeline sniffed dramatically. "I should be here in case Clara needs me."

"Sure, you do that." Lola sounded exhausted, and we'd only been here for an hour. "I need to consult with Anders anyway."

"Why?" Madeline demanded. "Is something going on between you two?"

"No," we both said again.

"Well, you two are on the same page, at least." Her lips pursed, and somehow, I realized she knew that we were lying.

God, the only thing worse than staying in London was going to be staying here while avoiding Lola's nosey mother. Hopefully, a new grandbaby would distract her.

"We'll get you a coffee." Lola patted her mother's arm and then pointed toward the lift. "Ready?"

Before either of us could object, Lola grabbed me and dragged me toward it. She stayed a careful distance from me while we waited for it to arrive. When it did, she stepped casually inside and pressed the button for the lobby. But when the doors closed, she whirled around and shoved me against the wall.

"What the—" I started, but she kept her palm pressed to my chest, pinning me to the spot. "I thought there were rules in London, boss."

"There are. Now, tell me what the hell is going on, Your Highness."

CHAPTER EIGHTEEN

LOLA

Anders was determined to push all my buttons. I pushed my own: the stop button. The lift shrieked to a stop somewhere between the second and third floors.

"Should you do that? People need to use lifts in the hospital," he said.

"Then you better get to the point and tell me what's going on," I demanded. "What did Alexander want to talk to you about?"

A slow grin—the kind that made my stomach do somersaults—spread across his face. "Are you curious, boss? I'm not sure if it's against the rules to tell you."

"It's not," I said flatly. "The rules exist to keep us out of trouble and on task." At least, that's what I kept telling myself. The truth was that being stuck in an elevator with him was putting all sorts of ideas in my head. Ideas that were definitely against the rules.

"But I might get in trouble for telling you."

"Fine. I'll just ask Alexander myself." Not that I would

convince him to tell me anything. I rarely spoke to him directly. Messages were generally relayed through Clara, but she was in no position to help me right now.

"Go ahead." He reached out and brushed a strand of hair out of my eyes. "Or you could try asking me nicely."

"Seriously." I planted a hand on my hips, edging away so he couldn't touch me. But I only shuffled a few inches. "Will you please tell me what's going on?"

"You don't sound like you mean that *please*." He crossed his arms across his broad chest, and instantly, a memory of running my fingers down the hard muscles I knew lay beneath his shirt flashed to mind.

I forced myself to get focused. "You want me to beg?"

"I wouldn't dare ask that," he said, taking another step toward me. I tried to back away, only to be met with the lift's metal wall. "Unless it involves you on your knees, boss."

I gasped, doing my best to scrounge up an appropriate level of disgust at what he was suggesting. The trouble was that his words sent my imagination into overdrive, and my soaked knickers proved it. I couldn't be offended because all I could think about was doing exactly what he was suggesting. Did he know that? Judging from the smirk he wore, he did.

"You look scandalized," he murmured, leaning down so that his face was well within kissing range. I caught my breath as he studied my face for a minute. "Would it help if I got on my knees first?"

Oh my...

I shook my head feebly. "We can't. The rules..."

"Fuck the rules," he growled. "Except rule number 5. I like that rule."

"Do you know what will happen if we get caught? You won't be able to sneeze without being on a tabloid," I told him, but Anders's hands found my waist. My eyes closed as he kneaded my hips through the fabric of my dress.

"Then we don't get caught. Easy," he whispered, bringing his lips to my neck. He kissed it softly, and I felt goosebumps ripple across my skin. "Why don't you let me take this off so that I can enact rule number 5?"

"Let me be clear there is no way I'm letting you get me naked in this lift, just so we can shag," I said as firmly as I could between gasps of pleasure.

Anders continued to explore my neck. "I can work with that. Since you're always changing the rules, maybe we need to make number 5 simpler," he murmured into my ear. A second later, his hands slipped entirely under my skirt. His palms slid over my ass, coming to rest on the waistband of my thong. And then, without warning, he snapped the elastic and yanked the ruined underwear off me. "How about I'm in charge when this is naked?"

His palm moved to cover my sex, and I moaned. "Not fair."

"I can be fair." He reached for his trousers and undid the buckle. "Is this what you want?"

"Yes," I said, completely giving in to the moment. Any minute now, some maintenance guy was probably going to check to see why our lift had stopped. I didn't care.

"Ask for it," he muttered as he unzipped his fly. "Beg for it, boss."

"Please give it to me," I whispered, staring into his blue

eyes. A moment later, I felt his thick crown brushing against my seam.

"This?" he asked, guiding it slowly up and down my wet entrance.

"Yes," I bit my lip. My muscles tensed, waiting for him to push inside me. When he didn't, my whole body began to tremble from the effort.

"You want my cock?" His words pressed as his body did the same.

"Yes," I snapped.

"Careful, boss," he said with a low chuckle that sent tiny ripples of electricity pulsing through me. "I'm in charge right now, and I want to hear you say it. Tell me what it is that you want. I want to hear that pretty, posh mouth of yours begging me to give you your every filthy fantasy."

I swallowed. Wetting my lips, my mouth had gone suddenly dry, I looked defiantly up at him. "Please give me your cock."

"I want to," he said, dropping his forehead against mine, "but I didn't bring anything with me." Despite that revelation, he pushed its tip past my seam and began to rub it against my swollen clit.

"I'm on birth control," I said without really thinking. I wasn't sure I could think if he was going to keep doing that.

"Are you sure?" Anders asked slowly as if he was deciding his own answer to the question.

I already knew that he was a lost cause. There was nothing short of me telling him to stop that would put an end to this. The trouble was that I was beginning to suspect I'd lost my inhibitions along with my knickers. "Please," I repeated in a breathy voice. "Please give me your cock."

"Fuck," he said, hooking an arm around my waist. "How can I say no when you ask me like that?"

One hand slipped back down under the curve of my buttock and hitched me just enough to brace me against the wall. With the other, he guided himself down and positioned himself at my entrance. I whimpered as he nudged inside me.

"I love the little noises you make when I'm about to fuck you," he said in a raspy voice. He pushed in an inch. "Holy shit. You feel fucking amazing."

He was taking his time, but I was on the edge. Not only could we get caught at any moment, but I could also no longer conceive of stopping. I didn't care what happened. I just wanted him to fuck me. He might be in charge when my knickers were off, but I could still give him some encouragement. "Fuck me, Your Highness. Please."

Anders groaned and shoved inside me so hard and fast that he lifted me another few inches off the ground. I dug my nails into his shoulders as he thrust inside me. He was right. It felt good. Too good. I'd never let a man go bare inside me, and now that I knew what I was missing, I wasn't sure how I'd ever go back. Everything felt different. Raw and primal and blistering hot.

Moans burst out of me with every thrust until they were coming so hard and fast that filthier requests replaced them. "Don't stop fucking me," I begged. "Fill me up. I want to feel you come inside me."

Anders matched my frenzied pleading by plunging deeper and faster inside me until my limbs tightened. He groaned as my orgasm shattered through me, and my channel spasmed around him. "I love how you come on my cock, boss," he muttered, not stopping. "I love filling you up."

Another smaller orgasm rocked through me as I felt heat spill inside me. A moment later, we collapsed against each other, still joined together. I wrapped my arms around his neck, clinging to him, sweaty and spent.

"I'm going to put you down now," he said gently after seconds stretched into minutes. "Careful."

He placed me on my feet, and I felt a gush of liquid against my thigh.

I looked around the lift for the remaining scraps of my underwear. Anders swiped them off the floor and handed them to me with a grin. They were beyond saving.

"Sorry."

"You don't look like you mean that," I said dryly. "I need to find the loo or it's going to be pretty obvious what just happened."

He reached up and tucked my hair into place. "You look fine."

"Anders." I sighed, a little embarrassed to point out the real problem. "I sorta have...down my leg."

"What?" He looked puzzled, and then his mouth formed an o-shape. "Really?"

Before I could stop him, he lifted my skirt to check.

I covered my face with my hands, wishing I could turn invisible.

"That is so fucking hot," he said in a rough voice that scraped across my already sensitive nerves and sent butterflies dancing in my stomach.

I peeked out at him from between my fingers. "I'm glad you think so, but I'm the one who has to get to a bathroom without dripping all over the floor."

"We can't have that," he agreed. "It would be dangerous. Someone could slip and fall. Thank god we're in a hospital."

"Anders!" I smacked him on the shoulder.

But he just grinned and lowered onto one knee. "Let me see what I can do."

My core clenched as he took the scrap of lace I'd once called knickers and drew it gently up my thigh. There was something insanely sexy about the purpose on his face.

"That's better, but you're so wet." He shook his head. Tipping his face up, he smiled wickedly at me. "No knickers means I'm still in charge, right?"

"I'm not sure if I agreed to that rule," I said slowly.

But Anders chuckled. He drew the lacy scrap across my swollen sex. "This doesn't count as having knickers on, by the way."

Before I could ask him what he meant, he shoved the fabric between my folds, nearly sending me over the edge. I braced myself against the wall. "What?"

"Trust me," he ordered. Slowly he worked them deeper until they were half wedged inside my sore entrance. It shouldn't be erotic, and yet, I felt completely wanton as he stood and surveyed me with a smirk. I shifted a little, and my eyes widened.

"Can you keep those right there, boss?" he asked, lifting my chin with his index finger.

"It feels funny." I moved again, and my eyes rolled a little.

"It looks like it feels good," he said softly.

"It does, a little," I admitted.

"Good. You're going to stay like this. No arguments," he said when I opened my mouth to protest. "No knickers means rule number 5 is still in play, right?"

I whimpered, unable to resist nodding.

"And every time you feel that lace, every time you take a step or sit down or try to arrange your legs to hide it, I want you to remember why it's there." His eyes smoldered into mine. "Can you do that for me?"

"Yes," I breathed.

"Good." He kissed me softly. "Every time you remember what we did, I want you to remember that you just broke your rules." My eyes narrowed, but he wasn't done rubbing in his victory. "And I want you to remember that you begged me to break them."

CHAPTER NINETEEN

ANDERS

"This is a bad idea," I muttered, a couple of hours later as we waited in the hall for our turn to see Clara. The flowers I'd bought earlier were beginning to wilt.

Lola chewed on her lower lip, shifting nervously on her feet. I'd never seen her so rattled. Fuck, I hadn't even known her long enough to think things like that, but somehow, I felt like I did.

"Hey, everything is fine," I reminded her. It turned out that my brother wasn't just being a massive prick. He had a damn good reason for how he'd acted overnight. The baby was premature and had needed a life-saving surgery.

"I know what Alexander said, but it feels off to me." She sighed.

"It was a long night," I said quietly. We'd taken turns doing coffee runs. Every once in a while, we'd found an excuse that suited Madeline Bishop enough to sneak off and fuck somewhere. It seemed both Lola and I needed a little life-affirming activity during the grim waiting period. But now, I was more than willing to let my anxiety go. Lola wasn't.

After a few more minutes, she groaned. "My mother forgot about us," she announced. Before I could stop her, she opened the door and peeked through it. "Can we join you?"

I didn't hear an answer, but a moment later, Lola was walking inside. I followed cautiously behind her.

"Give her the flowers," Lola ordered.

I locked my jaw, doing my best not to call her bossy in front of her whole family. Although, they probably already knew. I wondered if they knew how hot and cold she could be. Like right now, she was as cold as ice, even though half an hour ago, she'd been molten as she rode my cock in an abandoned room.

"I know how to bring a woman flowers," I growled.

"Thanks." Alexander intercepted them before I could get closer to his wife.

"Can we see the baby?" Madeline asked.

"Only from an observation window."

Madeline looked miffed, but to my surprise she didn't argue.

"That's fine." She took her husband's arm and started toward the door. "Lola?"

Lola looked to her sister than to me, a battle waging on her face.

"I should..." Alexander started, equally stressed.

"Anders will be here," Clara said to my surprise.

But what shocked me was Alexander's silent nod of

approval. Since when did he trust me with his wife? Or maybe he knew that there was no way I was going to try anything less than twenty-four hours after her giving birth.

Or maybe he'd figured out what was going on with me and Lola.

"Georgia's in the hall," Alexander said. He gestured for Clara's family to follow him, lecturing them about his expectations. Maybe he wasn't just a controlling prick where I was concerned.

Maybe he was a controlling prick.

Too bad Clara didn't seem like the type that might submit, because releasing some of that dominant streak might do Alexander a lot of good.

"How are you?" I asked tentatively, picking up the flowers Alexander had left on a chair and taking them to her bedside table.

"I don't want to talk about it," she said in a small voice. "How are you?"

"You really want to know?" I frowned, my frustrations getting the better of me. "Your sister is driving me nuts!"

Clara's eyes widened, and I realized she was holding back laughter.

"She's thrown out half my clothes, insists on taking me to fancy dinners to practice my etiquette"—I held up a pinky—"and she keeps talking about a plant-based diet. I don't mind some veg with my rashers, but I'm not about to become a bloody vegan..."

By the time Alexander returned, I'd managed to make her smile.

"Clara needs to feed the baby, and well, obviously..." He pointed toward the door.

Magically, no one argued. Instead, Madeline rushed over to plant a kiss on her daughter's forehead.

"We'll visit tomorrow," she promised.

I looked expectantly at Lola. She had to be fucking exhausted. We'd been up all night, fucking and worrying. But she studiously avoided my eyes.

"Your room is ready," her mother told her as we stepped into the lounge.

I raised an eyebrow. My bossy handler still lived with her parents despite her trust fund. That surprised me.

Lola sighed and looked at me. "I need to go to bed."

I didn't dare tell her what I was thinking—that she didn't need to go to her bed. She needed to go to mine.

"Can I talk to you for a second?" I asked.

She glanced at her mother, who rolled her eyes but shooed us away. "Quickly. Your father is bringing the car around."

When we were alone, I dragged her into a dark hospital room. "Why don't you come with me, boss? I might get into trouble in London by myself."

"Anders." She swallowed, and my mouth tracked the movement of her throat. "I can't. If I leave with you, my mother will know."

"Just tell them you have to tuck me in," I coaxed, wrapping an arm around her waist.

"You don't get it, do you?" she said. "I. Am. Exhausted."

"Then we'll sleep," I suggested.

There was a moment of hesitation, and I knew I wasn't going to like what she said next. "I need to think."

I went still. "About what?"

"Last night was..." She didn't need to finish that sentence. Every adjective ever created applied to last night. "But there was a reason I made rules."

"Rules are meant to be broken," I said.

But she shook her head. "What happens if you break the rules on the track?"

"Disqualification."

"Or worse, right? You've crashed before. You know what can happen if you break the rules."

"I didn't break any rules when I crashed," I said tightly.

"That's not the point."

"What is the point?" I asked, letting her go.

"What we're doing is dangerous. I have to think clearly. It's my job to think clearly." She twisted her hands together, looking at me like she expected me to understand.

But I didn't. I wasn't built like her. "Your control isn't going to keep you safe, boss."

"And being reckless will?" she challenged.

"You know what." I pointed a finger at her as I backed away. "Go run home and hide, but every time you feel that soreness between your legs, every time you soak yourself thinking about me, remember this moment."

I was nearly to the door when she spoke. "The moment where you were a total asshole?"

"The moment where you quit before you started the race." I left her there without another look.

. . .

It wasn't a flat or a house or an apartment. It was a bloody castle. Somehow on the ride from the hospital to Kensington Palace, I'd convinced myself it wouldn't be too bad. It wasn't as if my brother had asked me to shack up at Buckingham. It wasn't that bad, at least.

But it was close.

I shifted away from the window as Brexton Miles—my new bodyguard or whatever the hell he was—drove us past the gates and into the private parking reserved for royals who lived inside. Since the Palace itself sat on the edge of a large green spot open to Londoners and tourists, more than a few people were milling near the fence, hoping to catch a glimpse of royal life. I was not about to let them catch one of me.

"Relax, those windows are tinted," Brex said as he pulled into a spot and turned off the engine. "Once we're to the gate, no one can really see the passenger, and no one starts paying attention until a car pulls up to the gate. But if you want to keep a low profile, you can ride in the back. I won't mind."

"I would." I wasn't certain what would be worse. Someone catching Brex delivering me to the palace, or being so snobby I sat in the back while he drove me. "I'm not sure why Alexander thinks I need security."

"He has his reasons," Brex said smoothly. Apparently, he was as uninclined to share as my brother. "Don't worry. No one can see you now."

I got out of the Range Rover and surveyed this side of the building. From this angle, it didn't look as foreboding. I could almost pretend it wasn't a palace. Grabbing the overnight bag I was suddenly glad I'd packed, I asked, "So, who lives here?"

"Edward just moved out," he told me. "Henry was here for a while, and Alexander kept an apartment here before he met Clara."

"So basically no one?" I said flatly.

"There's some staff. A few more guards. But in terms of the family, you've got the place to yourself." He grinned at me. "Except for me. I'll be upstairs."

"Well, hello, roomie." I stared glumly at the brick walls as he led me into the private entrance. "It's not quite as grand as I expected."

"What did you expect?"

"I don't know, dragons or moats or some shit."

Brex laughed. "We keep the dragons at Buckingham. It's the only way to keep poor boy in line."

"Why do you call him that?" I asked, curiosity getting the best of me.

Brex started up the stairs, and I followed. "He walked into our unit, and I shouted something about who was getting stuck with poor boy."

"Let me guess..." I couldn't help laughing along with him.

"Yeah, it was me. But poor boy had a bit of a death wish, so he saved my ass a few times."

"Really?" I frowned. It was hard to imagine Alexander doing anything that didn't benefit himself.

"Look." Brex stopped in front of a door marked with a golden number four. "He's not as bad as you think he is. He's just a man."

"A man who gets off ordering everyone around," I grumbled.

"Would it help if I told you he was doing that with the best of intentions?"

I raised an eyebrow. "I doubt it."

"You sound like Clara."

"She puts up with it," I said sourly.

"Nobody challenges Alexander more than Clara," he corrected me. "And thank God for that. He'd have gotten himself killed, or burned the whole country to the ground by now if it weren't for her."

"I guess I don't know him."

"You don't," he said firmly but not unkindly. "But maybe you should try."

"I suspect he isn't very interested in getting to know me."

"A piece of advice?" Brex said as he unlocked the door and opened it for me. "Don't assume anything where he's concerned. He's got you here because he cares about you."

Now I knew that wasn't true, but I kept the thought to myself. Alexander only cared about the scandal that followed the public revelation of my paternity. I was just collateral damage he needed to find a place to store. I stepped inside the apartment and whistled.

At least it was a very nice storage box. The apartment itself looked like you'd expect a royal residence to look, complete with silk curtains and expensive furniture. However, a massive television sat in the living room, so that was a modern perk. I continued to explore. Opening one door, I found a large bathroom with a tub big enough for two, and a walk-in shower I could fit a car inside. A dozen ways I could get Lola naked and wet flashed to mind—if she didn't overthink everything and keep her distance. I imagined she'd try for a while, especially after I'd persuaded her to break them in the lift and then again and again in other rooms and alcoves. I could almost hear her breathy gasps as she begged me to fuck her.

Maybe it wouldn't be that hard after all.

My dick, on the other hand, was another story. I adjusted it as inconspicuously as possible as I moved to the attached bedroom. The king-size bed's four-poster frame just gave me more ideas.

I was going to need to smooth things over with Lola as quickly as possible. If I was going to be stuck here behind security gates in a freaking palace, I might as well enjoy myself.

I turned and found Brex standing in the doorway. "Anything else I can show you?"

"Food?"

He beckoned me to follow him. Brex led me into a gourmet kitchen that was compact but had all the necessary equipment.

"You cook?" he asked.

"Not really," I admitted.

"I'll make sure they keep you stocked up. You can order out, but it's best to go through me. I can grab you whatever."

"Thanks." I already knew I wouldn't be taking him up on that offer. There was no way I was going to treat a grown man as my errand boy. No matter how nice he was. "They can just drop me some cereal."

"They'll bring your meals," he said. "There's always too much food around here anyway."

I put my palm on the kitchen island's granite counter and

immediately imagined spreading Lola across it. It turned out there weren't many places I didn't want to screw Lola Bishop. Right now, the only one I could think of was the toilet. But I could probably be convinced to give it a go.

"What about guests?" I asked, trying to sound casual.

"How many?" he asked suspiciously. When he saw my face, he explained. "Sarah had a party a few weeks ago at Buckingham. It didn't go over so well."

"I don't really know anyone around here, but I imagine Miss Bishop will want to practice my tea parties," I said.

Brex surveyed me, his eyes twinkling like he knew that 'tea parties' was code for wild, hate-fueled sex. Maybe we hadn't made it out of the lift without attracting anyone's attention.

"I'll put her on the list."

"Better get her a key or whatever, too." I shrugged. "I learned the hard way she'll find a way to let herself in."

"That sounds like a story."

I smirked. "It is."

But I didn't offer to tell it. Brex seemed like a cool guy, but he was Alexander's man, not mine. I already had Lola reporting my every move—well, maybe not my *every* move—to Clara. I didn't need any more spies.

Still, Brex might be useful. "Do you know what Alexander wants to talk to me about?"

"Nope."

"Could you guess?"

"I could."

But he didn't.

I supposed we'd both be keeping each other at arm's length.

That was for the best. I could stay here. I could eat their food and fuck in their bed. But I wasn't about to let anyone, including myself, believe I was one of them.

"Let me know if you need anything or want to leave the premises," he told me as he headed toward the door.

"I don't really need a babysitter."

"I am a very cool babysitter," he assured me as he stepped out. He smirked at me. "I won't interrupt any tea parties."

Yeah, he knew exactly what was going on with Lola and me. "I'd appreciate keeping the tea parties on the down low."

"Yes, Sir." He nodded at me. "Good night."

I shut the door behind him, not even bothering to lock it. Dragons or not, no one was getting inside this place. Now that I had a home base in London, I just needed to figure out how to get Lola inside it.

But plotting would have to wait. I didn't bother to undress. I threw myself on the bed and drifted off to thoughts of exactly what I was going to do the next time I had Lola alone.

I woke up in the early evening in a wrinkled suit, starving. Padding into the kitchen, I opened the fridge and found several plates of food wrapped up and waiting. Apparently, the staff here were very discreet, or I was sleeping like the dead. Given the last twenty-four hours, it was probably the latter. I peeled off the wrap from some kind of chicken dish and smiled. It wasn't exactly what I wanted to be eating, but it would do. I found a fork and dug in without bothering to heat it up. I was just finishing my cold dinner when I heard my phone alert. Pulling it out of my pocket, I saw it was from Lola.

Maybe she wasn't as mad as I thought.

> Boss: Are you still sleeping?

> Wide awake.

> Want to grab a drink?

Yeah, she was thirsty.

CHAPTER TWENTY

LOLA

> Your Highness: On my way.

I stared at the message for a second before putting my mobile back on the table. I'd lost my mind, but after the longest night ever, I needed a break from Madeline Bishop. That was how I'd wound up here with two of my university mates. They were how I'd wound up texting Anders. Clearly, I should have slept longer.

"Well?" Lucy asked, taking a sip from her straw. Her eyes glimmered, framed by a thick, black fringe. She shifted on her barstool, crossing her long legs carefully since her micro skirt barely covered her. A few men paused to admire her, but she ignored them. "Is he coming?"

"Yes," I said with a sigh.

"Brilliant." Next to her, Beatrice smiled wickedly. Tonight, she didn't look like a young aristocrat. In her short purple mini-dress, she blended in with the others at the club. Her honey-blonde hair was pulled into a high ponytail, and she watched the crowd with smoky eyes. "I've never shagged a prince."

"Who says you get to shag him?" Lucy asked. "It was my idea. Lola, back me up."

"I'm staying out of this." Inviting Anders was the last thing I wanted to do. It had definitely been their idea. They continued to argue over which one of them had dibs while I nursed a vodka soda and tried to ignore my stomach flipping nervously. The last thing I needed was for Anders to show up and give away the fact that we'd been at each other like rabbits for the last two days.

The trouble was that the last thing I wanted was for him to take an interest in either of my friends. Not that I could tell them what had happened between us. I wriggled in my seat as I remembered the last time I'd seen Anders. My knickers were no longer shoved inside me. I'd slept, showered, ate, but new underwear hadn't erased the dirty pleasure I'd taken from what he'd done. It was strange to be both unbelievably pissed at him and desperate to have his hands on me again. Not that I could let what he'd said slide. If he thought I was just going to drop my boundaries every time he snapped his fingers, I needed to show him that I wasn't that easy. That was made trickier by continually proving I was exactly that easy.

"He is single, right?" Lucy asked.

"What? Yeah," I said quickly.

"Good, I'm done with emotionally unavailable men," Beatrice said seriously.

"Since when?" Lucy giggled.

"Since Holden turned out to be a bigger dick than his brother," she said.

"I tried to tell you he's still hung up on Kerrigan...oh shit," Lucy gasped and grabbed my hand.

I looked up to see what had caught her attention. "What is it?"

"At the bar," she called over the pulse of the music.

I craned my neck to get a glimpse and found myself staring at the worst mistake I had ever made. Chad Hazlitt. While the rest of the world had been obsessing over my sister's wedding details, I had been crying myself to sleep over the black-haired dick at the bar. Two years of on-again and off-again had flipped back on so strongly that I'd known something was up. I'd been mortified to discover he was angling to be my date to Clara's wedding. He was a social climber, a manipulative boyfriend, and a selfish lover. And for some reason, I'd been completely mad for him. Even now, the sight of him squeezed my chest until I thought my heart might shatter.

"Do you want to go?" Beatrice asked, looking concerned.

I shook my head. "I'm over him. Besides, Anderson is on his way."

"Ohhh! Make him pretend to be your boyfriend," Lucy suggested.

"No way!" I wasn't going to put myself in his debt. Things were confusing enough between us already without adding fake relationships. Plus, it went firmly against rule number 6. I couldn't risk being photographed with him.

"Good," Beatrice said, shrugging while Lucy glared at her. "Anders is coming to flirt with me."

Lucy rolled her eyes. "Lola's need to rub her awesomeness in Chad's face is way more important than our need to get laid."

"Maybe for you."

"Why do I need a man to help me prove that?" I asked. "I run a successful business. I have amazing friends."

"And you're smoking hot," Beatrice said, nodding her approval.

"Just keep your options open," Lucy said, which started the debate up again.

I checked my phone while they bickered, hoping that if Chad looked up, he wouldn't notice me. But if he did, I refused to risk him catching me looking at him.

I had a new message. My heart fluttered when I saw Anders' name. That wasn't good. Maybe introducing him to my friends was the right move. The last person I needed to give me butterflies was, well, Chad. But Anders was a close second.

> Where are you? This place is crazy.

I smiled despite my determination to keep this friendly.

> We're at a table near the bar.

> I don't see you.

> I'm in a gold sequined dress.

I perched precariously on the stool, lifting myself as high

as I could to search for him. I spotted his blond mop across the room and waved.

The song changed to something slower. The seductive rhythm drew several groups away from the seating area, clearing a path so that I could see him. He wore dark denim jeans and a tightly fitted white T-shirt that I distinctly remembered throwing in the donation pile. Seeing him in it made me so glad he'd taken it out. As he moved, it strained across his muscular body, and my brain began playing a reel of memories featuring his abs.

"Is he here?" Lucy shrieked.

I caught myself frowning and quickly flipped it over. The point was to occupy Anders with one of my friends, right? I just needed a little breathing room, and I would be able to think clearly again. Because a relationship with Anders was off-the-table, even if the sex was mind-alteringly hot. After another thirty seconds of waving, I gave up.

"He doesn't see me!" I shot off another message, but this time it refused to send. I groaned and slid off the stool. "I'll be right back."

I took a few steps toward Anders, smoothing down my short skirt as I walked. He disappeared behind a group moving to the door. I zig-zagged toward him, clearing a large group just in time for Anders to look up from his mobile's screen. He froze when he saw me, but only for a moment. Then his gaze raked down me, slowly, from the breasts he'd expertly sucked last night to the strappy Louboutins I'd picked out for a night at the clubs. He took his time returning his eyes to their normal position. Under his hungry gaze, I felt exposed, like he'd just slowly stripped me down to nothing but bare skin and high heels. Suddenly, I found myself wishing he had.

He cut across the floor, heading directly toward me. When he reached me, he leaned in, his lips brushing my earlobe. "Please tell me that your pussy is naked under that."

I lingered a split second longer than I should, soaking in the dirty request, but refused to answer him. Let him wonder.

"This is supposed to be girls' night," I told him, stepping away to put some distance between us. "So behave."

"Girls' night?" he repeated, his eyebrow quirked. "Why am I here?"

"They want to meet you." I started to reach for his hand but changed my mind. That would send the wrong message. Instead, I waved for him to follow me.

Lucy and Beatrice shared a devilish look as we approached the table. Lucy opened her mouth, but Beatrice beat her to it.

"You must be Anderson."

"Anders," he corrected her, but he took her offered hand and shook it.

"Lola has told us so much about you," Lucy said. It was possibly the most cliché small talk of all time, but Anders smirked.

"Has she?" he asked meaningfully. He glanced over at me, eyebrow lifted.

I shook my head slightly, hoping neither of my friends read into it. But Beatrice tilted her own and watched us.

"All good things," Lucy said, still completely oblivious.

"That's a shame." He glanced at the table. "Can I buy you all another round?"

My friends nodded enthusiastically, and I muttered, "Sure."

Considering I couldn't keep his hands off me when we weren't drinking, there was no point resisting a little booze.

"I need to go to the bathroom," Beatrice announced. She stood and grabbed my hand. "Come with me."

I didn't have much of a choice since she proceeded to drag me toward the loo. She bypassed the line entirely, catching the door as someone stepped out. Smiling sweetly at the next person waiting, she said, "Sorry. It's an emergency. We'll just be a minute."

The girl started to protest, but Beatrice shut the door and locked it behind us.

"I can't believe you just cut, like, fifty people." Still, I was impressed. It wasn't something I would ever do. I waited for her to use the toilet or the sink, but she just stood and tapped her foot.

"What is it?" I asked slowly.

Beatrice smiled as she delivered my words back to me. "I can't believe you didn't tell us that you're screwing Anderson Stone."

CHAPTER TWENTY-ONE

ANDERS

I stared over my shoulder, waiting for Lola to reappear. The club was packed, which made keeping up with her friend's small talk difficult. We also didn't have a bloody thing in common, which made it even harder.

"So then I transferred from Oxford to the University of London," she yelled over the music. She paused and took a sip of her drink. "Where did you go to uni?"

"Didn't," I called back, trying to remember her name. "I started racing when I turned eighteen."

"Oh." She looked pleased at the idea I was some uneducated barbarian from nowhere. Or, at least, that's what I imagined the attraction was. "I have a confession. I've never driven."

What a surprise. Did city girls ever get behind the wheel? I plastered a smile on my face. "No kidding."

She shook her head. "You could teach me how to drive."

Not bloody likely. Before I had to concoct an excuse, Lola reappeared with her other friend. I couldn't remember her name either, and I wasn't going to sit here all night, trying to think of it. "Hey, what's your name again?"

"Lucy," the girl at the table chirped brightly.

I turned to the friend with Lola, who pursed her lips as if she was insulted.

"Or I can call you baby or some shit?" I offered.

"Tempting," she called back. "But I wouldn't want to cause trouble. I'm Beatrice."

Trouble? I cocked my head about to ask her what she meant when Lola grabbed me.

"Let's dance."

"Oh! I'll come," Lucy said, but Beatrice stopped her.

"No, sweetie, Lola needs to tend to her charge."

Something told me I wasn't going to like this Beatrice. Lola dragged me onto the dance floor just as the music sputtered from a club beat into something slower. I expected Lola to panic and run, but she sighed. "That's better. I can't hear anything in here."

"Then, why did you come?" I asked. My hands found her waist as we swayed.

"You met my mother," she said with a laugh. "I'd do anything to get away from that house."

"I can't believe you live with your parents," I admitted.

"London real estate is expensive." She shrugged.

"I couldn't live with my mum. I love her," I added quickly, "but I need to have my privacy."

"In other words, you need to be able to have women over at all hours?" she guessed.

"You sound jealous, boss." I moved a little closer.

"Don't," she said quickly. "Beatrice already figured out something is going on."

"Ahhh." That explained the comment earlier, but I didn't see what the big deal was. "So?"

"We're trying to be discreet, remember?"

"I think I fucked all the discretion out of you earlier." I grabbed hold of her skirt's fabric and yanked her a little closer. "About my earlier question. Please tell me that your pussy is bare underneath this."

Lola glared into my eyes defiantly, but her throat slid. She could try to deny it all she wanted. We both knew the truth. "This? In case you didn't notice, it barely covers my ass."

"Oh, I noticed," I said darkly. The number was more than tempting. "In fact, I can't stop thinking about how easy it would be to lift it and spank you."

"Spank?" she repeated with wide eyes.

"Did I stutter?"

"I'm not really sure—"

"I am," I cut her off. Leaning closer, I whispered in her ear, "And I promise you're going to enjoy it."

"Anders." She pulled herself out of my arms and placed a hand on my chest. "The rules."

"The rules again?" I rolled my eyes. I'd expected some pushback after this afternoon, but I didn't understand why she was fighting it.

"The rules," she said more forcefully. "They're just as much for you as they are for me. In fact, they're more for you. You're the one who needs to watch your reputation."

"People finding out that I fucked you will only improve my reputation, boss."

She stared at me, mouth open. Somehow I'd managed to shock Lola Bishop into silence. After a second, she stomped back toward the table, but she only got a few steps before she stopped. I caught up with her. "Look, I'll behave myself—"

"Shh!" She lifted a hand. "Shit!"

I followed her gaze to where her friends were sitting. A tall, dark-haired guy had joined them, and they were all talking like old friends.

"Someone you know?" I guessed.

"Unfortunately."

"Want to dance some more?"

She shot a look at me. "I think we've danced enough."

"Fine!" I threw my hands in the air. "I'm getting another drink."

I crossed to the bar and ordered another whiskey. Turning, I watched as Lola made her way to the table. Her old friend stood and awkwardly hugged her. Then he stepped back and looked her up and down appraisingly. White-hot anger shot through me as I watched him study her. Lola shifted uncomfortably, and he said something. Lola's face fell. It only happened for a moment before she regained her composure.

A moment was all it took.

"Raincheck!" I called to the bartender. Striding back across the crowded room, I caught sight of an increasingly agitated Lola through the crowd.

Dark-haired dickhead was talking. I didn't have time for small talk and smaller dicks. "Well, if you'd asked me to go to—"

"Hey, boss," I cut him off, grabbed Lola, and kissed her

roughly on the mouth. She went limp in my arms, completely surrendering. When I drew back, her eyes were bright, and her lips swollen. I glanced over at the dickhead, acting like I'd just seen him. "Oh, sorry, were you saying something?"

"Just...just catching up," he said, making an admirable recovery.

At the table, Beatrice held a hand over her smile, but Lucy looked confused.

"Are you—" she started to ask, but then she yelped. "Ouch!"

"What Lucy was wondering was, are you two leaving?" Beatrice asked me sweetly. She turned toward dickhead. "These two can't keep their hands off each other. It's gross, really."

"It's true." I reached down and squeezed Lola's ass. "This dress doesn't help."

It was like I'd found her mute button. She just kept staring at me like she couldn't process what I'd just done.

"Lola?" I prompted gently. "Do you want to introduce your friend?"

That snapped her out of it. "Actually, this is my ex, Chad."

Chad? Fucking Chad? I forced a smile and reached out to shake his hand.

"Anders."

"Yeah," he said, slowly shaking it. "I know who you are. Wait...you two are..."

"Scandalous, right? But I'd have to be a goddamn fool to let her get away." I looked at him and laughed like I'd slipped up. "Oops. No offense."

"None taken," he said sourly.

Oh, Chad was offended. Chad was very offended.

"Now, as Beatrice was saying." I turned to Lola. "I would like to get you home and discuss the terms of that agreement we were debating."

"Agreement," she said in a daze. Then her eyes flew open. Her tongue darted over her lower lip as she realized what I meant. Maybe she was going to let me spank her after all. "Oh, that. Yeah, we need to run."

"So soon?" Beatrice said innocently.

Chad shuffled his feet, still looking between us like we might be playing a joke on him. "It was good to see you."

Lola lifted her chin and smiled at him. "I'm sure it was."

That's my girl.

I threw an arm around her waist, tucking her against me. "Let's go, boss."

"Lead the way."

I wasn't stupid enough to believe I was getting away with this, but if I was already in trouble, I wanted it to be worth it. Sliding my palm down, I cupped her ass as we walked out the door.

As soon as the night air hit us, Lola sped up until we were around the corner and away from the line of people waiting to get in.

"Anders, do you know how many people saw that?" she demanded. I stepped closer, but she pressed a palm to my chest to stop me.

"I think what you meant to say was 'thank you.'"

"Someone will have seen us." She began to pace, which looked a bit dangerous in the heels she was wearing.

"Yep," I agreed.

"Someone probably got a picture."

"Also true."

"And they're going to sell it for a lot of money."

"Look," I stopped her. Grabbing ahold of her shoulders, I forced her to look me in the eye. "I meant it earlier. Being seen with you is only going to help my reputation."

"Don't you mean fucked by you?"

I tensed my jaw. She had me there. "Yes. No. Anything to do with you only makes me look better."

"And why is that?"

"Because you're pretty much the strongest, smartest, sexiest woman I've ever met," I blurted out, "and I would be fucking honored for people to think you're mine."

And then she did the last thing I expected.

CHAPTER TWENTY-TWO

LOLA

I kissed him.

I wasn't planning to. In fact, I'd been hellbent on putting a stop to whatever was going on between us. But then he'd had to go and say that. If it was a play, I'd fallen hard for it. But it didn't feel insincere. It felt like the most genuine compliment anyone had ever paid me.

So, I kissed him—and kept kissing him.

A sort of growl vibrated in his chest as Anders caught on to what was happening. A second later, he had me against the glass window of a shop. Its lights were off. It must be hours past closing time, but I didn't care. He could have hoisted me up in broad daylight and had me while the shopkeepers watched.

I snaked my arm around his neck, trying to drag him closer. He chuckled, his mouth brushing over mine, unwilling to reduce contact even though we were both breathless.

"What was that for, boss?" he murmured, moving his lips to nibble at my neck.

A wave of delicious shivers rolled across my skin from the foreplay. "You know what it was for."

"This could get complicated," he said softly.

I knew what he meant. Sex wasn't complicated. It was just...sex. Insert A into B until C! Whatever was going on between us wasn't that simple. We both knew it. Anders was giving me an out or maybe buying enough time for one of us to come to our senses. The trouble was that I didn't want to come to my senses. Not one little bit. I wanted to lose control entirely.

"I can handle complicated," I purred, letting my free hand slip to the bulge straining against his jeans.

"Is there anything you can't handle?" he asked in a strained voice as I stroked my palm over his erection.

"No."

Anders narrowed his eyes, studying me for a second. "I'm not sure you're ready for everything I want to do to you."

Fuck.

I practically felt my knickers dampen at the suggestion in his words. So far, he'd displayed an impressive oeuvre of sexual talents. I couldn't imagine how he could top some of them. I was certain I wanted to find out. "Try me."

"Are you sure?" His tone took on a husky, smoky darkness that sent a different kind of thrill racing through me. "You seemed scandalized when I wanted to spank you earlier."

I caught my breath, hanging off his every word, as he began to paint a picture of exactly what he wanted to do to me.

"Because I want to take you home and pull up that shitty

excuse for a dress and bend you over the nearest flat surface. And then, do you know what I'm going to do?"

I bit my lip, not daring to interrupt his plotting.

"I'm going to turn your ass pink with this." He slid his palm over my rear. "And when it's as red as your cheeks are right now, I'm going to fuck you until you beg me to come. But Lola..."

I couldn't breathe. I didn't want to—not until he finished that sentence.

"That's only the beginning of what I'm going to do to you." He lifted my chin with his index finger, propping it up so I was looking him in the eyes. "I'm going to tie you up and fuck you with my mouth until you beg me for my cock."

My tongue darted over my dry lips.

"Is that okay with you, boss?"

"Yes," I whispered.

"Yes?" He lifted an eyebrow.

"Yes, Your Highness."

"That's a good girl." He kissed me. "Are you ready to go home and play by my rules?"

I almost came on the spot. Instead, I nodded.

"Good, because the car is here."

I almost jumped out of my skin when I looked over to see a Range Rover idling at the curb. I recognized that car—or, at least, the fleet it belonged to—and hesitated.

Anders took my hand. "Are you coming?"

I would be soon, if I just went with him. But this was the complicated part. "Where are we going?"

"You'll chicken out if I tell you," he warned me, "and

then you won't get any of the multiple orgasms I'm planning to give you."

I stared a moment longer at the Range Rover. Did it really matter where he took me? We'd just kissed in front of dozens of people. Whatever was happening between us wouldn't stay secret for long. I'd learned that lesson from watching my sister navigate a high-profile romance. And, besides, wherever it was he had in mind would be more private than snogging in the middle of the street.

"Lead the way, Your Highness."

His wicked smile convinced me—or, at least, the parts of me driven by hormones—that I'd made the right decision. We walked hand-in-hand to the SUV. Anders opened a door and stepped to the side. I peeked in, and my stomach clenched when I saw Brex behind the wheel. So much for keeping things quiet. Brex would probably report what happened directly to Alexander, who would tell Clara and then...

I shook my head to clear the paranoid thoughts. He'd already seen us together. There was no point in trying to hide now. I started to climb into the back seat when Anders stepped closer, offering me a hand to ensure I didn't lose my balance. My heart skipped a beat, and I found myself returning his wide smile. Anders shut the door behind me and started to go around the car. He paused to wait for oncoming traffic, and I discovered Brexton's amused eyes watching me in the rearview mirror.

"Good evening, Miss Bishop."

"Hi, Brex," I said, skipping the false formalities. I glanced over my shoulder to find Anders still waiting for a slow-moving cab to pass. "If we could keep this between us..."

"Keep what?" He pretended innocence. "As far as I'm concerned, I picked Anders up from having a drink with friends and took him home."

Home? Something about the way he said it coiled my stomach into more knots. The other door opened before I could ask him where *home* currently was for Anders. Anders slid in next to me and placed a hand on my knee.

"Ready?" Brex asked.

Anders nodded.

There was no point in pretending I wasn't curious. I was already in the car, and now that it was moving, I was unlikely to go anywhere. "So, where are we going, exactly?"

"You didn't tell her," Brex said, his eyes on the road.

Anders' hand crept up my thigh a little. "I wasn't sure she'd come."

"And now?" I prompted.

"I'm not sure you won't jump out of the car."

"It's moving."

"Yes, which makes it even more worrying," he teased.

I glared at him and turned my attention to the streets outside, watching for clues. His fingers darted higher and retreated. We both knew Brex too well to give in to temptation in the backseat, but that didn't mean we were any less tempted. Every inch of my body wanted his hand to move higher to the throbbing center between my thighs.

"Do you two want me to stop anywhere? Grab a bite?" Brex asked. "Some condoms?"

I nearly choked, inhaling a shocked breath at the question.

"We'll be fine," Anders said dryly.

"It's no trouble," Brex added.

I rolled my eyes and decided to ignore them. Outside, it began to drizzle. Misty rain gathered on the windows as a thick fog rolled through the streets. The moody darkness called to me, my mind returning over and over to the ideas Anders had planted in my head. Spanking and ropes and who knew what else. I wasn't exactly a prude, but I'd never done anything like that. I'd never thought about it—until he'd made it sound too delicious to refuse. What would it be like to be restrained and at his mercy? A hard throb at my core told me I wanted to find out. I squeezed my legs together, trapping Anders' wandering hand in the process.

"Something preoccupying you?" he asked, leaning close—too close since we weren't alone.

"Just wondering where we're going," I lied. I felt like we'd been in the car forever. For all I knew, it had only been five minutes. Time seemed to slow to a standstill when satisfaction was at the other end.

"We're here," he told me. There was an edge to his voice that hadn't been present at the club. Looking up, I realized what had him on edge.

Brex pulled to the private entrance of Kensington Palace and rolled down his window to speak to a guard.

No wonder Anders hadn't told me where we were going. There was no way I would have agreed to spend the night with him at one of the Royal residences.

"Don't worry," Anders said as if reading my mind. "None of the family are living here at the moment."

I sighed with relief, but anxiety still prickled through me. "What about..."

"The staff is very discreet," Brex assured me. "And I never saw the two of you." He parked the car but didn't get out. "I assume you don't need to be seen inside."

"I've got it from here," Anders said smoothly. He jumped out of the backseat and made it around the boot of the Range Rover before I'd opened my door. Anders helped me to my feet and held out a hand.

For a moment, I stared at it. There was complicated, and then there was royally complicated.

"Don't be scared," he murmured.

I looked up at him, surprised to see his softer side watching me. I had no idea how many sides Anderson Stone had, but I suspected I hadn't seen them all yet. Placing my hand in his, I took a steadying breath. "I'm not."

The rain picked up in intensity as we walked toward the door. Anderson glanced over, sweeping a disapproving look over me.

"What?" I demanded.

"You're going to break your ankle on wet pavement, and then we'll wind up at the hospital all night."

Before I could remind him we'd found a way to do it at the hospital earlier, he scooped me into his arms and carried me inside.

It turned out Anders could be the picture of a gentleman.

That was, until the door shut behind us.

CHAPTER TWENTY-THREE

ANDERS

I had Lola Bishop alone. It was exactly where I wanted her. Kicking closed the door, I carried her to the small kitchen and placed her gently on the counter. Lola licked her lip expectantly, but I paused. I took a step back to appreciate the sight in front of me. Her too-short skirt bunched at the hips, revealing her bare thighs. They were pressed into a modest line that traveled to the taunt hem of the skirt. Lola crossed her legs at the ankles, drawing attention to her toned calves and the *fuck me* heels she wore. She was pure modesty and raw sensuality mixed in an unholy communion.

"You've got me. Now, what are you going to do to me?" she asked.

"It's not what I'm going to do to you." I chuckled darkly, enjoying the way she shivered at the sound. "It's where I'm going to start. But are you sure you're ready?"

She wriggled on the marble counter, her fingers curling around its edge for balance. After a second, she nodded.

"Good." I chewed on my lower lip, tilting my head to try to get a glimpse up her skirt. "Spread your legs, boss."

Lola hesitated as if she was staring at a charging bull and trying to decide if she should wave red or white. Then she complied. Her skirt popped past her hips into a bunch at her waist as she opened her thighs. A triangle of sheer black mesh covered her pussy—covered in the loosest sense of the term.

"Very nice," I said softly. "Although, I don't know why you bother with knickers at all if they don't cover anything." I stepped closer and ran my palm across the top of her thigh. "Or is it so you don't drip everywhere when you see me?"

Her eyes snapped open, her mouth twisting indignantly. I placed a finger over her lips before she could protest.

"This might as well be naked." I slid my free hand higher and dipped a thumb over the damp fabric. "So, rule number 5 is in effect. Is that a problem?"

Annoyance flashed over her, but she remained silent.

"Good. Because there's nothing wrong with telling me I'm right." I brushed the finger over her lips. "Let me be clear. I want you to be wet when you see me. I want to know that your body wants my cock the second you see me. Do you know why?"

She shook her head.

I leaned in and kissed her earlobe. "Because," I whispered, "I'm hard every second I'm with you." I heard her swallow, which sent thoughts of her mouth in a stream to my dick. I reached down to adjust it. I was beginning to run out of room in my pants. "Feel it."

She released the edge of the counter and ran her palm over the front of my jeans. A low moan spilled from her.

"That's for you," I told her. "Every inch of it, and it's been that hard since I saw you at the club. Now, tell me why you need to wear these."

"Because I'm wet," she whispered shyly.

Fuck. Lola was gorgeous when she was bossing me around. She was a fucking *goddess* when she was vulnerable. My dick twitched under her hand, and she gasped with surprised delight. It was everything I could do to not take her on the spot.

"Why are you wet?" I asked her in a firm tone. She was used to being in charge. That was going to be hard for her to give up. Not that I wouldn't occasionally enjoy letting her take control and ride me. But under her polished, commanding presence, I glimpsed the woman she kept hidden from the world.

It was the woman who pleased her family to feel needed. The woman who made herself indispensable so she wouldn't be left out. The woman underneath the armor she always wore.

That was the woman I wanted to touch—the woman I wanted to free.

This wasn't just about fucking her. I wanted to strip away that heavy armor until it was only her and me. I wanted to dismantle her fortifications piece by piece with my hands.

"Because I want you," she admitted finally.

"No." I shook my head. "You're wet because you know it pleases me. It pleases me to know that you're ready for my cock. Because it means you trust me to give you what you need. Do you trust me?"

She nodded slowly.

"This is important." I took her chin between my fingers and forced her to look me in the eyes. "Do you know why I need control?" She shook her head slightly, not breaking eye contact. "Because I won't settle for stealing a minute of pleasure from you. From the moment I touch you, there is nothing else. No more rules. No more worrying. No more responsibilities, or obligations, or reputations. There is only you and me. I can give you that, but you have to trust me."

"I trust you," she murmured.

"Have you ever used a safe word?" I asked her seriously.

She inhaled sharply. "I don't really know..."

"There are layers to trust and layers to pleasure. I want to peel back every one of your layers, but I need to trust you first."

"What does that have to do with...a safe word?" She blushed a little as she said it.

"I need to trust that you'll always tell me to stop if it's too much. I can't take you the way I want until I know you can do that."

"What if I forget?" She turned her face to brush her cheek against my wrist.

"Let's keep it simple. If you're nervous or want to slow down but not stop, say yellow. If you want to stop immediately, say red. Can you remember that?"

"I think so." She giggled and bit her lip.

"So impertinent," I muttered. I moved away and snapped my fingers. "Take off your clothes."

Lola slid off the counter and leaned down to undo the strap of her shoe.

"Leave those on," I stopped her.

She pressed her lips together as she straightened. There was no resistance to my commands. No hesitation. She wanted the vision I'd dangled in front of her, but was she ready for it?

Lola reached under her arm and unzipped her dress. She wiggled out of it, allowing it to drop to the floor. She kicked it off and paused to preen as I studied her appreciatively. Her nipples beaded in the open air. She hooked her thumbs around her thong and drew it slowly off. Stepping out of it carefully, she tossed it at me.

"More impertinence," I murmured. "Are you trying to push my buttons, boss?"

"Maybe," she admitted, fluttering her eyes at me.

I closed the space between us. Thanks to her heels, she was nearly face-to-face with me. "You don't have to work so hard to get what you want with me," I explained. "It's my privilege to give your body what it needs. Got that?"

Another quiet nod.

She was starting to understand, but it would take time before she submitted immediately. Even now, as she stood nude before me, she wasn't ready. "Now, I'm going to finish undressing you," I told her, grabbing her hip and guiding her around to face the counter. "Bend over."

She folded over, clutching the edge of the counter as she presented her ass to me.

"Put your hands flat on the marble." Grabbing hold of her hips, I gently urged her forward. Her palms slid across the hard surface. Pressing a hand to her shoulder blades, I encouraged her to relax. Her breasts flattened on the marble as she gradually settled into position. I took my time, erasing all but the final strands of her tension. Those were bound to her like a second skin. They would come off together.

I brought my palm to her bare ass, and she drew in a sharp breath. I didn't spank her. Instead, I rubbed circles, preparing her. I continued as I opened the drawer next to us. I closed it when I found silverware. Tension began to creep back into her limbs as I opened the next drawer. But I found what I needed inside it.

Lola turned her head, pressing her cheek against the counter as I placed the wooden spoon next to her. Her eyes widened. "Yellow..."

I snorted as I brushed hair from her face. "Noted, boss. Now, about what you're wearing."

"I'm naked," she said with confusion.

"No, you're not." I trailed a finger down her spine, and she trembled. "But you will be soon. May I undress you now?"

She stared at the spoon for a second before she answered softly. "Yes."

I didn't start with the spoon. I wasn't even sure I would use it this time since it had been an immediate yellow. Showing her was about setting expectations. The sooner she accepted what her body needed, the easier she would accept who she needed to be in the bedroom.

I lifted my hand and brought it down with one hard clap on the lower curve of her rear. Her ass bounced as I smacked it, and she gasped. The imprint of my hand lingered angrily on her fair skin, and I rubbed it out slowly as I waited. She made no other noise. No safe word came. Crossing my arm, I delivered another smack to the opposite side. This time, she flinched a little but made no noise.

"Perfect," I praised her, rubbing out the sting. "More now."

She tensed as I stepped back and positioned myself to deliver a series of spanks. She clung to that tension for the first five. On the sixth, her arms gave, and she slipped lower. By the tenth, her eyes had closed, and her mouth hung open. Her backside glowed red, and my dick twitched as I gently rubbed the heat from her skin. Lola barely moved. Her chest rose and fell so rhythmically that she looked like she might be sleeping.

It was better than I'd imagined. Most women I'd dated enjoyed a little spanking now and again, but usually just for fun. There'd only been a few who seemed game for more. But none of them had relaxed into it as she had. Until this moment, I'd only experienced this at a very private club I'd talked my way into a few years ago. Some of the women there responded like this. Was it too much to hope that I'd finally found a woman I not only wanted to talk to and fuck, but one who filled the empty half of me?

I already knew that Lola Bishop could hold her own with me. She was a spitfire at my side. She fucked like a goddess. She took absolutely no shit. She was nearly everything I'd ever wanted. She nearly completed me.

But as I stared at the angry lines of my palm lingering on her porcelain skin, I couldn't help hoping that I'd found the last piece of me. And maybe she'd found the part of her she didn't realize was missing.

My submissive. Her Dominant.

There was only one way to know. I reached for the spoon.

CHAPTER TWENTY-FOUR

LOLA

There was nothing. I was dimly aware of my stinging skin, of Anders' hands on my backside, of the cool counter I was sprawled across. I'd never felt so free.

Then I felt the slightly rough surface of a spoon glide across my rear.

"Remember your safe words," Anders said, sounding distant.

I didn't bother to reply. I didn't want to. Wherever this man tried to take me, I would go. He continued to draw it across my skin as if giving me a chance to stop him. I didn't move.

A loud thwack splintered my peaceful calm, and I gasped. My fingers shot toward the edge of the counter as the biting burn filtered through my bliss. And then his hand was back, soothing the ragged edge the spoon had left behind.

"Two more," he said, his voice strained and husky. But he didn't lift it again. He waited.

I bit my lower lip and relaxed a bit, if not quite as deeply as I had when he was using his hands.

"Good," he murmured, sounding pleased.

I forced myself to take a deep breath as his careful hands lifted from my ass, knowing what came next. The second strike hit the same spot, and I barely swallowed my gasp, but I didn't move this time. There was no warning for the third, and I turned my face to the counter to cut off a cry.

I didn't want Anders to stop. I didn't want him to question. And I didn't want him to ask permission.

This time, his lips pressed to the tender skin, kissing away the feverish heat from the spanking. I sighed, both pleased and sad that it was over. His mouth continued to move across my skin before dipping between my legs. Strong hands urged my thighs open gently, and then a warm tongue lapped against my swollen sex.

It was absent the fierce hunger he'd shown in the hotel. Instead, it was languid and leisurely. He was savoring it. Between the lingering heat on my skin and his coaxing strokes, I slowly coiled around his touch. But there was no rush, even as my body began to tremble well past the point of climax. There was no crest. No plummet. Just constant, uninterrupted ecstasy. It was something more than pleasure, and there was no end in sight.

Despite the rolling waves of bliss, my breathing grew ragged, punctuated by tiny, involuntary gasps. The longer I came, the more aware I was of the orgasm Anders seemed to be pulling from my very soul, and the more the ache inside me deepened. I could barely stay upright. My knees weakened, but he held me firmly, refusing to stop his exquisite torture.

And out of the darkness, I realized every ounce of my body was centered on him.

But it wasn't enough. It wouldn't be until...

"Anders," I moaned his name. "Please. Please fuck me."

He drew back, cursing under his breath when I nearly toppled over. He swept me into his arms, where I writhed and twisted, convinced that I was about to implode as he carried me out of the kitchen.

A moment later, Anders placed me softly on the bed, and I reached for him, panting harder now.

He reached behind his neck and hooked his T-shirt, drawing it off with one swift motion. I licked my lips as my eyes trailed down his stacked abs and landed on the hand currently unfastening his belt buckle. He yanked it free, the leather cracking the air like a whip. The sound triggered me to moan. I didn't quite understand it, but Anders' wide mouth curved when he heard it.

"You are so fucking perfect," he muttered, pushing his jeans to the ground. His quads flexed as he stepped out of them. Reaching past the waistband of his pants, he stroked himself. "Should I find something?"

My tongue darted over my lower lip as I considered the question. It was oddly respectful, given that he'd just had me folded over a kitchen counter and paddled me with a wooden spoon.

"I know what we've already done—and what you said," he continued softly, "about being on birth control, but if you'd rather avoid the mess..."

My eyes fluttered away from him, my cheeks growing as hot as my rear end had been minutes before. Each second took me further away from the total oblivion I'd experienced in the kitchen, but pleasure still thrummed inside me, begging for one final explosive release.

"Boss?" he prompted. "If you'd rather not—"

"I liked it," I blurted out.

He stilled.

"Feeling you bare inside," I rushed on before I lost my nerve. I couldn't believe I was admitting this to him. "I liked being full of your..."

"I see." A muscle tensed in his jaw. He glanced away, and for a second, I thought he was upset, but when he turned back, his eyes were on fire. "I'm not sure I can control myself, Lola."

I blinked, shaking my dazed head. "I don't want you to."

"I'm trying to tell you," he said, sounding more strained than ever, "that I can't be gentle or loving. Not right now. Not after that. I just want to fuck you like a goddamn animal."

"Oh..." I inhaled sharply and met his burning eyes. "Then fuck me, Anders. Don't hold back."

He froze as if considering for a split second before he was on me. His body crushed against me, and my thighs parted willingly. Anders seized control instantly, reaching between our pinned bodies and shoving his cock inside me. Reaching over our heads, he grabbed hold of the headboard for leverage, and then he delivered exactly what he'd warned he would. His hips bucked, thrusting hard, and I exploded like he'd hit some invisible button. The never-ending orgasm ripped through me, and I screamed his name. Anders drove harder, forcing every last fragment of my climax out. Finally, I hooked my arms around his neck, completely spent.

But he didn't relent. He fucked me so hard that it hurt. His cock knocked against my womb, battering it with ruthless abandon. The agony stretched me open, and I found something new—an unholy union of torment and release. I nearly choked as it gripped my body, and I splintered around the new center of my existence.

Anders smashed his lips to mine as he spilled inside me. The kiss slowed as he settled into his release. Then it deepened into something far more serious than any line we'd crossed tonight. An arm slipped under my back, and he rolled us to our sides, but he didn't pull out. I wrapped my leg around him to allow him to linger inside me. When we finally broke the kiss, he pressed his damp forehead to mine.

"Thank you," he murmured, surprising me.

I snorted softly. "I think I just orgasmed for twenty minutes straight. I should be thanking you."

"Never." He brushed the tip of his nose against mine. "It's just one of the many services I offer."

"Exclusively, I hope."

Anders tensed, and I realized the implication of my words.

I backpedaled as fast as I could. "I'm sorry, I meant—"

"Don't," he cut me off. "Don't take it back."

"I don't want you to feel like..." What didn't I want him to feel like? That I expected exclusivity? I didn't really have the right to demand that after all the rules we'd established.

"I meant what I said earlier." His words were rough around the edges. "I'd be honored if you were mine."

I swallowed, uncertain how to feel about this. There was something between us—something that extended beyond the physical. But whatever it was, was it worth the hell we'd endure in the public eye? "Anders, you don't want my world," I reminded him.

"I don't want *their* world," he corrected me. "But I'm stuck in it anyway."

"So, what does that mean?" I squirmed away, finally disentangling our bodies so that I could look at him. "You might as well fuck me if you're stuck here?"

"That's not what I meant, boss," he said, sighing heavily. "If I thought I could drag you back to my house and keep you there, I would. But I know that's not going to happen."

"I don't know." I couldn't help smiling. "A few more nights like this, and I might be open to the possibility."

He grinned back at me. "Don't tempt me. There is plenty more where that came from."

My thighs squeezed together as a pang shot through my core. "Even more of what happened in the kitchen?"

"Is that what you want, boss?"

"I'm not sure that nickname really fits anymore." I flushed as I admitted the truth. "Not if I'm going to let you do things like..." I didn't have the vocabulary for the place he'd shown me tonight.

"Dominate you?" he offered carefully.

"Um, I guess." It felt stupid to suddenly be so shy, given what had just happened between us.

Anders gazed at me, his eyes piercing straight through me. "I dominated you," he said, the words thick on his tongue, "and you submitted to it."

"Was I supposed to?" I asked, a little shaken by this revelation.

"Fuck, I wanted you to." He leaned closer and kissed me. "But only if you want it, too."

"I do," I confessed. Just admitting it soothed the nerves clawing at me. He was right. I hadn't just allowed him to dominate me. I had submitted. It might all be new to me, but I understood what he meant. "It was like I went somewhere else, but not to get away, if that makes sense."

I chewed on the inside of my cheek as he breathed heavily, not responding.

"Would you let me take you there again?" he finally asked.

"Right now?" I squeaked. Even as I lay in his arms, I felt soreness creeping through my body. Not just from where he'd spanked me but between my legs as well. It felt a little like losing my virginity all over again—but a lot more satisfying. "Wait! I should just say yes, right? That's what I'm supposed to do."

"No," he said quickly. "You're always the one in control. You call the shots. You say the safe words. You set my boundaries."

"So, I really am in charge still?" I teased.

"You're still the boss." He propped himself up on one elbow. "But roll onto your stomach, and let me check your rear."

"I thought I was in charge?"

"Part of my job is to take care of you after..." He forced a thin-lipped smile. "I should have done that before taking you to bed. I owe you an apology,"

"I asked for it," I reminded him. "But you can take care of me now." I wiggled away to give myself enough room to turn onto my stomach.

"Good girl," he murmured as he shifted to inspect me. "Fuck."

I peeked through the hair curtaining my face. "What?"

"I might have left some marks," he admitted, gently touching my skin.

"Like bruises?"

"It looks like they might be." He pulled the hair away from my face and studied me. "I'll show better control next time."

I pressed my lips together, feelings tumbling through me as he stared down at me with earnest eyes. "What if...I don't mind?"

Anders went completely still. When he finally opened his mouth, he had to pause and swallow. "For now, let's see how you feel in a day or two. You might change your mind if it hurts every time you sit down."

"I doubt it," I said absently. My eyes flashed to his when he inhaled sharply.

"A few days," he repeated, "and then we'll see." He turned and swung his legs off the bed.

"Where do you think you're going?" I asked.

"To run you a bath," he said seriously, "and make you something to eat."

"Is that part of taking care of me?"

He nodded.

"Man, I should have found a Dominant years ago."

Anders narrowed his eyes, the muscles in his neck tightening.

"Whoa," I breathed.

He took a deep breath. "Sorry. Just the thought of you..."

"I didn't think you were the jealous type." How did he continue to surprise me?

"Neither did I." He leaned down and kissed my shoulder. "Neither did I, boss."

CHAPTER TWENTY-FIVE

ANDERS

The day was alive with an energy that thrummed through me like a live wire. Lola and I had parted ways hours ago, but even as I settled into my new home, my thoughts kept returning to her. The breathy sound she made on the verge of climax, the way she could go from ice-cold queen to sexy-as-hell spitfire within moments, how it felt when she looked at me with those wide, willing eyes. I had spent all of forty-eight hours in Lola's presence, and one thing was clear: I was in trouble. I thought I was taking a break from racing and distracting myself with a no-strings-attached flirtation. I was wrong. Lola Bishop was not a distraction. She was an obsession.

"You sure about this?" Brex asked me, drawing me from my thoughts.

I shook my head slightly to clear the steam from my brain. "Yeah, I shouldn't have left the car here yesterday. I wasn't thinking."

"That will happen when you're distracted." Brex grinned

over his shoulder, flashing me his pearly whites. "How was the tea party?"

I bit back a laugh at the secret code we'd stumbled upon regarding my forbidden relationship with Lola. "Best tea party I've ever been to." I shifted in my seat, leaning closer to the front seat's center console. "Remind me why I can't sit up there with you. I feel like a dick back here."

"Do you really want to be on every tabloid in the country?" he asked.

He had a point, but still. "Maybe the new baby will be a distraction."

Brex's shoulders tensed, and I knew I'd said the wrong thing.

"Sorry. I shouldn't wish all that fucking attention on anyone." Especially a fucking kid. I was a dick.

"Don't be," he said quickly, his eyes watching me in the rearview mirror. "It's just the way it is."

"Does anyone ever stop to think maybe it shouldn't be?" I mused, sliding back in my seat with a groan.

"Now, you really sound like your brother," Brex teased.

Part of me wanted to ask him more—about Alexander, about the hints he'd been dropping that maybe things weren't so perfect for my royal family members. But Brex was a company man, and I knew he wouldn't tell me, even if he was nice.

"Shit," he said under his breath. "There's even more of them now."

When we'd left the hospital, I'd been astounded by the number of people filling the streets surrounding the hospital. There were press and reporters everywhere, but most of those swarming the streets were simply citizens with banners and signs and flowers. I might have thought it was impossible to fit any more people safely around the hospital, but the crowd apparently didn't. They'd crammed closer together, and there wasn't an end to the onlookers in sight.

"I'm guessing that it's pointless to talk you out of this," Brex said.

"It's a Ferrari," I responded. I didn't need to say more.

"Somehow, that makes it worse." He maneuvered us past the security blockade set up to control the hospital's private entrance. "I guess there's no point in telling you to keep a low profile."

"Low profile and Ferrari don't really go together," I said, tacking on, "but I'll try."

"I'll follow you back to Kensington once you're in your car," he informed me as he pulled into the car park where I'd left my car yesterday.

I blew out a stream of air, hesitating but finally asking, "Do you have to?"

"Do I really have to answer that?"

That was answer enough. Like it or not, it seemed I had a new personal bodyguard. "My own security, a sexy publicist—I can see how this whole royalty thing can go to your head."

"Careful, or you won't fit that head of yours in that car." Brex whistled as he studied the Ferrari, which, thankfully, looked untouched.

I snorted and climbed out of the backseat. Pausing, I gestured for him to roll down his window. "Mind if we go home the long way? I need to stop for something."

"More condoms?" he guessed. Since he was the one who'd driven Lola home, I couldn't exactly lie.

But I wasn't about to tell him that she'd let me go bare, that I'd pumped her full of me, and that I couldn't stop thinking about it. How good she felt with nothing between us. How undeniably we fit together in every way.

"Nah." I swallowed against the lump in my throat. "I just thought maybe I'd get her flowers."

I waited for him to laugh, mock me or rib me like my pit crew might do back at the track. Instead, he nodded solemnly as though he deeply approved of this gesture. "There's a shop in Kensington, around the corner from your place. I can go inside."

But I shook my head. "I need to do this myself," I said in a strained voice.

Now Brex looked torn between his approval and his duty. Finally, he agreed.

Dropping into the Ferrari's low-slung seat was like coming home. I hit the ignition, and it roared to life with what used to be my favorite sound in the world. I still loved its animalistic purr, but it didn't even occupy the top ten spots anymore. All of those were now held by Miss Lola Bishop. It wasn't just the tiny gasps and moans holding those spots. It was the frustrated groan when I made a tasteless joke or the small huff of annoyance when I challenged her. Along with a half dozen other intimate noises she'd made just for me.

I shifted in my seat, suddenly aware that my pants felt very tight.

It was not normal to feel this way about a woman I barely knew.

No, that was bullshit. I knew Lola. I knew little stuff, like how she liked her coffee, and big stuff, like the feelings she masked so carefully from the world. And maybe someday I would know all the rest—if I didn't fuck it up before then.

I steered the Ferrari carefully out of the car park's bumpy entrance, more aware of its low frame than the crowds. But as soon as I was on the street, I realized what Brex meant.

The waiting crowds went from curious to rabid. A few managed to get past the security blockades, rushing toward my car. Some of them had cameras. Clearly paparazzi. But most of them just looked like ordinary people, and they were screaming my name.

There was a time when I would have wanted this. Not because I wanted to be famous, exactly, but because attention like this would mean I'd done it. I'd risen high enough on the circuit to have fans. People who followed me not because of my DNA but because of my driving.

My fingers clenched on the steering wheel. I hated this, and no amount of handling or prep would ever get me used to this.

I glanced in my mirror, slightly relieved to see Brex was right behind me.

I hated that, too. The relief. It meant I wasn't just getting used to this, I was submitting to it. And there wasn't a submissive bone in my body.

When we finally rounded the street, driving far enough away that the crowds grew sparser before petering out altogether, my phone rang. I glanced at the dash and smiled.

I accepted the call. "Hey, Mum."

"Where are you at? You sound like you're driving," she said warily. "You aren't on the track, right?"

I resisted the urge to roll my eyes because, somehow, I was sure she would know if I did. "No, I'm in London."

"I wondered..."

I waited for her to continue, but when she didn't, I frowned. "What does that mean?"

"There are just some stories in the press."

"Do you mean the tabloids?" I asked. "Because you can't believe their bullshit."

"They're just reporting that you went to the hospital with Clara's family." She paused, and I knew she was waiting for me to confirm or deny.

"I did." There was no point in lying to her. Plus, I never lied to my mum. Once again, she'd know. "They sent Lola Bishop to, uh, give me a makeover."

"A makeover?" She sounded strained, and for a second, I thought she was shocked, then I heard her muffled laughter.

"It's not funny. She tried to throw out half my clothes."

"Remind me to send her a thank you note," Mum teased. "But a makeover doesn't explain why you're in London if she was sent to you, or..."

"Or?" I prompted.

"Or why there's a picture of you two kissing in a club last night on TMI."

"Fuck." It had been dark in there. I don't know how anyone got a good shot of us.

"Anders," she said disapprovingly.

"Sorry, Mum, but sometimes fuck is the only response. I mean, how clear is this picture?"

"They're pretty sure it's you," she said flatly, "and I'm your mother. *I* know it is. So, it seems like Lola is doing a little more than giving you a makeover."

I wasn't about to tell her how much more, especially since Lola was probably having an aneurysm right now. "Can we talk about this later?"

"Only if you promise to bring her home to meet me."

"It's not really like that," I hedged.

"You've met her family, right?"

"Yeah, but—"

"Then it's settled. I'll make you both dinner when you're back in town."

There was no point in arguing with her. She would just wear me down with guilt until I agreed. "Fine. Look, I need to go. There's traffic."

"Drive safely," she said, switching on her worried voice, "and don't take phone calls in the car! I love you."

There was no point in reminding her that she had known I was driving this whole time. "Love you, Mum."

As soon as I hung up, the reality of her news hit me, and I found the car slowing. A blast on the horn from another driver shook me free from the daze.

I'd known from the first time I kissed Lola that this was inevitable, but I'd fooled myself into thinking we would have more time before the shit hit the fan. Ignoring my mother's demand, I dialed the newest number on my phone.

It rang once before Brex answered. "Everything okay?"

"Change of plans," I told him. "Do you know where Lola Bishop lives?"

There was a pause before he answered with a heavy "yes."

"We need to go there right now." I waited for him to ask why.

Instead, he sighed over the car's speakers, sounding exhausted when he said, "Follow me."

CHAPTER TWENTY-SIX

LOLA

"What were you thinking?"

The lecture had been going on since I'd walked through the door. There'd been no point in denying I was involved with Anders when she had photographic evidence. Plus, I'd been caught doing the walk of shame. I'd barely convinced her to let me change. As it was, she'd followed me to my room and yelled at me through my entire shower.

"I can handle this," I told her.

My mother paused her pacing to sigh deeply, her favorite guilt trip. "The last time one of my children told me that I was attending a royal wedding a few months later."

"What a burden," I said flatly. "It's like you don't even remember how thrilled you were when they got married." I remembered. I'd been dragged hat shopping for weeks.

"It's not the same."

Of course, it wasn't. It never was when it came to Clara

and me. "What's the problem? He's not a prince? Or is it that he's not in line to the throne?"

She stopped muttering under her breath and lifted horrified eyes to mine. "Is that what you think?"

"I don't know what to think," I admitted. "Believe me, this thing with Anders caught me off-guard, too."

So much for being discreet. Despite all my rules and caution, it had taken days before we got caught.

"So, there is something between you two," she whispered.

I dropped my head back, letting the sofa cushions cradle it, and tried to decide how to answer. Twenty-four hours ago, I would have denied it. Now? "I don't know. Maybe."

I waited for her to dig. That's what Madeline Bishop was good at, slowly wriggling deeper and deeper until you confessed everything just to get her to stop. Instead, she sank into a linen wingback across from mine. Silence stretched through the sitting room.

Usually, I felt safe coming home. It was home, after all. I'd never fancied the idea of living alone in a flat. I much preferred the comforts of my parents' townhome in Kensington.

"I wish Clara hadn't married Alexander," she finally whispered.

She might as well have dropped a bomb. I jumped to my feet. "What are you talking about?"

I couldn't believe this was coming out of her mouth. My parents were wealthy. My father had made a fortune selling one of the first internet dating websites. But even with millions of pounds at their disposal, neither was happy. Dad was always chasing his next big idea, while my mother sought validation for her new station in life. My sister marrying Alexander had given her that.

At least, I'd thought it had.

"She's never safe," she murmured, her eyes distant. "My grandchildren are never safe. They can't have normal lives. They belong to the people of this country. I know that. I don't want that for you, too. I know how hard you've worked to make something of your own."

I couldn't think of a damn thing to say. She'd never shown much ability to think beyond herself, and yet, here she was, saying the exact thing I'd been thinking.

I didn't want that for myself, either. There was a time when I'd thought I might, but I'd watched Clara struggle with her role. My sister was the sweet one, and her strength lay in her composure and quiet resolve. Those weren't traits I was blessed with. I could handle things. I could spin things. But I had worked hard to build a career and make a name for myself that felt like it belonged to me.

"I don't know what happened," I confessed to Mom. "He's infuriating. He doesn't listen to a thing I say. He doesn't care what anyone thinks about him. He is the last guy I should be with."

But just saying that made my chest ache. It was all true. I believed every word, but none of it stopped me from wanting him.

My mother laughed quietly, her lips curving into a knowing smile. "It's worse than I thought."

"No." I shook my head. "It isn't. I just needed to get him out of my system."

"Some men don't ever get out of your system," she told me. There was a twinge of sadness in her words.

I hoped she was talking about my father, but I didn't dare to ask. I wasn't sure I could handle it if I found out she wasn't. Not after years of watching him patiently put up with her mood swings.

"It's not like that," I lied.

My mother pulled a face and waved her hand like it didn't matter. "No, you're right. It's too soon to know. I just want you to be careful."

That's exactly what I needed to be, and I'd known it the entire time. There was only one way to be sure it happened, though. "I'm ending it with him."

"Really?" Her lips twitched.

"Is that so hard to believe?" I shrugged. Clara could find someone else to whip her bastard brother-in-law into shape. "I barely know him."

"That's a relief." Now she was full-on smiling, but it was oddly smug and self-satisfied. "Because I was worried you were falling in love with him."

"In love?" I sputtered. Maybe the last few years had warped her brain entirely. "I don't know him, remember? I can't be in love with him."

"I suppose you don't believe in love at first sight. That doesn't surprise me. You're so like your father."

"Of course I don't. Do you?"

Love at first sight? That shit belonged in fairytales. It didn't happen in the real world, and there was no way I'd fallen for Anders at first sight. He'd been a sweaty, cocky, swaggering jackass. Not some knight in shining armor. Not someone I could ever fall in love with.

Who cared if my heart raced faster than his stupid car when he looked at me? It meant nothing that even now, part of me ached for him to walk through that door and kiss me. The same part that hoped he would take me upstairs and do far dirtier things to me in the dark. That was my real problem.

"It was lust," I announced. "Lust at first sight. He's hot."

"He is very attractive." She nodded.

"But even if there was something more," I said, choosing my words carefully, "we have completely different lives. He races cars and lives in the middle of nowhere. I've got Bless and London and friends. We lead completely separate lives."

Except for when he was moving inside me. Then we were connected in a way I'd never experienced before. But that was just sex. Great sex. Mind-blowing sex. The kind of sex that makes you think crazy things like you want to fall asleep in his arms or go dancing with him.

Thankfully, as soon as I got enough distance, my head usually cleared up.

"I guess it's not a problem," she said. "I suppose I worried for no reason."

"Not a problem at all. The story will blow over, and everything will go back to normal."

My mother nodded, this time looking genuinely relieved. "Good."

"Good," I repeated, but the word sounded hollow to me. It didn't feel good. It felt wrong.

Before I could process why that was, the front bell rang. I turned toward the sound.

"Let someone else get it." She waved it off.

But it was probably reporters. There was no way any tabloid was letting this story die for a while. Why would they? The king's illegitimate brother and the Queen's sister? It was like printing pound notes. My mother knew that, and I loved that she wanted to protect me. But I wasn't about to live my life in hiding. "I'll take care of it."

"Are you sure?" she said carefully.

"I got this." I truly believed I did as I walked through the foyer. I'd handled attention since Clara's relationship with Alexander went public. When the media realized nothing was happening with Anders, they would lose interest eventually. It was just a matter of time.

I braced myself as I opened the door. But there were no camera flashes or screaming paparazzi. I was totally unprepared to find Anders on the doorstep in a black T-shirt and jeans, which made me seriously rethink my plan to make him wear more suits. He grinned, drawing attention to the stubble I'd felt between my legs this morning.

I clenched my thighs and tried to act unruffled by his sudden presence. Secretly I was glad he couldn't feel my heart speed up, that he didn't know about the hungry tick at my core.

I shook my head, but I still felt dizzy. I poked my head out the door, looking around the street for signs of reporters. There was only his Ferrari, and a black Range Rover parked on the street. I waved half-heartedly, knowing Brex was inside. But the lack of other cars didn't mean we had privacy.

"What are you doing here?" I grabbed his arm and yanked him inside. I whirled around to remind him that we had rules, but before I could, he kicked the door shut and slammed me against it.

The kiss drove every rational argument I was about to make out of my head. I melted into it.

He groaned against my lips. "I'm here to tell you that we can stop hiding from now on."

He'd seen the report and drawn a very different conclusion than I had.

"We can't." I shook my head, even as I wound my hand into his hair and pulled him closer. "We have to stop."

"No one tells us what we have to do," he growled, his mouth cruising along my jaw. "No one tells us to stop, so unless you want me to stop, boss, I don't give a shit what anyone says."

His hands moved over me, skimmed my hips, and drifted to my waist. I felt the heat of his palms searing through my clothes. I wanted to touch him, too. I wanted to feel his skin. I wanted to press my lips against his hard chest and run my fingers over the dips and planes of his abdomen. More than anything, I wanted to taste him.

But the fastest way out of this was to be firm. "I would savor this moment because it is the last time you'll touch me."

"What are you talking about?" He pulled away, wary eyes studying me.

"We got caught," I reminded him. "You didn't want media attention. Well, this won't be reporters showing up at the track. This will be a circus. We have to end things."

"End things?" he echoed, his gaze zeroing in on me. "Is that what you want?"

My mouth went dry.

"Just say the word, boss," he pressed, fingers hooking under my waistband and drawing me close enough that I smelled the mint toothpaste on his breath. "Is that what you want?"

I nodded, even as I said, "No."

CHAPTER TWENTY-SEVEN

ANDERS

"I could get used to this." I paused in the doorframe and watched as Lola applied makeup in the mirror.

Her lips lifted in a smile, but she didn't turn toward me. "I thought you hated it here."

"It's growing on me."

This time she froze and slowly swiveled in my direction. "It is?"

London. Her. Yeah, I could handle that. Dealing with a media circus and living in a palace with a bodyguard? Not so much. Brex was an okay guy. He'd managed to get us from Lola's house back to my apartment at Kensington Palace without anyone snapping a single photo. Thanks to him, the paparazzi hadn't managed to get a clear shot of us together.

Yet.

We had holed up at my temporary flat for days, enjoying what was probably a very short reprieve from media attention. But right now, in the relative calm before the storm, I liked London. I liked the food, the energy, the noise. But I liked it most of all because Lola Bishop was standing in my loo in nothing but a pair of lacy red knickers.

I took a step forward. "What are you doing?"

"My makeup." She frowned at herself in the mirror.

"I know that much, but why? Do you have plans I don't know about?"

She sighed and dropped her mascara back into the case. "I'm going out."

"Going out where?" I asked. "I thought we were staying here naked for as long as possible."

"Tempting." She grinned, biting her lip in a way that gave me ideas. "I'm going to visit my sister. She's back at Buckingham with the baby." She hesitated. The smile fell from her face, and instantly, I wanted to put it back in place. Lola was gorgeous every moment of the day, but when she smiled, it took my breath away.

"Should I come with you?"

"I don't think so," she hedged.

I lifted an eyebrow. We hadn't known each other that long, but I could already read her. Mostly because she didn't bother to hide from me. "Something wrong?"

She took a deep breath. "I'm going to tell her about us—if she doesn't already know."

She fell silent and watched me, waiting for a reaction. To be honest, I waited for one, too. Finally, I shrugged. "She's had a lot on her plate, but I get it if you want her to hear from you."

"You're okay with confirming it?" she blurted out, looking more ruffled than I'd ever seen her.

"Why wouldn't I be?" I stalked toward her, the bathroom

tile cold on my bare feet. I'd thrown on jeans to grab a take-away order from Brex. As far as I was concerned, food was the only necessity worth leaving bed for if she was around.

"Because it's going to sound like we're in a relationship," she said, aiming those piercing blue eyes at me.

I caught her around the waist and hauled her against me. "And that's a problem how?"

"It's not...exactly." Her breathy voice sent blood flooding to my groin. When she lowered her lashes, I nearly came undone. "This was supposed to be about sex and nothing more, remember?"

"Lola." I pressed my index finger under her chin and lifted it. "I think it's time to officially lose the rules."

"Even rule number 5?" She blushed.

Fuck me. The color staining her cheeks made me think of other places I wanted to turn that pretty shade of pink. "We can keep 5 if you want."

"If I want?" she repeated. I didn't miss the amusement in her voice.

"Yeah." I slanted my head over hers. "It's okay to admit you like that one, boss."

"We can keep that one," she said, popping onto her tiptoes and brushing a kiss over my lips. "I should get dressed."

"You should," I agreed, even as I lowered to trail kisses down her neck.

"Anders." Her voice was light, but her eyes were serious when I lifted my head to meet them. "I like my life. I like my job. I like London. But I like you, too. Maybe a bit more than I expected. And I'm not sure what that means."

I nodded. I knew. I didn't need her to explain it to me. I took her hand and pressed a kiss to her knuckles. I understood. I did. I had my own fears and reservations. I deserved the same from her.

"I've made mistakes in the past. I've been blind to things I should have seen, but I'm not anymore. I haven't bothered with a lot of relationships because I like my life, too, and my job. But I would be a damn fool if I ignored that something's changed. Something with you and me."

Maybe I didn't know what was going on either. Maybe I was hitting the gas when I would usually be pumping the brakes. I didn't know exactly what that meant, either. But I wouldn't hide it from her. Not when she saw me so clearly.

"No more rules, except number 5." She smiled, and I felt like I'd won a prize. "Fine by me."

"Now, about you getting dressed." I plucked at the waistband of her lace knickers. "How committed are you to that plan?"

"I'm not sure they'll let me in Buckingham looking like this," she said dryly.

"Maybe you should stay here," I suggested.

"I can't stay naked in your bed forever." But fire flared white-hot in her eyes as she spoke.

I wondered if this thing between us would ever cool down or if it would stay this hot and demanding forever. Fuck, I hoped it would. I hoped she would always look at me like she was looking at me now: hungry, ready, waiting for me to do whatever the fuck I wanted with her. I hooked my thumbs under her knickers and pushed them free.

"They definitely won't let me into Buckingham like this," she simpered.

"That, boss, is the point." I ran my hands over her hips and slipped them around to squeeze her perfectly plump ass.

"Why is only one of us naked?" she asked, taking on a businesslike tone.

I hushed her with a smirk. "Rule number 5 is in effect."

"My apologies." She ran a tongue over her red lipstick. "It's too bad you're in charge."

"Oh?"

"I was thinking..." She caressed my hard dick through my jeans. "But I'm not supposed to be thinking, am I?"

I swallowed down a groan. Lola wasn't just a natural submissive. She was a tease in the sexiest way possible. Even when I bent her over my knee or ordered her onto the bed, she drew it out and made me want her even more.

"No," I said with a smile, brushing a thumb over those red lips. "You don't need to think, because I know exactly what you want."

Her mouth parted, and she sucked the tip of my thumb softly. It seemed what she wanted and what I wanted were exactly the same thing.

"On your knees," I ordered her gently.

Her mouth split into a wide smile. She locked her eyes with me, never breaking contact as she lowered onto the floor. But as soon as she was on her knees, she paused and waited with wide, innocent eyes.

"Unzip my pants," I said gruffly, gathering her hair into my fist.

Those eyes stayed on me as she followed my order, and it

took effort not to let my own close when I felt her cool, soft hand wrap around my cock.

"What do you want?" I asked her.

"This," she whispered, stroking me slowly, "is what I want."

I groaned as she pumped my dick with one hand and tugged my jeans lower with the other.

"What do you want?" I repeated more forcefully.

"I want your cock." She licked those red lips, and my cock twitched.

"Take it, then."

She didn't hesitate. She lifted her head and opened her mouth to welcome my cock. I held on to the fistful of her hair while she worked my dick, licking and sucking. It had been a long time since I'd had a blowjob this good. Maybe I'd never had one this good. Probably because it had been so long since I'd wanted anyone as much as I wanted Lola.

"Fuck," I growled, my grip tightening on her hair. "That's my good girl. You look so fucking beautiful with your red lips wrapped around me."

She moaned something I couldn't understand. Using her hair, I pulled her off.

"Do you need to tell me something?" I asked softly.

She licked her swollen lips, her red lipstick slightly smeared and her eyes bright, and whispered one word. "More."

Need gripped me like a vise, but I forced myself to stay in control. "You sure about that, boss?" The vise tightened as she nodded. I swallowed. "You won't be able to say your safe words."

"Don't need 'em," she purred.

I was about to point out that this was the exact scenario she needed them for when she plunged her mouth back over me, taking me halfway down her throat. Instantly, I forgot my objection. I thrust my hips up to meet her, pushing my dick deeper until her lips were buried against me. She choked and then moaned, the sound vibrating through my cock.

"Fuck, that's a good girl. Just like that." I was going to lose it. Need barreled down my spine as I continued to thrust into her mouth, as she continued to take it, staring up at me with something that bordered on adoration.

And it was that look that made me pull her off. Lola started to protest, but I ignored her, scooping her off the ground and carrying her to the bed.

"Hand and knees," I gritted out as I placed her on it. She scrambled obediently into position, putting that perfect ass on display. "I fucking need you," I said by way of explanation. I dipped a finger inside her, discovering she was soaked. I slicked my cock with her wetness. "What do you need?"

"You," she moaned. "You. I need you, Anders."

Me? She needed me. Not my cock. Not His Highness. She'd used my name, and I'd heard the truth we both feared hiding behind her words.

"I need you, too, Lola," I whispered and shoved myself inside her.

Her head arched up, a cry escaping her lips as I pushed the last few inches.

"You okay?" I said, waiting a moment for her to adjust.

She mumbled something reassuring as she rocked her hips just enough to send a clear message. I grabbed her hair, yanking her back just enough that I could see her face as I started to move. I took it slowly, feasting on the breathy pants and gasps escaping her until it was too much, and I began to thrust harder and faster. Lola got louder, her eyes rolling back a little as I claimed her, one hand holding her, the other guiding her hips to meet my punishing pace.

"I need you to come, Lola," I urged her. "I need to feel you coming on my cock."

A tortured noise gargled from her, and I felt her tightening around my shaft. Her whole body shook as she fell apart and took my release with her. I emptied myself inside her, savoring the primal noises she made as I took her. When the last of our pleasure was wrung out, we collapsed onto the bed in a sweaty heap.

"That was..." she mumbled.

"Yeah." I brushed her hair off her shoulders, my fingers lingering on the silky strands as I remembered how it had felt as I held it moments ago. "It was."

We didn't need words to describe what just happened. Hell, I wasn't sure there were words to describe it. It was instinct. Raw, primal instinct that neither of us could control when we touched. I wasn't sure I wanted to control it.

And Lola lying next to me with her smeared makeup, her skin damp with sweat, was the picture of every fantasy I'd ever had. But she wasn't a fantasy. She was here in my bed. And I would be damned if I ever let her go.

"What's that look for?" she asked with narrowed eyes.

"You look well-fucked." I moved so I could kiss her forehead.

"I feel well-fucked." She wiggled closer to me, and I breathed her in, never wanting this moment to end.

"You might have to redo your makeup," I said.

She giggled. "I figured."

It was a perfect moment, so naturally, it couldn't last. Across the room, in my abandoned jeans, my phone began to vibrate.

"Are you going to get that?" Lola asked.

"Nope." I kissed her again. God, she was fucking perfect.

The phone started ringing again, so I kissed her again. It quieted for a second, and then the sounds of incoming texts began to barrage us.

"I think someone needs to talk to you," she said with a laugh.

I cursed under my breath as I climbed out of bed to grab the phone and turn it off. But as soon as it was in my hand, I saw who was trying to reach me. My thumb slid over the screen. I read the messages, each one further deflating me.

"What is it?" Lola sat up and reached for a sheet.

I looked up at her, forcing a grim smile. "I guess we're both going to Buckingham. My brother wants to see me. Now."

CHAPTER TWENTY-EIGHT

LOLA

This wasn't the first time I'd visited Buckingham Palace, but for some reason, I was fidgeting like a schoolgirl. There was no bypassing the crowds outside the castle. Not with a newborn royal inside. I cringed down in my seat, shielding my face as the crowds swelled closer from their spots on the sidewalk.

"Ashamed to be seen with me?" Anders teased. He might be joking but his hand squeezed my knee tightly, and I knew he was as anxious as I was. Maybe even more so.

Clara wasn't going to be angry that I'd started up something romantic with Anders.

Alexander probably wouldn't be as understanding with his half-brother.

"They can't see you," Brex called from the driver's seat. "That window tint might as well be made out of obsidian. Alexander values his privacy."

As if to drive that point home, there were double the number of palace guards.

"This is excessive," Anders said, noticing the same thing. "Does he really think someone's going to kidnap his newborn?"

Brex's eyes flashed to the rearview mirror. "I'd advise you don't ever use the word kidnapping around your brother."

Anders rolled his eyes, muttering something like *overprotective prick* under his breath. But something in the way Brex spoke sent cold dread sluicing through me.

"He has a right to worry," I murmured to my...boyfriend? We seriously needed to sort a few things out later. "He's probably a wreck. Give him a break. The baby just had surgery."

Anders dropped his head and shot me a sheepish smile. "I promise to be on my best behavior. You will have no regrets telling Clara you're my girlfriend."

Girlfriend. My heart did a silly flip-flop. How had we gotten from at each other's throats to this in the last week? It seemed impossible, but something about Anders made me want to do things I normally wouldn't, like go to bed with a racecar driver or fall in love with one. I swallowed as I considered whether or not I was doing just that.

He stretched out his arm and his fingers brushed against mine. "That good enough for you?"

"Perfect." And as Brex pulled up to the palace gates, I squeezed his fingers.

The guard pulled open the gate, but before we could drive forward, the press rushed the car, their cameras flashing in our eyes. The guard didn't hesitate to move them back, but some of the harder-nosed reporters got around him. Soon, the crowds pressed in from all sides.

"This is fucking ridiculous," Anders muttered.

I barely heard him. I was too focused on the way his thumb brushed the back of my hand. Gentle. Soothing. A reminder that he was here to protect me. It shouldn't make me giddy. Not with an out-of-control crowd rushing the Range Rover.

But it did.

"Just give them a second. Everything's fine," Brex told us.

Looking out my window, I saw more guards move in and begin to clear the crowd.

"Everyone wants their shot," Brex said, continuing down the newly cleared drive and past the gate.

"We're just normal people. Why do they give a shit?" Anders asked. He slumped back in his seat and gave me a tired grin.

"Do you say that about the fans at the track?" I asked him. Things might have changed between us, but I still had a job to do. I needed him to see that being a royal wasn't a punishment. Getting him to fall in line with Alexander's craziness might be a little harder now that we were involved, but I would do everything I could to help Anders transition into his new life with as little pain as possible.

He shook his head, and I shrugged, my point already proven.

"This is their racetrack. They're fans."

Anders raised an eyebrow and stayed quiet. He wasn't a fan of Alexander, but other people were. He needed to see that. Even if he didn't want to be a royal, there was still a chance that he could be the type of prince I thought he might be. The kind that handed the princess a sword and let her slay her own dragons, then kissed her and live happily ever after.

But first, he needed to see that this wasn't all bad.

Brex pulled up to the front entrance, and more guards rushed forward to usher us inside. Anders was out of the car almost before Brex could put it in park. To my surprise, he rushed around the car, shooed a guard away, and opened my door. I bit back a smile as he offered me his hand.

I took it, lacing my fingers with his and climbed out. It felt right. Him and me. Even here. The place I'd thought things might fall apart.

Brex came up beside us, grinning at our joined hands. "So, I'm not going to have to keep sneaking you two around, huh?"

"Let's just get this over with," Anders said, looking suddenly gloomy.

"Right this way, Your Highness." Brex bowed a little and gestured to the side entrance.

Anders glowered as we followed him, and I realized a nerve had been struck. That was my first course of action. I needed to get him comfortable with being a member of the royal family. The question was: how?

Before I could come up with an answer, Brex led us around a corner and directly into Alexander's path.

My brother-in-law was a formidable man. He didn't give off the same English gentility his father had. Rather, he was like a hurricane. You never knew when he would descend or how much damage he'd inflict until it was all over. Today, he looked especially stormy. His shirtsleeves were rolled to his elbows, stubble dusted his chin, and judging from the circles under his eyes, he wasn't sleeping.

"That took long enough," he barked at Brex, and I flinched. Sometimes I wondered what my sister saw in him. The fact that he was the King of England might sway many women, but not Clara. I'd never quite understood them, even though they obviously loved each other.

"Half of London is outside," Anders interrupted, going rigid. "He did the best he could."

Alexander stopped, regarding his brother with calculating eyes that dropped down to where I was holding hands with Anders.

"Interesting," he muttered.

I wasn't sure how to take that.

Anger rippled off both of them, and I wondered if they would get in another fight. Before they could, I dropped his hand and stepped between them.

"I wanted to check on Clara and the baby. Is now a good time?" I asked calmly.

A muscle twitched in Alexander's jaw. "William is sleeping, but I'm sure Clara would love to see you. It seems you two have some things to catch up on."

I ignored the pointed remark and turned to Anders.

"Join me when you're done talking?" I asked him softly. Alexander stiffened as though he disliked this request, but he didn't say anything.

"Sure," Anders said. His eyes strayed over my shoulder to his brother.

"Behave," I whispered.

"Only if he does, boss." He winked at me, and then before I could stop him, he pressed a quick kiss to my lips.

Maybe it was the fact that we were in mixed company, but my whole body flamed to life at his touch, especially my cheeks.

"Clara is in our quarters," Alexander said stiffly.

I nodded, glancing between the two of them before I slowly made my way toward the apartments the royal family kept at the palace. Part of me wanted to run before the next bomb detonated between them, but I wouldn't let anyone—not even Anders—see me ruffled.

When I reached the gilded ivory doors, I stepped inside and released a long sigh.

"Do I want to know?" a curt voice interrupted my moment of solitude.

I looked up to find Georgia, Clara's personal bodyguard, slinking from the shadows like she belonged to them. She was in her usual black leather. It seemed not even the joyful arrival of a baby could get her to soften up.

"Anders and Alexander." I didn't need to say more. Georgia snorted and nodded.

"Those two..."

"Exactly." I nodded toward the hallway that led to the bedrooms. "Is she in the nursery?"

"Resting," Georgia told me. "The nursery has been turned into a medical suite until William has recovered."

I gulped, imagining the tiny human I'd seen through the glass at the hospital, still surrounded by wires and machines. "How is she holding up?"

"She's tough." Her eyes flashed and I found myself surprised because Georgia looked impressed.

"Should I wait?"

"She's awake." Georgia hesitated for a minute before adding, "She's having a hard time sleeping."

Of course she was. My sister had a toddler and a newborn recovering from heart surgery. She might have guards and nannies and doctors but she was still a mother. She had to be worried sick.

And I was about to give her something else to worry about.

CHAPTER TWENTY-NINE

ANDERS

My brother's office was as devoid of personality as he was—a cold, masculine remnant of the establishment he now headed. The only personal touches were a few framed pictures of Clara and their kids. I picked up the photo of Clara from the polished desk. She was smiling in front of the London Eye, eyes shining, her arms full of red roses. It was the exact opposite of Alexander, spontaneous, joyful, alive.

"Put that down," my brother said harshly, stalking into the room and looking as pleased to be here as I felt.

I replaced the photo and leaned against the desk, crossing my arms. "You summoned me?"

"We need to talk." He didn't bother to look me in the eye. I understood why. The only trait we remotely shared were our father's eyes.

Did he hate looking into my eyes and seeing that as much as I did?

"About what?"

"A couple of things, it seems." He took a chair by the unlit fireplace and gestured for me to take the one opposite.

My muscles tensed, and I stared at him, waiting for him to make more demands. It was always orders and commands with him. Not just when it came to me—he acted that way with everyone. And that was why we'd never see eye-to-eye.

He cleared his throat, still studiously avoiding my eyes. "I'm giving you a title."

I'd considered what he wanted to talk to me about. I'd assumed it was some new rule I needed to follow, or concern about my relationship with Lola. *This* had never crossed my mind. Even now, it was the last thing that seemed possible.

He finally looked at me, impatience knitting his eyebrows as he waited for my response.

"Why?" I finally blurted out.

His calculating gaze looked past me again. "You're my brother. It makes sense."

"Bullshit." I jumped to my feet. This made no sense, and we both knew it. "I'm a bastard. Your father never married my mother. He hid me away—"

"Lucky you." His voice dripped with acid.

"Is this some new attempt to piss off Parliament, or the whole of England?" I demanded.

He ignored me. "You will also move into the line of succession, although pretty far down it." It sounded like he was reading off a list of my fucking nightmares. "You can use the moniker His Royal Highness, Prince Anderson of..."

His momentary hesitance was the moment I needed. I seized it.

"You're just making this up as you fucking go," I

accused. My hands balled into fists as if waiting for a chance to take a swing. It wouldn't be the first time things had come to blows between us. "What the hell is this about?"

But he didn't rise to meet my fury. Instead, he folded his hands in his lap and looked blandly at me. "There's no need to fight it. It's already been done."

"And if I refuse?" Royals could walk away. I was pretty sure that some had done it over the years.

"You won't." His eyes sparked, giving away that he wasn't nearly as composed as he was acting. "You are now His Royal Highness Anderson Stone, Duke of Edinburgh."

"Fuck you." I couldn't think of anything else to say.

"Lola will be pleased," he muttered, and I hated him even more. He didn't know her, but it was clear he thought he did.

"Don't fucking talk about my girlfriend," I snarled.

"So, she is your girlfriend?" he asked. "I thought she was supposed to handle you. I didn't know that included fucking you."

I took a step toward him, my breath ragged as I tried not to lose it. "Say that again."

He smirked at me. "People are going to say a lot of things you don't like about your relationship. It's part of the package, and something you need to get used to now you're a member of the royal family."

I didn't want to think about that. Not now. It was all I could do not to punch him in his smug fucking face right now. Was this what it was going to be like to be part of his family? Alexander making decisions without my permission, and then acting superior all the time?

"I'm not discussing this with you." I turned on my heel and grabbed the door. "And don't think I won't walk away."

"You actually think you have a choice, don't you?" He sounded amused in a hollow, tired way, but I didn't turn around. I didn't want to see his face. "Believe me, *none* of us have a choice. But I'm actually doing you a favor."

"I really don't give a fuck what you think, Alexander." I moved toward the door. I'd wait for Lola outside. I couldn't stand the idea of being in the same building with him.

"There's another option," he said, and I paused. "Break up with her."

I turned slowly, his words like a slow burn on my skin. My fists clenched at my sides. "Why would I do that?"

"Because you hate me, you hate this life, and you're going to force her firmly into it," he said, and I wanted to punch him again. "And if she becomes part of this family, she will never be safe. They'll follow her, photograph her, belittle her, endanger her. You will spend every minute hating yourself for making her into the thing you hate the most."

"And what is that?" I growled.

"One of *us*."

Our eyes locked and there was no avoiding it now. No avoiding those eyes we shared. No avoiding that we were more similar than we wanted to admit. No avoiding that we were bound by blood, like it or not. And right now, I definitely *did not*.

"I'll never be one of *you*."

He laughed, the sound devoid of any mirth. It rang through the air like a death knell. "You already are, *brother*."

"Over my dead body." I moved closer to him. He didn't

flinch. Why would he? We were the same. The same rage boiling inside me burned inside him. He might be my brother, and I might have a title and whatever bullshit that came with that unwanted title, but he was still a prince, and I was still a bastard.

And I had the feeling he knew it.

"It's already done," he repeated, "and now you have to decide if you want Lola to suffer this unbearable fate you seem so eager to avoid."

Despite my anger, I recognized the truth in his words. It was no wonder my father had hidden me away. This was the fucked up world that I would have been forced to inherit.

"Let's get a few things clear." I managed to keep my fists at my side, but it was difficult. "I choose my own path. You can give me a title—"

"And a security detail now that you're in the line of succession," he interjected.

Was he fucking kidding? I tamped down the anger flaring inside me. I'd deal with that later. "You can give me a title," I repeated, "but I will never be your family. I will never be your brother."

He stared at me, no emotion on his face. Then, he shrugged. "Fine."

Fine? That was all he was going to say. "What is the fucking point of all of this?"

"Do you really want to know?" he asked coolly.

I nodded, not trusting myself to speak.

"Duty."

I waited for him to say more, but he didn't. Instead, he tilted his head toward the door. "You can go."

"Am I dismissed?" I bit out, shaking my head. "Since I'm royalty now, I guess I won't get in trouble for telling the King of England he's an asshole."

His shoulder lifted, but he showed no sign that he cared what I thought of him.

"Your apartment at Kensington—" he began as I walked toward the door.

I didn't turn. "I'm going back to Silverstone."

"I don't think that's a good idea."

I shrugged, giving him a taste of his own medicine. "I don't give a fuck."

I left before he could say another word.

I blew into the corridor. Brex looked up from his phone, frowning when he saw my face.

"Where's Lola?" I asked him, still seething.

"Still with her sister, I think."

"I need to get out of here. Now."

He pocketed his phone and nodded. He didn't ask why I was pissed. Maybe that was a side effect of always staying in the shadows, or maybe he knew Alexander well enough not to be surprised that ten minutes alone with him would have me fuming.

"I can take you back to Kensington and return for her," he suggested, falling into step beside me.

"I'm not leaving her behind, and I'm only going back to Kensington for my shit. I leave for Silverstone tonight," I informed him. The longer I stayed in London, the more control Alexander would assume he had over me. I needed to send a clear message.

I was not his puppet. He couldn't pull my strings.

"Did Alexander–" he started.

I turned on him. "I assume you're the one who's getting the shit deal of watching me, so I want to be clear. Alexander can assign babysitters and sign papers and hand out crowns, but he cannot tell me what to do."

"I'll take that as a no," he said flatly.

"Are you going to try to stop me?"

A muscle tensed in his jaw, but he finally shook his head. "I'm your bodyguard not a warden. A man makes his own choices. I'm just around to make sure you don't get killed."

My chest heaved as I studied him. He meant it. Well, it was something. "Good," I said. "Now show me where Lola is."

CHAPTER THIRTY

LOLA

"Please tell me that you're alone." Clara sounded exhausted as she opened the door. Before I could answer, she wrapped her arms around me and hugged me tightly. Even a few days after giving birth, she was radiant, despite the circles under her eyes.

"I am," I promised, squeezing her back. "Everything okay?"

It wasn't like her to hug me like this. Our family wasn't really the hugging type. Maybe it was because our father was British, and my mother was more worried about wrinkling her clothes than showing affection. Either way, it had been a while since my sister had greeted me this warmly.

"No reason." Her smile looked forced, and I knew she was lying. But I couldn't blame her. She had a lot to worry about. Maybe she was simply relieved I wasn't likely to add to her headache.

Except I was. I *totally* was.

My sister had sent me to coach Anders, to get him in line. Instead, I'd made things more complicated than ever.

I forced my anxiety deep inside me and pasted on a smile. "How are you feeling?"

"Okay," she said, yawning. She adjusted the belt of her silk robe.

"Are you sure about that?" I raised an eyebrow.

Clara threw her hands up. "Fine, I'm tired, but that's normal."

"And how is my nephew?" I asked, my stomach doing cartwheels. There was more security than ever at Buckingham. Was it because they were worried something might happen to little William in his sleep? Surely not. If that were the case, he would have stayed in hospital longer.

"Perfect." She gestured to a chair by the fire. "Belle is in with him now."

"Is she practicing?" I teased. My business partner, Clara's best friend, was expecting a baby in a few months.

Clara nodded, but I noticed how her throat slid uneasily. "None of us want to take our eyes off him. Alexander barely lets either of us out of his sight."

I didn't find that surprising. My brother-in-law was the dictionary definition of overprotective.

"Well, Anders is distracting him now," I told her. My foot tapped a nervous beat so loudly that Clara glanced at it, her eyebrows knitting together. I hastily crossed my legs. It was bad enough I had to tell her. Did I have to look like a mental case doing it?

"Anders." She blinked and then nodded. "I suppose that makes sense."

"Why?" I asked, narrowing my eyes.

"It's nothing important," she said breezily—another lie. I wondered what my boyfriend would have to tell me after his meeting.

"Speaking of Anders." I cleared my throat. "There's something I need to tell you."

Clara tensed, her whole body going completely still. "What?"

Did she already know? I'd thought with the media circus surrounding William's birth and his subsequent surgery, she would be out of the loop. But had she heard? Was that why she was acting strangely?

There was only one way to find out. "I might be...I mean, I am...it just happened, by the way, and I didn't plan it, but..."

"What happened?" Clara pressed, her lips tipping into a frown.

I blew a stream of air through my lips. Now or never. "Us."

"Us?" She blinked, looking confused. "I'm sorry. I don't follow."

"Anders...and me," I forced myself to add.

"You and Anders what?" She stared for a moment, and then her eyes lit up. "*Ohhhhh.*"

I buried my face in my hands, wishing I could disappear. "I'm so sorry. You asked me to help him, and then I..."

"You what?" she asked seriously.

"You know." I couldn't bear to look at her.

"Lola, I'm a married woman. What would I know about it?" Her tone was rich with amusement. I looked up to see the first genuine smile on her face since I arrived.

"You suck," I informed her.

But Clara laughed. The sound was like music. I'd always admired my older sister, admired her poise, admired her kindness. We were so different. "I suppose I should have seen that coming."

"Oh?" I arched an eyebrow.

"Well, you know he had a thing for..." she trailed away, biting her lower lip. "It's not important."

I scooted forward in my seat, shaking my head. "You can't leave something like that hanging out there!"

"It doesn't matter." She folded her hands in her lap, looking the part of the benevolent Madonna. "Is it serious?"

That was the question. "It's barely been a week."

But even as I spoke, the truth tightened around my heart.

"In my experience, when you know, *you know*." She blew a loose strand of hair from her face. "Time isn't really that important. My life divided in two the first time Alexander kissed me, and I didn't even know his name."

"Only you could not recognize the future King of England," I teased, but I still felt heavy. "We're not in love." Love. Why had I jumped to that?

"You sure about that?" Clara asked softly.

I was not, and judging by the understanding smile my sister wore, I didn't need to say anything. "What do you think of Anders?"

"It doesn't matter."

"It matters to me," I pressed.

"I like Anders." She paused, chewing on her lower lip. "But there was this thing that happened."

"He had a crush on you?" I guessed.

Her shoulders sagged with relief. She tucked her legs under her and nodded. "I'm glad you know."

"That I'm the consolation prize?"

Clara's mouth fell open. "No, Lola–"

"I'm joking," I stopped her. I thought of how Anders looked at me in bed, how his eyes devoured me, the confidence of his hands. My whole body warmed, heat creeping onto my cheeks. "Believe me. He doesn't make me feel that way."

"I can see that. You're the color of a phonebox." Her lips twitched, then she sighed. "Thank you."

"For what?" I asked.

"Taking my mind off everything. It's been hard," she said darkly.

"Clara, is there anything–"

A sharp knock cut me off.

"Yours or mine?" she said dryly.

Georgia peeked inside, wearing a look of utter annoyance. "Everyone decent?"

We nodded. I doubted she would bother asking if it was Alexander out there. He probably wouldn't have even let her knock.

"Mine," I said. On cue, Anders stepped through the door. He looked past us, his entire body tense.

"You ready?" he asked, not bothering to meet my gaze.

Clara and I shared a look.

"Uh." I wasn't sure what to say. Glancing at my sister, she nodded. "Sure."

He stalked into the hallway without another word.

"What did Alexander want to talk to him about?" I asked Clara as I stood. Whatever it was had riled Anders up.

"I'll let him tell you." She reached for my hand and squeezed. "Try to talk him into it. It's for the best."

"Now you're freaking me out." I leaned down and gave her a hug, wondering what Anders' new family could have done to upset him this much.

I found Anders waiting for me by the door to the royal quarters. He grabbed my hand. I practically had to run to keep up with him as we left Buckingham. Brex was waiting near the car, but as soon as we were outside, I pulled away.

"What is going on?" I demanded.

"I don't want to talk about it. I need to get out of here," he said cagily, his eyes shifting around the space.

I crossed my arms and glared at him. "I'm not going anywhere until you tell me why you're so angry."

"It doesn't matter."

"It clearly does," I argued. "Or you wouldn't be reverting to caveman mode."

"You want to know?" he growled.

Did I? What could have upset him this much? Alexander had a talent for pissing people off, but this was next level. I paused before finally nodding.

"I'm getting a title," he seethed.

I blinked as I processed this. "So?"

It was the wrong thing to say. Anders threw his hands in the air, starting to curse. "Because I never wanted any of this, and now I'm being forced to be one of them."

His words hit me like a lead weight. I wasn't sure why I was so surprised. Maybe it was because he seemed to be getting used to the fact, or maybe because I'd been stupid enough to believe our relationship might change his mind.

"*I'm* one of them," I said softly.

"I didn't mean you." He stepped toward me, but I backed away.

"This life that you hate—that you don't want—*is my life*, Anders." Why couldn't he see that?

"You aren't one of them. You're like me." He shook his head, his face twisting with disdain. "They don't want us."

Is that what he thought brought us together? A trauma bond? Not that we struggled to know where we belonged, but that we weren't wanted at all?

"No. You don't want *them*," I corrected him, lifting my chin, even as my voice trembled. "And if you don't want them, you don't want me."

CHAPTER THIRTY-ONE

ANDERS

Every word coming out of my mouth was wrong, but I couldn't seem to shut up. Lola's lip trembled, drawing my attention to her mouth, which caught the attention of other parts of my body. Now definitely wasn't the time for that. I had to get her to understand where I was coming from because there was only one thing I didn't want to walk away from: *her*.

My eyes met hers, and I could see her straining to hold back tears. I hadn't wanted to hurt her, but I couldn't force myself to stay here. "Lola, I'm sorry. Everything is messed up. I didn't mean to make you feel that way, but I'm not sure…"

I couldn't finish because I didn't want to walk away and risk losing her. But I didn't fit in here, even if she did. It was probably best to walk away, but I knew that I didn't want to stop seeing her.

I stepped closer to her, trying to read the expression on her face. Was she angry? Hurt? If she was upset, I was probably only making things worse.

I couldn't stop myself from touching her. I skimmed my thumb along her bottom lip. I wanted to kiss her, but I resisted. I wasn't about to get caught doing that by my asshole brother, so I pulled away.

"I don't belong here," I said softly.

She shook her head. "That's all in your head. No one gets along with Alexander, but if you give the others a—"

"I will never belong here," I cut her off before she latched on to her own wishful thinking. "I can't do this, boss."

"You don't belong?" she repeated, blinking back tears. "Are you saying you're leaving?"

I didn't know how to answer her. I didn't want to shut her out. I didn't want to say goodbye.

"I don't know what I'm saying. But this title shit is crazy. I didn't sign up for this life." I shook my head, wishing I could clear out the confusion and rage muddying up my brain. "I'm not sure what to do."

"Let me know when you figure it out," Lola said defiantly. There was no doubt now that she was angry...with me.

Somehow it was worse to see her pissed off than crying, mostly because I'd learned a few things about Lola Bishop. How she bit her lip when she came. The exact way she took her morning tea. And that when she got that look of determined anger on her face, she'd already made up her mind.

"Lola, I..."

"Make sure to inform me when you reach your decision. Because I'm not waiting around for you forever." She stood there, staring me down. Her eyes hadn't lost their shine, but they were as hard as glittering sapphires. She turned away. "Just go. I can get another ride to my place."

"Maybe we should talk about this," I started, but she held a hand up.

"You don't want this life. You made that clear from the start." Did I hear a tremble in her voice? "I'll do what I can to get Alexander and Clara to back off."

"You don't need to do that."

"Consider it my parting gift." She squared her shoulders, looking like a defiant queen.

I wasn't sure what to say. This wasn't what I wanted. Any of it. The title. The life. Walking away from her. But I needed to get out of there because I was losing the battle against my desire to hold her, to pull her into my arms and never let her go.

But I couldn't do that to her. We barely knew each other. Maybe this would be better for both of us. Maybe she'd finally see the light.

I refused to change, and the man I was didn't deserve her.

"I'm going by Kensington if you need anything," I muttered.

"I'm sure someone can pick up my things later."

Our eyes locked and it was like she was looking into my soul. Could she see how torn I was? How part of me wanted her to ask me to stay? The same part of me that knew she never would. I saw the truth of that in her eyes. Clear. Bright. Determined. She'd meant everything she said, and there was no sign of doubts.

Footsteps echoed on the marble floor, and I glanced over my shoulder to see Brex approaching. "You ready?"

"Just a sec," I told him. "We're saying goodbye."

His eyebrows lifted. We'd managed to surprise the bodyguard. "I think you already did."

Turning back, I spotted Lola slipping back inside the royal apartments. Just like that, she was gone.

"Fuck." My head fell, wondering if there was any point to going after her. I knew how that would end. "Let's get out of here."

I HADN'T BROUGHT enough belongings with me to need more than a few items from the apartment in Kensington. Lola, on the other hand, had shit everywhere. I tried to look past it as I shoved things into a duffel bag. But reminders of her plagued me. Her lipstick on the bathroom counter. A pair of lacy knickers on the floor. The cold remnants of morning tea in the kitchen. A few hours ago, we'd been rolling around in the still-unmade bed.

Now, it was over.

I zipped up my bag and carried it to the door.

"Got everything?" Brex asked from his lookout spot at the door.

"Yep." I threw the bag over my shoulder. "You aren't going to try to talk me into sticking around."

"That's not how this works. I go where you go, and you're leaving, so..."

I refrained from rolling my eyes. I liked Brex, but right now, I wanted to be alone. Alone in the darkest, most destructive way possible, and something told me that he would probably put a cramp in my plans. "Not going to try to talk me out of it?"

"Why?" He shrugged his broad shoulders, not a hint of his usual grin on his face. "If she couldn't, what chance do I have?"

He made a good point, but I didn't admit it.

"How bad is traffic this time of day?" I asked him.

"We'll get an escort out of the city," he said as we made our way to the private parking lot where my car waited.

"Is that necessary? I don't want to draw any attention."

"Well, unless you want to dig a tunnel out of London, we're going to need a little help to get you past the paparazzi."

There were still a few intrepid souls parked at the Kensington Palace gates, hoping for shots of me or Lola. But most of the media's attention was on the new royal baby. "There's only a couple of them," I reminded him. "I can lose them."

"I've seen you drive and I'm sure you can. But you might lose *me*. I'll be following behind you in the Range Rover."

At least I'd finally get a minute alone.

I threw my bag in the passenger seat and slid behind the wheel. I tried not to think that she should be sitting in that seat. But Lola had been clear. She thought I was some sort of coward, that I was running away from my title instead of embracing it.

I didn't care. I wasn't going to spend my summer playing Alexander's games and having tea parties. My shit wasn't exactly together, but no one here could help me. My brother had written the book on being fucked up. What was I supposed to do? Stick around and learn how to be miserable from the best? And wreck my life even more in the process?

I'd been in this city for a little over a week, and it was getting under my skin.

London was full of pretty buildings, but underneath it was crumbling. Just like my unwanted family. Every soul here was hoping they could hold on just a little bit longer.

But I refused.

I fired the engine and peeled out of the parking lot. When I reached the gate, several black sedans were waiting.

My phone rang over the car's speaker, and I punched accept.

"Just follow them. They're taking us on the most secure route."

"Great." I ended the call. Secure route? That sounded fun. For the first time in days, I thought about the track, about the rush I felt when I was out there alone, pushing my car to the limit. That's where everything had gone wrong. I should never have taken a break from racing. I could see that now. Behind the wheel was the closest thing I had to a place in the world.

And now even that was being taken from me. I couldn't even drive down the street without being surrounded by security. I'd lost my identity, my career, even Lola. But I didn't have to.

The streets were congested, but traffic was moving. I kept my eyes on the road, waiting for my moment. I hadn't walked away from her for this. When we reached Paddington, I saw my chance. The light was about to change, and my entourage slowed, but I swerved around the cars in front and ran through the light. I didn't bother to look into my mirror to see if they were following. I knew they were.

Without stopping, I turned left onto a side street, narrowly avoiding a group of pedestrians crossing. It was an asshole move. One of them screamed at me, but it had done the trick. The others couldn't risk following me until the crossing cleared. My phone began to ring again, but I reached over and turned down the volume. The street opened like a sign from the gods, and I sped toward the A40 and my escape.

CHAPTER THIRTY-TWO

LOLA

I don't know how long I stood in my sister's sitting room. Long enough to start crying, stop crying, and start crying again. At the first opportunity, Anders had bolted. I leaned against the papered wall, feeling its rough texture against my flattened palms. I might have thought this was all a dream if it weren't for that stupid wallpaper. I was wrung out. Hollow. Empty.

And I'd only spent a week with him.

I couldn't bring myself to go back in and tell my sister the complete reversal of everything we'd just talked about. She'd had her own rocky moments with her husband, but I didn't want to hear about having faith or how it had worked out for her after a breakup. Just the thought of my sister and brother-in-law made me feel queasy. They were so happy, even if Alexander could be a controlling jerk.

Clara's words floated to mind. *In my experience, when you know, you know.*

So much for knowing. Maybe it was different for them. Maybe I wasn't really in love with Anders.

In the hallway, the door to the nursery opened, and Belle walked out, patting her own small bump. Her pale golden hair was curled in the humidity, her face radiant and joyful. Even in the dim hall, her blue eyes sparkled in delight, and her skin glowed as if she was lit from within.

Great. Another happy person.

I swiped at the evidence I'd been crying, but my hands came back streaked with mascara.

She startled when she turned and spotted me. Clutching her chest, she laughed—until she spotted my stricken face.

"Lola?" She rushed toward me. "What's wrong?"

I opened my mouth, but then I closed it as I realized there was no way I could tell her without breaking down again.

I was in love with a man who I'd known for a week—albeit a week of being knocked sideways by emotions that swung wildly between annoyance, lust, and love.

"Lola?" She placed a hand on my shoulder, her eyes widening with concern.

A sob tore from my throat, and I flung myself into her arms. She smelled like flowers and cream, and her arms were warm and welcoming. I buried my face in her shoulder and let it all out. Not just the pent-up emotion about how Anders left but also all the fears and worries about how he had changed me.

Belle's arms tightened around me, and she rubbed soothing circles on my back. "Don't cry, darling."

"I'm not crying," I lied, pulling back and wiping my eyes.

Belle looked me up and down and placed an arm around my waist. She led me toward the couch, but I hesitated.

"You're busy. I'll be fine." The cracking sensation in my chest suggested otherwise, but I plastered a smile on my face.

Belle hugged me, shaking my head. She knew me too well to buy the bullshit I was selling. "If you need to cry, you can cry in front of me."

I shook my head. I didn't want to cry in front of anyone. Not even her.

"Is this about a man?" She let me go and looked into my eyes.

I forced myself to nod.

"A man that drives racecars?"

I groaned. "You saw the papers."

"I saw the tabloids," she corrected me gently. She sat down and patted the seat next to her. "It's true, then?"

"It was," I croaked. "We just ended things." And then the entire story spilled out of me. The irresistible attraction. The rules. Breaking the rules every chance we got. "And the worst part is," I sobbed to her, "I think I'm in love with him, which is just stupid. You can't fall in love in a week!"

"Like hell you can't," she said with a snort. "I think the right man makes you fall harder than the wrong one."

"Not you, too." I swallowed. I repeated the advice Clara had given me.

Belle laughed, shooting me a sympathetic smile. She picked up a throw pillow and squeezed it. "She's not wrong. I think you need to put it into perspective."

"Perspective?"

"I know it feels as if your world has just been shaken, but

it hasn't. You're still the same woman you were," she said firmly. "You're a total badass, and that didn't change."

"I don't feel like a badass," I admitted, dabbing my eyes with my fingertip.

"You will again, and if he is the right one, he'll come around."

I thought of what Anders had said about this world and about his future. "I don't see how we can work. He wants something entirely different than I do."

She smiled. "A funny thing happens when you fall in love. You start wanting that person more than anything else."

Maybe she was right. Maybe Anders would return and grovel. I wasn't counting on it. Not when he was so stubborn, and I wasn't about to do any groveling of my own. "I don't know what I'm supposed to do."

"I see." She took a deep breath and let it out slowly. "What would you be doing if nothing happened between the two of you?"

"Probably throttling him," I said dryly.

"Okay." She giggled. "Let me rephrase. What would you be doing if you hadn't met him at all?"

"Working. Hanging with friends. Working," I repeated.

"There's your answer." She reached over and took my hand. "Your life didn't end when you met him, and it didn't end when you broke up. It's right there waiting for you, and it's excited to have you back."

Begrudgingly, I smiled. "You're right. Thank you."

"Go home, call your friends, and go dancing. Do it for me since I can't."

"What about work? I've been letting things slip with

Bless." I'd been so consumed by Anders that I'd been doing little more than checking our company's emails.

"Bless will be there whenever, and I've still got things under control until this little one shows up in a few months."

"Thanks, Belle, really." I suspected Clara would have given me similar advice, but I couldn't face her so soon after telling her about my relationship.

Her eyes softened with sympathy. "I know you're not the type of person who needs to be attached to someone else to feel happy, but you deserve that happiness, Lola. You deserve someone who will fight for you, and if Anders won't, fuck him."

She was right. I knew she was right, but the emptiness in my chest lingered.

She squeezed my hand. "Call me when you get home safely, okay?"

"Of course." I shook my head, sending the tears spilling down my face.

"It's going to be okay."

"I know. I just remembered that I need to find a ride home. I came here with…him." I hated feeling helpless, but I was glad I'd stood my ground even if I was stranded. "Do you think they'll let an Uber pick me up?

"I think that might actually give Alexander a heart attack," she said with a laugh. "Hold on. I'll call my car service. Smith won't let me drive in my condition."

"What?" I couldn't help giggling at that. "You're barely showing, and he's already this overprotective. How do you put up with that?"

"The orgasms," she said, flashing me a wicked smile. "The driver is waiting nearby. It shouldn't take long."

"I think I'll step outside until he gets here." I gave her another hug and headed out. Belle was right. My life wasn't over. I just had to get my head back into the game.

The driver pulled into the private drive a few minutes later, and I climbed into the backseat. I gave the driver my address and settled into the plush leather seat.

I thought of what Belle had said. I didn't need Anders to love me. I deserved a man who would fight for me, and if he wouldn't, I didn't want him anyway.

CHAPTER THIRTY-THREE

ANDERS

I gritted my teeth and shifted up a gear before dialing back my differential. I'd barely made the same corner that had nearly flattened me six months ago. A month. I'd been back on the track for over a month—a month away from London and royalty and *her*—and I was driving like shit.

"Give it up, kid, and bring it in," he ordered me, his anger replaced by disappointment. I'd lost count of the number of times I'd heard those words in the last few weeks. He'd said it at least once a day since I'd gotten back from London and declared my pity party was over.

I hit the pit crew button on the wheel out of habit, even though I couldn't bring myself to respond to Wilkes. He was right. I needed to get off the track and clear my head before my bloodstain became a permanent fixture somewhere on the asphalt. But that didn't make it any easier to face the crew as I pulled into the pit.

I got out without a word and headed straight for the locker room.

"Where are you going?" Wilkes asked, following at my heels.

"We're done, right?" I snarled, not bothering to hold the door for him

He swore under his breath as it swung toward him. He caught it before it smacked him in the face and headed in after me.

"Are we going to talk about what's going on out there?" he asked.

I started peeling off my suit and shook my head. "What's the point?"

"The point?" he repeated and barked a laugh. "The point is that you're supposed to be a professional racecar driver but that last time you clocked wouldn't put you on the boards. It wouldn't put you in the same room."

"Thanks for the pep talk." I pushed past him, padding toward the shower. I already knew my times were shit. I wasn't sure why he kept pointing it out. I turned on the tap to *scalding* and stepped under it. Heat seared my skin, but the tension I felt in my muscles, my body, *my fucking soul*, didn't melt.

I half expected him to follow me and continue his lecture, but he didn't. I stayed under the water, wishing it was hotter, wishing it could wash away the memory of Lola. But she lingered—her smile, her touch, her scent that seemed to coat my entire body right down to my heart. It was beyond wishful thinking. It was stupid. Nothing could do that. I knew because I'd been trying everything I could think of for weeks.

Wilkes was waiting for me outside the showers when I finally emerged. I groaned when I saw him.

"You know, it's the strangest thing," he said as I wrapped a towel around my waist. "I'm looking at you, but it's like you left your head in London."

"Sod off," I muttered. Digging through my locker I found my pants and yanked them on.

"Being mad at me isn't going to help."

"It can't hurt." I shot him a smirk as I pulled my T-shirt over my head.

"You know what's going to hurt? Losing all your sponsors. McKinnons called and they want to send their people over to check out their investment."

I froze but didn't look over at him. McKinnons was the biggest sponsor we had left. Between my wreck, my hiatus, and my royal scandal, most of our sponsors had dropped me quickly and quietly.

"If we lose them—" he started.

"I get it." If we lost them, that was it. No car. No season. No future. "What did you tell them?"

"I gave them some bullshit excuse that they should wait a few weeks." He crossed his arms and leaned against the wall. "But I can't stall them forever. "

"I know that." The words tasted bitter because I meant what I said. I knew exactly how bad our situation was. The problem was that I couldn't seem to do a damn thing about it.

"Look." Wilkes straightened and took a deep breath that told me I really wasn't going to like whatever came out of his mouth next. "Maybe you should talk to Lola."

"Fuck you." I grabbed my phone and keys from the shelf and shoved them into my pocket.

"I don't think I'm the one you want to fuck," he said meaningfully.

"Fuck you," I repeated and instantly felt like a knob, so I added, "harder."

"How eloquent," he said. "Is that Chaucer or Shakespeare?"

I pushed wet hair out of my eyes. I needed to get it cut. I had needed to for weeks. I'd needed to do a lot of things for weeks. Scratching my chin, I realized that I didn't remember the last time I had shaved. I made a note to do it later, right after I wiped away the memory of today's laps with a few pints.

I turned to Wilkes and forced a smile.

"What are you doing?" he asked suspiciously.

"Smiling." But as I said it my lips fell into a frown.

"It looks like you're in pain," he said in a flat voice.

I gave up trying to look cheerful. "I get it. I need McKinnons. Don't worry. I got this."

"You do?" He lifted his eyebrows. "Because whatever it is you're doing, it's not racing."

His words hit me in the gut, and I sucked in a breath. He was right. "I know, but I'm fighting."

Wilkes studied me for a moment, his eyes unreadable. Even after all our years together, I never knew what he was thinking. Mostly because he was usually concocting some deep, life-changing insight that might help if I could see past my annoyance.

Finally, he shook his head. "You aren't fighting. You're

surviving. And that's a whole different thing."

"Profound," I said, rolling my eyes. "Is that a fortune cookie or Yoda?"

"You aren't going to fix this thing by pretending it's not happening."

"We won't know until we try, right?" I was getting sick of this, but I didn't have a choice but to listen to him. Not if I wanted to keep what was left of my career. Before he could respond, I walked away.

Brex was waiting in the parking lot, leaning against the side of the Range Rover parked next to my bike. Despite refusing to speak with Alexander or any other royal representative since I'd left over a month ago, I couldn't shake Brex. I'd given up trying and just gotten used to it. He wasn't so bad. Probably because he stayed out of my business, unlike everyone else I knew. And he didn't care that I drove my motorcycle as long as I let him follow me in the SUV.

He shot me a wide grin as I approached and grabbed my helmet.

"Don't ask," I said before he could ask me how things had gone today.

"Got it." He shoved his hands in his pockets and tilted his head. "I assume we're going to the pub then."

"You assume correctly." I put my helmet on and straddled the bike, reconsidering. "You know, you don't have to go with me. Nothing's going to happen."

"But I enjoy your company," he drawled. "It always cheers me up."

"Prick," I called as he climbed behind the wheel.

He shrugged. "Bastard."

Touché.

The ride to the Dark Horse went too quickly. There was something about being on the back of a bike that cleared my head. Or, at least, it gave me a break from thinking about the laundry list of fuck-ups I was racking up day after day. I didn't bother to wait for Brex to pull in before I headed inside the bar.

There were three or four regulars inside. For a Tuesday, that was practically a record. Brex came in behind me, his mobile pressed to his ear and his face stony.

"Got it," he said in a clipped tone. Then his face softened a little. "You too, poor boy."

Great. He was talking to Alexander. With any luck, my older brother would also find a way to show up and tell me off. That would really take this day from bad to shit.

I sat down on my usual stool, and two beers appeared before me.

"Thanks, Joy." Brex flashed a winning smile at the barkeep as he took the stool next to mine.

Picking up my glass, I took a long drink before turning to him. "What was that about?"

"The call?" he asked, and I nodded. "Going over some reports. Nothing to worry about."

"As long as Alexander isn't planning to chain me to the wall in Buckingham," I said miserably.

"At least you'd be in London," he said, taking a sip.

"Not you, too," I groaned. "Look, Lola and I are ancient history."

He grinned at me. "Who said anything about Lola? I didn't. Is she on your mind?"

"Nope." I held up a hand. "Keep your Jedi mind tricks to yourself."

"I'm just saying—"

"Can we not talk about Lola?"

He put his drink back down on the bar before finally nodding. "Whatever."

"Whatever," I agreed. "Now, let's get pissed."

"Maybe we should order some food," he suggested gently.

I raised an eyebrow. "Who put you up to this? Wilkes or my mother?"

"I'm just looking out for you."

I gulped down the rest of my pint and slammed the empty glass on the counter. "In that case, get me another."

Brex hesitated, and for a moment, I thought he was going to say something. He'd been doing that more and more lately: falling silent like he was about to unload on me. But in the end, he shrugged and lifted his hand. "Another pint for my mate, Joy?"

She beamed back at him.

"Have you guys picked out colors for the wedding?" I teased him.

"Shut it." He rolled his eyes. "I'm not in the market."

Somehow, I suspected that had less to do with Joy being at least seventy and a certain gorgeous, if somewhat terrifying, Indian partner of his.

"Me neither," I said, clinking my glass against his in a toast.

We were such liars.

. . .

By ten, I was pissed out of my mind. I cupped my half-full pint with both hands to keep myself from falling off the barstool. Brex had disappeared a few minutes ago. Maybe hours ago. Usually, I didn't let it get that bad, but today had sent me into a spiral. Any minute, we would lose our last sponsor and my career would be over, my crew would be out of a job, and Wilkes would never stop looking disappointed.

I could almost picture his sad, concerned face.

I blinked, and it became clearer.

"Joy, another round," I yelled in her general direction.

"Joy, ignore that," Wilkes barked.

I swiveled to him in surprise. "You're real."

"Well-spotted." He sighed and put his arm around me. "C'mon, let's get you home."

"Brex is here," I told him, waving off his help.

"I know. He called me."

"Snitch," I muttered, but I let Wilkes help me out of the bar. Brex was waiting by the Range Rover.

"We'll get your bike tomorrow," Brex told me as he opened the passenger door.

"Go get some rest," Wilkes told me. "Try and make it through the day tomorrow, okay?"

I saluted him, earning another frustrated sigh. He shut the door, and I waited, watching as he and Brex spoke with their heads together outside the car.

"Just came in for a drink," I muttered. "What a crock."

They were humoring me, but I wasn't stupid. And tomorrow I was going to tell them.

. . .

BRIGHT LIGHT BURST through my eyelids, and I bolted upright. A couple of things were readily apparent. I was home and in my own bed. I blinked, trying to adjust to the light. Grabbing a pillow, I tried to smother myself with it.

"Never again," I announced into the pillow. It wasn't the first time I'd said I would cut this shit out, but it was the most recent.

I wasn't expecting anyone to answer me.

"Until tonight?"

I froze at the sound of that voice, still holding the pillow over my face. Had I actually smothered myself? Was I dead? Lifting the pillow, I peeked out from under it and found Lola Bishop staring back at me.

CHAPTER THIRTY-FOUR

LOLA

I'd gone mental.

There was no other explanation for why I was standing in Anders' bedroom.

Except that I had been summoned once again to get him under control.

But that wasn't the real reason I was here. I just wasn't about to admit to anyone, even myself, that I was here because I fucking cared. Not when caring had left me with a broken heart for the last five weeks, two days, and two hours. But who was counting?

He sat up quickly, his broad chest and chiseled abs on full display. His T-shirt was wadded on the floor next to his bed, but thankfully, his jeans were still on—even if they were undone like an invitation. I turned my head away, hoping the flare of heat I felt didn't make it onto my cheeks.

"Are you real?" he mumbled.

"No, I'm the ghost of Christmas past." I rolled my eyes and dared to glance back at him. He looked like shit. Really hot shit. Like *damn-him-for-still-looking-like-sex-on-a-stick* shit. But shit, nonetheless. His hair was an artful mess, his chin deliciously stubbled, purple circles rimmed his eyes, and I could smell last night's drinks from here. But the smirk, the body, the whole package was still fully intact.

I felt a deep pang in my chest. He was drowning. It was obvious. I wasn't stupid enough to believe that had anything to do with me. He had left London after he'd made it perfectly clear he wanted nothing to do with my kind of people. No, this has more to do with what was going on in his own head and on the track. Wilkes had told me as much when he'd called.

"I need a drink." Anders threw his legs over the side of the bed. Apparently, he wasn't remotely curious as to *why* I was here.

"Good to see you, too." I circled around and blocked him from getting up to leave. Crossing my arms over my chest, I swept my eyes over him, careful to keep my concern tamped down. But that wasn't easy.

He sighed and ran a hand through his mussed hair. "Why are you here, boss?"

My body went molten, clearly recalling exactly what the man behind that voice—that damn nickname—could do to me. But I wasn't going to let him see that, especially since he clearly hadn't spent the last month replaying the nights we'd spent together while sadly getting himself off. Nope, only I had been that pathetic. Going to work and closing deals, growing Bless like crazy, and then going home to mastur-cry into my pillow.

"I have a challenge for you," I told him.

"Oh yeah?" His tongue licked over his lower lip, and I knew exactly what he was thinking.

"Not that kind of challenge, Your–"

"Don't call me that," he snarled, and I took an involuntary step back. He hung his head and fumbled an apology. "Sorry. Just don't fucking remind me that I'm one of them."

Them. It hit me in the chest like he'd thrown a knife at me.

"Got it." There was no need to remind either of us of the life he hated so much. Instead, I reached into my pocket, pulled out a key fob, and tossed it to him.

"What's this?" He turned it over in his hand, his thumb brushing over the McLaren logo.

"I finally bought a car." I shrugged, determined to act like this was no big deal and not like I was having an internal panic attack. "Teach me how to drive."

"You came here so I could teach you how to drive?" he asked slowly.

"I figured you were the best person for the job, and you offered, remember?"

"I did." His eyebrows knit together, and I realized he was looking for a way out. "It's just, um..."

"You're busy." I swallowed, but the lump of wounded pride in my throat didn't budge. Reaching down, I swiped the fob from his hands. "Never mind. See you later, Stone."

"Lola, wait!"

I was already out of the room. So much for my brilliant plan. When I'd gotten the call that Anders was a hot mess, I'd been foolish enough to believe I could help him. But he didn't want me or my help.

I stopped in the hallway outside of Anders' room and tried to steady my racing heart. It didn't matter. At least, it shouldn't matter. Anders was nothing more than a mistake. He'd left London without so much as a backward glance. Whatever I'd thought was happening between us until then had been in my own head. We had our own lives to lead. I just wished I could be as blasé about all of this as he seemed to be.

And that was the problem.

I hadn't really come here to help him. I'd come here to fix me. Part of me had wanted to see that he was a wreck—to see that he missed me as much as I missed him. But this wasn't about me. It was about his career.

I sighed and forced myself to straighten up. Anders was standing there, looking hesitant. His jeans were buttoned, but he hadn't bothered to put on a shirt or shoes. "Ready for that driving lesson now?"

"Forget I asked." Wilkes could find another way to handle Anders. I was done with this, done running to help whenever anyone called.

He followed me down the hallway, and by the time I reached the stairs, I felt the warmth of his body behind me.

"Wait," he said, spinning me around by the shoulders. "I don't want you to leave like this."

I waited, my eyes locked on his. It was up to him to make the next move. I'd shown up for him twice by my count; now it was his turn.

"Let me teach you. I said I would." He squeezed my shoulders, and I tossed a frosty look at his hands. Anders pulled away, holding them up in surrender.

"I don't want to inconvenience you." I let a chill seep into my voice, even though his touch had lit a fire inside me.

"You could never inconvenience me." He groaned and trailed a hand down his abs. I tried not to stare. "I wasn't expecting you. That's all. I'll teach you. We can start now."

"Maybe you should put some clothes on."

He glanced down to his bare feet, and a grin hooked across his face. "I don't need clothes to drive, boss."

Oh holy...

I blinked and pinned an unimpressed frown on my face. "You need them if you're going anywhere with me."

"I thought you liked—"

"Let's get one thing straight. I came here to learn how to drive this car. I want to be able to take it to the country on the weekends."

"The country?" he repeated.

Was my lie that flimsy? Probably.

"My boyfriend lives out there," I said, doubling down on the lie. Not only was it a good excuse, it was one he wouldn't question, and maybe he'd keep me at a distance. The last thing I needed was to fall into his arms again.

Boyfriend. His lips formed the word, but he didn't seem to process it. His throat slid, but he shrugged and kept that cocky grin on his face. "Okay, no problem. But if I'm going to teach you, it's my rules. Not yours."

I was afraid he would say that, so why did a thrill leap through me at the idea of letting him be in charge?

You know why, a little voice inside me chided.

"I can agree to that *behind the wheel*," I added.

"Not going to make me follow your old rules?" He lifted an eyebrow.

"Why would I do that?" I said blandly and hoped he bought it. "We're friends now, right? *Just friends?*"

Our eyes met, and we stared at each other for so long that I lost track of the seconds. I didn't want to be friends with Anderson Stone. I didn't want to be in the same room as him. My heart hammered in my chest, calling me out on yet another lie.

The truth was that I didn't want to get my heart broken again. Not when it was finally starting to heal. But I was here now, and I had to find a way to get out of this unscathed.

"Friends," he agreed, but he looked away like maybe he didn't like the sound of it.

This was going to be complicated.

CHAPTER THIRTY-FIVE

ANDERS

"Beautiful," I muttered as I circled the car parked in my drive.

"What?" Lola called. She was carefully maintaining her distance. I just wasn't sure what scared her more: me or the car.

"It looks good," I said casually, and she bit her lip, something flashing in her eyes.

It looked a hell of a lot like disappointment. But Lola hadn't come here to be called beautiful by me. Not when she had a fucking boyfriend who lived in the country. He sounded like a total wanker—an opinion I'd managed to keep to myself.

Besides, Lola wasn't beautiful. She was in a whole different league than beautiful. Stunning. Gorgeous. Cockteasingly perfect. I couldn't quite find the right words to sum her up. Maybe they'd never been invented. And maybe it was the time apart or the very definitive boundary she'd just erected between us, but I couldn't stop myself from stealing looks at her.

She was dressed casually by her standards. A white T-shirt and jeans that hugged her ass in a way that made me believe life really had a meaning, and she quite possibly was it. She'd traded her heels for a pair of red trainers the exact shade of her lipstick and her new McLaren GT. Seeing her behind its wheel looking like that might fulfill every male fantasy I'd ever had.

And it was going to make keeping my hands to myself much more difficult.

It was for the best, though. I couldn't afford to be any more distracted than I already was, not with Wilkes breathing down my neck about sponsors.

"How does it handle?" I asked her.

She shrugged, flattening her luscious red lips into a frown. "How would I know? I don't drive, remember?"

"How did you get it here?" A terrible thought occurred to me. She had a boyfriend, and the wanker was important enough that she'd bought a car to be able to see him. That must be serious. She hadn't even bought a car for me, and I was a professional driver. I glanced around, half expecting him to pop out of the bushes.

"I had it delivered, and I took the train down," she said, laughing at my confusion. "You would have heard them drop it off earlier if you weren't passed out at noon."

"It's Saturday," I said with a slight growl, even though I was pleased that the new boyfriend wouldn't be joining us. "I was up late."

"Oh?" Lola's laughter died down, and her curious eyes flickered over to me. "Out with someone?"

I tensed, aware of the question in her eyes. Was she asking because she was jealous? Or because she hoped I had moved on, too?

"Just went to the pub. It was a long week," I muttered, trying to keep my voice steady but failing.

Lola smiled, her curiosity shifting to a coyness that made my balls tighten. "I figured. But I can't resist winding you up."

I grinned back, feeling the tension between us ease a bit. "Yeah, you definitely still know how to drive me crazy." I held up the key fob. "Now, let's teach you how to drive."

She reached for the keys, but I closed my fist around them. Her hand brushed mine, and the contact sent a jolt racing down my spine.

"What do you think we're doing?"

"Learning how to drive," she said, sounding puzzled.

"I'm not letting you on the street here." I laughed as her confusion turned to annoyance. "Simmer down, boss. I can't let you mow down any little old ladies or kids."

"Fine." She marched over to the car and pulled up the butterfly door. I followed behind her and leaned in.

"First rule, boss? One step at a time," I told her gently. "Now buckle up."

She stuck her tongue out and made a show of pulling down her belt. I closed the door quickly before that tongue gave me any bad ideas. She was officially off-limits, and I needed to concentrate anyway. The last thing I wanted was to unleash an unprepared Lola onto the streets.

And teaching her would give me a chance to make sure she knew what she was doing—to know she'd be safe.

But as soon as I climbed into the driver's side and closed the door, I was questioning my sanity. Her perfume filled the cabin, reminding me just how good she smelled.

"Something wrong?" Her eyebrows flicked up, but I grinned.

"Just thinking about where to start." I pointed to the wheel. "Steering wheel."

"I know that." She rolled her eyes.

I forgot how fucking sexy she was when she was being obstinate. "Ok, prodigy, what are these?" I pointed to two paddles attached to the wheel.

"Uh, windshield wipers?" she guessed.

I smirked. "Paddle shifters. If you want to drive the car in manual mode, you can use them. But they suck."

"When do I need to do that?" She leaned closer to look at them, her shoulder bumping mine. I leaned back in my seat to give her room to check them out and hoped she didn't look at my crotch. Not while I was sporting a semi with her this close to me.

"You don't," I said. "Some people like to drive in manual. It helps them understand their car better."

"Am I learning that, too?" She flashed a concerned look at me.

I almost couldn't believe it. Lola Bishop was scared. I didn't think that was possible. I kept this thought to myself. "Not now. Not unless you want to. I'm just telling you what everything is."

I ran her through the rest of the buttons on the wheel before moving on to the pedals.

"Ready?" I finally asked.

She shook her head. "There are still a hundred buttons in here."

"Don't worry about that." I waved a hand dismissively over the console. "You can learn how to work your radio later. For now, it's all about the basics. Don't get bogged down in the details."

Lola huffed. "So, that will be lesson number two?"

I winked at her.

"Where are we going?" she asked as I steered the car onto the road.

"The track."

"What?" she shrieked. "I just want to learn how to drive the car. Not race it."

"The parking lot will be empty."

"Fine." She sank back into her seat.

"So, um, how have you been?" I cringed at the awkward question. It felt all wrong. Acting like friends. Ignoring the sparks between us. Keeping my hands off of her. But I had walked out like a fucking coward and lost my shot. I was just lucky to be near her, even if she didn't want me anymore.

"Good. Work is crazy. Belle and Smith bought a house in the country, so I'm going out there for meetings all the time. Figured it was time to get a car."

I nodded, doing my best to remain casual. "So that's where your fella is?"

Fella? Fella? So much for acting cool, but did that mean her new guy was staying with them like family already?

"What?" She glanced over at me. "Oh, um, yeah. Sure. Two birds. One stone."

"Makes sense," I said through gritted teeth. It was clear she wanted to talk about this even less than I did. I wasn't sure what was a safe topic. "I approve of your car choice, by the way."

"Thanks." Her smile dazzled me. "It's not too much?"

"Most people start with something a little less…"

"Expensive?" she guessed.

"For starters," I said with a laugh, "but it suits you. You weren't meant to drive something ordinary, boss."

Her teeth sank into her lower lip, her eyebrows furrowing. Was it the compliment or the nickname?

"Sorry," I said with a deep sigh as I turned down the street that led to the track. "I didn't mean to sound so flirty."

"It's just your default setting," she teased, lifting one shoulder. "Don't worry about it. I'm immune to your charm now."

"Good," I said, even as a pit opened inside my stomach.

"Good," she echoed absently.

We might be friends now, but it was clear small talk was a problem for us. I pulled into the track's car park and stopped.

"I thought we were going on the track," she said, looking around at the empty lot.

"You have to walk before you can run. We'll start here."

I opened the door and stepped out, trying to clear my head. I needed the fresh air. I needed to get her scent out of my brain. What the fuck was I thinking when I said yes to this? I couldn't do this. How was I supposed to act like we were just two friends hanging out? She had to feel the same tension I did. It wasn't just coming from me. She was giving off the same signals.

And now I'd volunteered to sit in the same car with her for hours—potentially days—and act like I didn't want to fold her over the hood of her new car and have my way with her. She watched me from inside the car, so I forced a smile and gestured for her to get out. She obeyed, following me to the bonnet, her hips swaying and her curves accentuated by the tight jeans she wore.

"Let's get started," I said, trying to sound nonchalant. "First lesson: keep it simple. I want you to get used to the feel of the car."

I led her over to the driver's side and circled to the passenger side while she adjusted the seat to her body. As soon as I got in the car, she looked at me nervously, excitement and trepidation warring in her eyes.

"Check your mirrors," I said in a strained voice. God, she looked good behind the wheel.

"All set?" I asked.

She nodded, her fingers clutching the wheel.

"Good. Now, put your foot on the brake pedal and hit the ignition."

The car roared to life. She bit her lip, and I nearly groaned.

"Put it in drive, and take it nice and easy," I said, my voice gruff. She followed my instructions, glancing over at me with a goofy grin once she had the car in drive.

She took a shaky breath and did as she was told. A second later, the car jolted forward a hundred meters before we slammed to a stop.

"Easy, boss," I coaxed her, but she was already shaking her head.

"This was a stupid idea," she muttered. "I can't do this. What was I thinking?"

"Hey." I reached over and tilted her head to face me. "Lola Bishop can do anything. I've seen it for myself. This is just a stupid car. You've handled much worse."

She managed a half smile. "Oh yeah?"

"Yeah. Like me," I reminded her. "A car's a lot easier to handle than I am."

For a moment, neither of us looked away. Her eyes softened, her mouth parting slightly. Without thinking, I leaned closer, close enough that I felt the heat of her breath on my face. Fuck, I wanted to kiss her. I was going to kiss her.

I forced myself back into my own seat and took a deep breath. "Let's try this again."

CHAPTER THIRTY-SIX

ANDERS

"This is awkward," Lola announced.

"What?" I asked as we turned onto my street, even though I suspected she meant coming home with me. To my house. To stay overnight. We hadn't really discussed it.

"I thought I'd be able to drive myself to my hotel," she admitted with a laugh.

"Oh." Fuck. Fuck. Fuck. "I just assumed you would crash here. I should have asked."

"No, I should have told you," she said quickly.

Well, she was right about the awkward part.

"I can take you over there and pick you up in the morning," I offered. "If you want another lesson."

She scrunched her nose. "I think I need a couple more lessons if I'm being honest."

She had managed to circle the car park at the track a couple of times, but we hadn't even attempted the actual track. She was far from being ready to take it out on her own.

"Maybe," I agreed. "As many as you need."

"Okay, just as long as I'm not a distraction."

"It's probably a lot safer to spend time with you at the track than with my team," I admitted to her.

"Is everything okay?" she asked, placing her hand on my arm.

My gaze fell on it for a split second, and she pulled back. "Sorry. I shouldn't pry."

"No," I stopped her before she got the wrong idea. "It's not that. I just haven't really talked about it. Brex is the closest thing I have to a friend, but that's more bodyguard privilege, I think."

"Where is Brex?" she asked. "I thought he would be around."

"I don't know," I realized. I'd been so distracted by Lola's unexpected arrival I'd forgotten about my bodyguard. I'd even managed to spend a day at the track, if not exactly on it, without thinking about sponsors or expectations or Wilkes' daily disappointment. "He's usually my shadow. Maybe I should call him. Mind if I grab my phone charger?"

"Sure." She settled against her seat as we reached my house.

But the driveway wasn't empty. "Shit."

Lola sat up and peered out the window. "Whose car is that? Is it Brex? Did I get you in trouble?"

"No, boss." I laughed as I shook my head. "Brex wouldn't drive a Peugeot."

"New girlfriend?"

Was that a catch in her voice, or was I imagining things?

Not that it mattered. "My mum."

"Your mum," she repeated, her eyes widening.

"I know. I'm embarrassed that she drives a Peugeot, too, but I can't talk her into letting me buy her a car." I turned off the engine. "I'll just be a second."

"Maybe I should come in." Lola chewed on her lower lip. Had she always done that, or was I just obsessing over her mouth? "I don't want to be rude."

I hesitated. My mother had asked to meet Lola before. When things hadn't worked out, I hadn't expected to ever have the chance to introduce them.

"Or not," she blurted out. "I don't want it to be weird."

She was worried about this getting weird. Maybe I wasn't completely out of her system, either. That was probably wishful thinking. "Come in. I know she wanted to meet you."

"Ok, as long as you don't mind."

I got out of the car and was halfway around the car to open her door before I realized what I was doing. My brain knew things were over between us, but it seemed the rest of me was having a hard time catching up. I shoved the uncomfortable thought deep inside me and trudged the last few steps to her door, and opened it.

"It's a low seat," I mumbled, trying to come up with an excuse for my gallantry.

"Thanks." She took the hand I offered, and a pulse of electricity shot through my skin at her touch. Her breath caught, and I knew she felt it, too. As she climbed out of the car, her hair fell in front of her face, a curtain of chestnut locks that hid her expression. She pulled away as soon as she was on her feet, but the heat between us was palpable. Our bodies hummed with the unspoken tension we'd both felt all day. The air crackled with energy as we stood there, silently daring each other to make a move.

"Better get inside," she said softly.

"Yeah." I forced myself to swallow the words on the tip of my tongue.

I'm sorry.

I miss you.

Give me another chance.

There was no point. I'd fucked up, and I would spend the rest of my life regretting letting her go.

We walked silently to the house. As soon as I opened the front door, the rich smell of tomato sauce hit me.

"Shit," I muttered.

"I made your favorite," my mum called from the kitchen, her voice growing closer with each word, "and I know you hate it when I surprise you, but—"

She rounded the corner and cut-off mid-sentence when she spotted us standing there.

"Oh, Anders, I am so sorry." She clapped a hand over her mouth. "I should have called first."

"It's okay." I put a hand on Lola's back, tipping my head toward her. "This is Lola. She needed my help with something."

Lola jumped forward like she'd been bitten by a snake. She covered it with a wide smile and held out a hand. "I'm so happy to meet you, Mrs. Stone."

"It's Rachel." Mum bypassed Lola's hand and went in for a hug. I stood by, rubbing my hand over my hair. "I'm so glad you're here. I hope you're hungry."

"Oh, um..." Lola glanced at me.

"Lola isn't staying. I was just taking her to her hotel."

"Hotel?" Mum said, looking between the two of us. "So, you two aren't..."

"No!" we both said at the same time.

"Anders is teaching me how to drive," Lola explained quickly. "I just bought my first car."

Mum continued to study us with a maternal suspicion that made me nervous. "Have you eaten?"

"I'll probably grab some room service."

"That's silly. It's late, and there is plenty of food." It wasn't an invitation. It was an order. "Stay, and I'll tell you embarrassing stories about Anders when he was a kid."

"Now *that* is tempting." Lola flashed me a grin, and I found myself hoping she would say yes.

"It's up to you," I said carefully.

Lola looked back at my mom. "I'd love to stay. Need any help?"

"It's all on the table, but maybe Anders can dig up some wine."

"I'm not sure if I have any."

"You do." Mum shot me a sweet and meaningful look that told me I was expected to find wine. Now.

No good could come of leaving my ex-girlfriend, if Lola even qualified as that, with my mother, but I knew better than to argue. "I've got a few bottles in the garage."

I headed to the garage, trying to sort through the mess I felt inside myself. Seeing Lola and my mother getting along like old friends made me realize how much I missed having her in my life. But I tried to push those thoughts aside and focus on picking out a good wine. I grabbed a bottle of

Cabernet Sauvignon, hoping it would meet my mother's approval.

When I returned to the kitchen, Lola and my mother were at the table, heads together and laughing.

"Please tell me you didn't tell her the dog story," I said as I carried the wine to the table.

Lola looked up at me, her eyes sparkling with laughter. "Oh, she did."

"It's a cute story." Mum reached to dish up a plate for me, but Lola stopped her.

"Let me. You cooked."

Mum shot me a look over Lola's head that clearly said she approved of this girl.

"It's not a cute story. It's mortifying," I informed them.

Lola passed a filled plate to my mother and then reached for mine. "You don't have to do that," I said in a low voice.

"Pour me some wine, and we'll call it even." She turned toward my mum as she dished up the plate. "So he didn't behave much as a kid either?"

"I was an angel," I said as I uncorked the Cab.

"Hardly," Mum said with a snort. "I didn't think he was going to live to see ten years old."

"Thanks for the vote of confidence."

Lola set the plate in front of me, and our eyes met again, lingering just too long. She cleared her throat and turned away.

My mother spent the next hour cataloging my entire youth in escalating order of the most embarrassing incidents of my life.

"It sounds like he kept you busy," Lola said after she

wrapped up the time I'd broken my leg trying to learn to skateboard.

"He did." Mum sighed and looked at me with the kind of love that made me feel guilty for all the shit I'd put her through. "He's alive, but it wasn't for lack of trying. He's still trying—and trying my heart." She turned to Lola. "Maybe you can talk him into a less dangerous career."

"I doubt that." Lola laughed, but it was a tad hollow. "He does what he wants."

"And he always has. Remember when you ran away?" She turned to me.

I rolled my eyes but nodded. "Yeah, but I don't remember why."

"Neither do I." She shook her head. "But you packed half the food in the kitchen, nothing else, mind you, and took off."

"My strategy needed work," I told Lola, who giggled.

"Just food, huh?"

"In my defense, growing boys are very hungry."

"I was in absolute panic," Mum told her. "I called all his friends. No one had seen him. The police were called, and do you remember where they found you?"

"The track." I rubbed my hands together. I could almost smell the air that day at Silverstone. "That day changed my life. I met Wilkes."

"Who, thankfully, told him that he would never be a racecar driver if he didn't listen to his mum," she cut in.

"Wilkes seems like a good one," Lola said with a smile.

"He is." I stabbed a meatball with my fork and sighed. Even all those years ago, he'd had my back. He had never given up on me. "I have no idea what he saw in a punk kid."

"What everyone else sees," Lola whispered, covering my hand with hers. "I just wish you saw it."

For a second, neither of us looked away. She saw me. She still saw me, and that's what hurt the most. I pulled my hand back and flashed my mum a grin.

"So, if you made my favorite dinner, does that mean..."

"There are biscuits in a tin in the kitchen," she said. "Let me clean up, and I'll get out of your hair."

"I'll help." Lola pushed back her chair. She grabbed a few plates and headed into the kitchen.

I stood to join her, but my mother caught me.

"I like her," she said quietly.

"We're just friends, Mum." I reached for a plate, but she clucked her tongue.

"She's in love with you, too, you know."

I closed my eyes and shook my head. "That ship has sailed. She's seeing someone else."

"So?" Mum shrugged. "That won't last if you tell her how you feel."

"I blew it," I admitted, looking to where Lola was filling the kitchen sink with water. God, she looked like she belonged there. Just like she looked like she belonged at my table, laughing with my mother. I could see a life with her so clearly that it hurt. But it wasn't just about how I had screwed up. She didn't belong in my world any more than I belonged in hers. And even if I hadn't been a total screw-up, we could never get around that. She was regal, and it didn't matter what a DNA test said. I wasn't royal.

"Neither of you is dead—even if you are constantly trying

to kill yourself on that track," she tacked on, squeezing my hand. "Win her back."

If only it was that easy.

CHAPTER THIRTY-SEVEN

LOLA

> Meet me out front in five.

I stared at the text as I rode the lift down to the lobby.

After last night, I had half-expected Anders not to come, especially after the completely silent ride back to my hotel. It hadn't helped to have dinner with his mom. He had already made it perfectly clear he didn't want me. But that wasn't the issue. Seeing him with his mom made it clear to me that Anders hadn't just checked out on me. He'd checked out on his life.

That meant what Wilkes had told me on the phone was true. Anders needed a purpose—something to drive him as much as racing once had—but I had no clue what that purpose was or how to help him find it.

"Miss Bishop," the doorman greeted me at the entrance. "Let me get that for you."

"Thank you." I stepped through the open door just as my

new McLaren roared to the curb, followed by a black Range Rover. "That's my ride."

He whistled, peering at it closer. "Buckle up."

"I will," I promised him. I waved to Brex before I climbed into the car.

Anders looked hotter than yesterday in a pair of fitted gray joggers and a T-shirt that showed off his biceps. But I couldn't help noticing the frown he wore with his clothes.

"What's up?" I asked cautiously. Was this the part where he let me have it for staying for dinner?

But his eyes flicked to the rearview mirror. "Our chaperone's returned."

"Is that why you're upset?" I breathed a silent sigh of relief. It would be a lot easier to figure out what was up with him if he wasn't mad at me.

"I didn't ask for this shit," he reminded me.

"I thought you liked Brex."

"I do." He groaned. "I don't like what his presence means."

A lump formed in my throat, and I fought back tears. I'd known coming back here would be difficult. I just hadn't expected to confront the reason we'd broken up at every turn. It was hard enough to be around him without being reminded of why he'd rejected me.

"You could always run away," I suggested, trying to keep my tone light. "It seems like you have some practice doing that."

He cocked an eyebrow, glancing over at me. "What does that mean, boss?"

His words were rough along the edge, and I realized he'd misunderstood the joke.

"When you were a kid and ran away to the track," I said, recalling the story his mother had told me last night.

His frown deepened. "What do you think I've been trying to do?"

"It's not going well?" I pressed gently. This was the real reason I'd come—to get inside his head and figure out what had him off his own game before he wound up wrecking another car.

"You tell me, boss." The corner of his mouth lifted into a grin. "I assume someone called you here. What did they say?"

"What?" I plastered a surprised look on my face. "I told you. I need you to help me learn how to drive."

"Right. You needed to learn to drive so you can visit your boyfriend." He practically spat the words.

I hated how the lie felt—and how I hadn't made the connection he'd just pointed out. But I couldn't risk telling him the truth. Not until I knew how he'd respond.

"I have other reasons, too." I shrugged. "But if I'm going to do this, it's because I want to do it."

"And you need a two-hundred-thousand pound car to do it?" he asked.

"I liked the color." I took a deep breath and spilled something I could only admit to him. "Maybe this is something I need to do for myself."

He thought for a moment before exhaling slowly. "I get that."

But I held back the rest of my thought. Maybe it was something I needed to do for the both of us. Anders might not love me, but I still cared about him, and I didn't want to see him hit rock bottom. Not if I could find a way to reach him.

"You know we could lose him in this car," he said, his eyes checking the mirror again.

"What's stopping you?"

"I don't want to set a bad example." His grin made my heart flip.

"I'm beginning to think you're all talk," I purred.

His eyes narrowed and he muttered something under his breath. The next thing I knew, we were flying down the road, and the Range Rover was a speck in the distance.

He took a corner hard, barely slowing down, and I grabbed his arm, my earlier bravado evaporating.

"Slow down!"

Anders chuckled and tipped his head toward the window. "We're here anyway, boss."

But this time, he didn't stop in the parking lot. Instead, he drove around until we reached a huge security gate.

"What are we doing?" I asked.

"You're doing today's lesson around the track," he informed me, and we waited for the gate to open. My heart shot into my throat. He couldn't be serious. I wasn't really going to drive my car around a racing circuit my second day behind the wheel.

"Is that safe?" I blurted out, earning another laugh.

"Trust me. There is no better place to learn than on a closed course. It has room to teach you everything you need—and you won't run over any pedestrians. You'll be the only one out," he said, reaching over and tucking a strand of hair behind my ear. "Try not to hit any walls."

"What about Brex?" I looked behind us, and the Range Rover was nowhere in sight.

"He knows where to find us."

Why did I find myself hoping that wasn't true? Maybe because this might be one of the last chances I had to have Anders all to myself. But that was dangerous thinking, the kind that would cost me my recently healed heart if I wasn't careful.

I settled into my seat as the gates opened, and Anders pulled onto the track and parked.

"I don't think I'm ready for this," I admitted when he came around to help me out.

He paused for a moment, a battle raging in his sky-blue eyes. Then, he cupped my cheek softly. I melted against him. "You got this."

"What if I don't?" I asked, my voice edged with panic.

"I'll be right next to you," he promised.

I shouldn't find that nearly as comforting as I did. That was the problem. Every second I spent with Anders proved to me I was wrong. My heart hadn't healed. I'd only learned to live with the pain.

"Let's do this." I lifted my chin and marched to the driver's side.

Anders slipped into the passenger seat as I checked my mirrors.

"You're sure this is safe?" I asked, my finger poised above the ignition button.

"You aren't racing. Just driving," he soothed me. "And we can stop anytime."

"Do I need a safe word?" I joked, immediately regretting it as memories hit me in full force.

His eyes flashed, but he wasn't angry. Instead, he shifted in his seat. "Just keep your eyes on the road," he said gruffly.

I did as he said, but out of the corner of my eye, I caught him adjusting his pants. It seemed I wasn't the only one remembering the last time I'd needed a safe word.

"Deep breaths, boss," he murmured.

I followed the advice as I placed my foot on the brake and started the car. He might have been right. The McLaren was a lot of car for a first-time driver. I took another deep breath and pressed my foot to the gas. We lurched forward.

"Easy," he advised. "Take it nice and slow."

Why did everything coming out of his mouth have to sound so pornographic? It wasn't helping me concentrate.

I focused on the road ahead, but as soon as reached the first turn, I slammed on my brakes.

"Why did you do that?" he asked.

"I don't know how to turn."

Anders bit back a smile. "Yeah, you do. Don't overthink it. As long as you remember where the brake pedal is, we're golden."

I nodded and started driving again, slowing down but not stopping when we reached the first turn.

"That's it," he crooned softly. "You've got this."

His words of encouragement spurred me on, and before long, I was cruising around the track with ease. It felt like...freedom.

When we reached the start of the track, I released the breath I had been holding and glanced over at him. His eyes twinkled in the sunlight, and the corners of his mouth curved upward. I grinned back.

"I did it!"

"Yeah, you did," he said, his voice thick with pride.

"I see why you love driving. I felt free," I whispered. I offered him a small smile. "Thanks for believing in me."

Anders reached out and brushed a strand of hair from my face, his thumb lingering on my cheek. The gesture was so tender and heartfelt that I almost forgot why we were here.

"You're a natural," he said softly.

His intense gaze flickered to my lips, and my heart skipped a beat as the air between us thickened. At that moment, I wanted him with a ferocity that left me breathless. The memory of our previous encounters came flooding back. The way he dominated me, pushed me to my limits, made me crave more.

Anders leaned in, his breath hot against my skin. "Do you feel that, boss?" he murmured, his lips hovering too close to mine. "That's the rush of adrenaline. That's living."

"This is why you race," I murmured, finally understanding.

"Nothing can touch it." He paused, his gaze raking over my face. "At least, that's how I used to feel."

I thought my heart was going to burst out of my chest. I should pull away. I should put a stop to this, but I not only could not, I didn't want to.

"What changed?" I breathed.

"Everything." His eyes dipped to my lips again. "I found someone who showed me what it really meant to feel alive." Suddenly, he drew back. "I'm sorry. We can't."

"Why not?" The question burst out of me.

"You have a boyfriend," he reminded me, "and you made it pretty clear we're nothing more than friends. *Just* friends, right?"

His question hung in the air between us.

My tongue darted over my dry lips as I gathered the courage to come clean. "Anders, I—"

A sharp rapping at the window startled us apart to find Wilkes standing there, looking white as a ghost.

Anders rolled down the window quickly.

"Thank God. I've been looking everywhere for you," he said, his words rushed and worried.

"What's wrong?" Anders asked.

"We're about to lose McKinnons."

I'd been around the track long enough to know McKinnons whiskey was one of his major sponsors.

"We can't lose them," Anders said, shaking his head, and maybe he loved me, but it was clear he loved racing, too. Without thinking, I grabbed his hand and held it.

"We'll figure something out," I promised him.

Wilkes glanced between us before letting out a heavy sigh. "Well, you better figure it out quickly because they're coming to the track tomorrow to make their final decision."

CHAPTER THIRTY-EIGHT

ANDERS

I hated the bottle staring back at me. We'd been locked in a silent battle of wills since I'd gotten home from dropping Lola and her car off at the hotel. Brex had driven me back to my place, not bothering to talk me out of a stop at the liquor store. He really wasn't such a bad guy.

I wasn't sure why I needed a bottle of McKinnons. The last thing I wanted to do was get drunk with tomorrow's meeting on the horizon. It wasn't like it would hurt, though. I hadn't had a decent lap time in months.

"Fuck you."

The bottle didn't respond.

"You don't get to decide what I'm worth," I screamed at it, wishing I believed it. But the truth was that if I lost racing, I would lose the last scrap of who I was—who I had fought to become for years.

I reached for it and twisted off the cap. I took a swig straight from the bottle, the amber liquid burning my throat.

But it tasted as bad as I felt. Whatever the answer was, I wasn't going to find it at its bottom.

Anxiety knotted my stomach as I walked to the window and looked out, trying to clear my head. I'd screwed up everything, and I had no one to blame but myself.

But the worst part wasn't being on the verge of losing my career. It was that Lola would be gone, too. Why would she want driving lessons from a failed racecar driver? She'd barely said a word when I'd dropped her off. Not that I'd been very talkative either. It was for the best. I'd barely had anything to offer her before. Soon I would have even less.

There was a knock at the door, and I frowned. It was probably Wilkes coming by to give me unhelpful advice. I couldn't blame him. He was about to lose his job, too.

I opened the door to find Lola on my doorstep, in shorts and a tank, sheer enough to reveal she was braless. She pushed past me, uninvited, and strode towards the living room.

"How did you get here?" I asked as I closed the door.

"I drove." She shrugged, her eyes surveying the room.

I stared at her. We'd only made it successfully around the track once today without any nervous braking. "By yourself?"

"Questioning your teaching skills?"

"I'm questioning leaving you with the car keys."

She ignored me and wandered over to the couch, but she didn't sit down.

"Do you always drink straight from the bottle like that?" she asked, grabbing the bottle of McKinnons from the table.

I didn't know what to say, but I couldn't bear the silence stretching between us. I could judge myself without her help.

"You shouldn't be here," I finally managed to say, trying to hide the desperation in my voice. "I'm not in the mood for company."

She shook her head. "Too bad, Your Highness."

"Don't call me—"

"Stop hiding who you are," she interrupted. "What is this going to solve?"

"I'm not drinking alone at home."

She raised an eyebrow, and I sighed.

"Not really."

"What are you doing with a bottle of whiskey then?" she demanded.

I shoved a hand through my hair. "You want to know?"

"Yes."

"Yelling at it," I admitted, letting my head hang.

There was a pause, and I couldn't bring myself to look up at her. She probably thought I was mental—*I* thought I was mental.

"And how's that working out?" she asked slowly.

"I think we were finally getting somewhere." I lifted my eyes to search hers for the answers I couldn't seem to find. "You can pour it out. I shouldn't drink. Tomorrow is going to be bad enough without being hungover."

"Good." She marched into the kitchen and returned a moment later empty-handed. "Now, why is tomorrow going to be that bad?"

"Why?" I echoed. "Where do I begin? Oh, how about: I'm going to lose my biggest sponsor."

"You'll get another one," she said fiercely, adding, "I'll help you."

"Not with my times. I've lost my flow."

"We'll find it." She planted her hands on her hips. "What other excuses do you have? Because I have all night to punch holes in them."

Fuck, I loved her. Any doubt I'd had—and most of that had been trying to ignore the facts—was gone. I wasn't sure I'd ever doubted it. No, I'd been scared of it—of her. Of this feeling that my whole life had changed the moment we met. And now, I realized what I was really afraid of.

"I fucked up," I said softly. "Leaving you was the biggest mistake I ever made."

Lola froze. The only movement was her eyes as they widened. "Oh."

"Don't worry. I know it's too late," I said swiftly, gathering the last shreds of my pride. "I know there's someone else."

"There isn't," she admitted, letting out a shaky breath. "I just said that so we wouldn't wind up back where we were."

Somehow that was worse. I was so pathetic that she'd needed an excuse to keep me from making a move.

"I deserved that." Suddenly, I wished I hadn't told her to pour out that bottle.

"I know you think your life is going to end tomorrow, but it won't." She moved a half step closer but didn't reach out.

Closing my eyes, I dropped my head and tried to bottle up the words swirling inside me. But it was no use. I couldn't keep it in. Not with her standing right here. Not when she deserved to know the truth.

"My life ended a month ago, boss," I whispered, daring to

look at her. "And the worst part is that it's all my fault. I threw it away."

"Anders—"

"I think I've been in love with you since the moment you walked onto my track." It felt better to admit than I'd thought it would. Not that it would change anything.

She opened her mouth and closed it again before shaking her head. "You are not in love with me."

My eyebrows shot up. After all this time keeping it in, now she was going to make me prove it? "Like hell I'm not."

"Compelling argument." She blinked rapidly and turned her head away, but not before I saw her tears.

I stepped forward and cupped her cheeks, gently guiding her eyes back to mine.

"I'm in love with you, Lola," I said, my eyes locked on hers. "I'm so in love with you it scares the shit out of me."

A sob escaped her, and she pulled away. "I didn't come here for us."

Her words snapped something inside of me. It was too little too late. I'd come up short once again, and I had no one to blame but myself. I swallowed, but the self-hatred continued to rise.

"Why did you come, then?" I demanded.

"Because I knew you were sitting alone." Her voice shook, but she continued, "And I knew you were telling yourself all those stupid lies, and I know because I've been where you've been. Alone and feeling empty and unwanted. But none of that is true."

"Really?" I hit back. "All evidence to the contrary, and you know what really sucks about it, boss? I know all those things are true because I made them come true. I had a career, and I blew it. And I don't even care about my stupid car. I've been sitting here, trying to give a shit about losing my last sponsor all night. But I can't because all I care about is that you're going back to London tomorrow, and that's it for us."

"Yeah, because we're incompatible, remember? You hate my world and everyone in it." She sniffed hard, the tears flowing harder now.

I shook my head, wishing I could make her see. "I hate being dissected and watched. I hate that everyone is just waiting for me to fuck up again. I hate that they're hoping I will. Because deep down, they all know I will. That's why I left. It's not about wanting their life or not wanting it. I just want something that's mine."

"Then take it," she screamed back at me. "We aren't like *them*. No one is going to hand us the world on a fucking platter, Anders! If you want something, you have to take it!"

Her words hit me like a punch in the gut. She was right. I'd waited my whole life to be told I was good enough—good enough to be a driver, good enough to have a family, good enough to be loved.

Two steps closed the distance between us. We crashed together, my arms drawing her roughly to me, our mouths colliding with an urgency that overtook my entire body. I poured everything into that kiss. I left nothing behind. She deserved that much. She deserved all of me, broken as I might be.

Lola gasped against my mouth. She grabbed my T-shirt, pulling me even closer. My hands cradled her head, deepening the kiss until I no longer knew where she ended and I began. I'd never felt like this before. Every touch, every moan, felt like a release. I finally knew why I'd fought so hard against my feelings for her.

Because loving her meant accepting the man she saw instead of the man I feared I was. I'd lived with that fear so long I'd let it control me. I'd nearly let it win. But it wasn't real.

This was real. She was real. *We* were real.

We broke apart and I pressed my forehead to hers, our skin damp with sweat. "I love you, Charlotte Bishop."

She laughed softly. "How formal of you."

"I felt the occasion called for it." I couldn't help but smile. Even if she walked away, I wouldn't waste another moment of happiness with her.

"What occasion is that?" she murmured.

"The first moment of the rest of my life."

Lola pulled back far enough to find my eyes and said the only words I needed to hear, "I love you, Anderson Stone."

CHAPTER THIRTY-NINE

LOLA

"Stop looking at me like that," I said, checking my blind spot one more time before I changed lanes. The McLaren's engine roared as I sped up. We were running late. Probably because we'd made the poor decision to shower together, which had resulted in getting dirty rather than clean.

Not that I regretted a single second.

Anders shifted in the passenger seat but didn't let go of my hand. "Like what, boss?"

"Like I'm going to kill you." She flashed me a smirk, her red lips drawing my attention away from the road. "I'm doing just fine."

"You are, but—stop!"

I slammed on the brakes in time to avoid hitting a car coming from the opposite direction. "That wasn't my fault!"

"I didn't say it was." He raised my hand to his lips and kissed the back of it. "It was your right of way, but, uh, you were going a little fast."

"Fast?" I snorted and shot him a look before returning my eyes to the road. My hands gripped the steering wheel more tightly, my whole body wound up from the near-miss. "You are one to talk, racecar driver."

"We'll see about that," he said grimly, his face darkening.

We'd been avoiding the subject of racing all morning, opting to stay in bed and celebrate our reunion until the last possible moment.

My heart sank as I realized that the moment was over. We were only a few minutes from the track and both of us were getting tenser with each passing second. I forced a smile and said, "I have faith."

"Sure." Anders sounded unconvinced.

Neither of us said anything the rest of the drive. He didn't even comment on my questionable driving. But a cloud had descended over our happiness, and it threatened storms. I couldn't blame him for being preoccupied. It had been easy to distract ourselves last night. Now we had to face those storms.

"We're here," I announced, mustering as much cheeriness as I could when we pulled into the track's car park.

He didn't let go of my hand.

My fingers twitched, wanting to stay in his grasp and wishing we could run back to bed together. But that moment had passed, and reality was calling.

As we got out of the car, Anders pulled me close and whispered in my ear, "What if I fuck this up?"

The vulnerability in his voice made my heart ache. But if he was unsettled I would be sure. He might question himself, but I really did have faith. I took a deep breath and popped onto my tiptoes, kissing him hard on the lips. "You've got this."

"And if I don't?" He searched my eyes.

"You've got me," I whispered.

He nodded, but the spark of excitement that had lit up his eyes for the last few hours was nowhere to be seen. Instead, he looked like he was about to face his worst nightmare. His face hardened into a stony mask as he took my hand and led me inside.

"I've got to get ready." He leaned down and kissed me, his lips lingering like he didn't want to go.

"I'll see you out there," I promised, grabbing his face with both hands. "I love you."

His mouth curved into a crooked grin. "I love you, too, boss."

As soon as he was in the locker room, I slumped against the wall. I'd meant every word I said. I knew he had it in him, but if he was going to find his flow, as he called it, it was up to him. He had been trying since we met, and part of me didn't want to admit that I might be the problem. Had I distracted him too much? Would I distract him today?

The glass doors down the hall swung open, and I looked up to find Brex walking toward me.

"He's getting ready," I told him, trying to smile but failing.

Brex nodded and threw an arm around my shoulder. "Is he as nervous as you are?"

"I'm the calm one," I said flatly.

"Fuck," he muttered.

I couldn't have said it better myself. I looked up at Brex. "Do you think I should go? Will it distract him if I'm here?"

"I think it will be a lot more distracting if you disappear," he said, shaking his head. "So, you two worked things out?"

"Yeah. I think so," I said breathlessly, "but don't report that back to your boss."

The last thing Anders needed right now was for his brother to butt into our relationship again. Not that we could hide it forever. For now, we needed to tackle one problem at a time. First, we needed to keep the sponsor happy. Then we could worry about the media and our families.

"My lips are sealed," he promised me. "It's not really my business anyway."

"You're the one who asked," I pointed out, a laugh escaping me.

"It's part of the job," he said, raising his eyebrows.

"Liar." I dropped my head on his shoulder and sighed. "I don't want to be the reason he ruins his career."

"Lola, from what I've seen, I think you saved his career."

"You really think that?" I asked.

"I know that," he said firmly. He took a step away and looked directly into my eyes. "I was there when he got into that fight with Alexander and when he wrecked his car and when he found out the truth about his father. He was a fucking mess until you came along."

"I think I just made things more complicated," I murmured.

"Nah." He shook his head. "You made them simple. Love does that. It wipes away all the other bullshit and makes you see things clearly. Even if he bombs today, he'll be fine. Cause he's got you."

A lump sat in my throat when he finished. I swallowed, but the raw emotion remained lodged there. "You sound like you're speaking from experience."

"Just observations. I spend a lot of time with love birds, remember?" he teased, but the joke didn't reach his eyes. I wondered who had taught Brex that important lesson—and why she had broken his heart. "Come on. We should head out there."

When we reached the pit, the crew was already assembled. Anders was there, dressed in his fitted black racing suit, and talking quietly with Wilkes, who had a hand on his shoulder. As we approached, Anders looked over his shoulder at me like he sensed me coming. He said something to Wilkes before he strode over to meet us.

"Good luck out there, man," Brex said, clapping him once on the back before shooting us a meaningful look. "I'll give you two a minute."

When he was gone, I let out a low whistle. "I'm having some serious waking fantasies about you in that racing suit."

"Yeah?" He smirked and leaned to whisper in my ear, "Later, I'm going to fuck you on the hood of my car in it."

I whimpered, and he laughed, brushing his hand along my cheek. Behind us, there was movement, and his hand fell to his side as he went rigid. Turning, I saw a group of men in suits enter the pit, one of them in the lead.

"Connor McKinnon," he muttered. "I guess I better go prove my worth."

He started to move away, but I grabbed his hand. "This

isn't about your worth," I told him. "This is about a car and a track and advertising. You're worth so much more than any of that, and fuck anyone who doesn't see that."

He stared at me a moment, the light returning to his eyes.

"Oh, and Anders." I dropped my voice so no one around could hear. "Rule number 5 is in play, so drive extra fast."

He groaned, swiping his tongue over his lower lip. "Now that is motivation, boss."

Anders leaned to kiss me once before he straightened and strode toward the sponsors. I stayed back as they spoke, not wanting to be in the way. But when he turned to get into the car, I dashed over to join Wilkes at the pit wall. McKinnon and his men had moved to the side behind barricades, set up to keep them out of the crew's way but close enough to see exactly how Anders performed.

"Here." Wilkes handed me a headset. "Want to sit in?"

I bit my lip as I took it. "Doesn't someone on the team need this?"

"You aren't on the team?" He raised an eyebrow. "As far as I'm concerned, you're the glue keeping our boy together."

I nodded, my pulse speeding up as I put the headset on. "Now what?"

"Your comms are off, so don't worry that you'll distract him," he informed me. He pointed to the monitors. "We're tracking everything. His wheels, the calibration of his steering, the wind. Everything. He's safe out there."

"Do I look worried?" I asked.

His eyes crinkled as he smiled. "A little. You'll get used to this. You ready?"

I nodded, and he turned, speaking into his headset as the

crew dashed about, finishing their final preparations. The team checked the car and the screens, but my eyes were firmly on the screen that showed Anders.

As the engine roared to life, a transformation took place. The fear in his eyes was replaced by a fierce determination, his face set in a grim expression.

And then he was off, hurtling down the track at impossible speeds. My heart pounded in my chest. My eyes darted to the camera that displayed his visor's camera and back to the monitor that displayed his progress. I didn't know how to read any of it.

"Fuck!" Wilkes let out a whoop, followed by, "Watch that corner."

I leaned toward the engineer next to me. "Is he doing okay?"

"Okay?" His eyes didn't leave the screen he was watching, but he shook his head in disbelief. "If he keeps his head, he's going to beat his best time."

My stomach lurched with every twist and turn, my pulse pounding like a jackhammer as the adrenaline surged through me. My entire heart was out there on that track, and I could scarcely breathe until he crossed the finish line. When he did, the entire crew cheered.

I yanked off my headset, trying to get control of my breathing.

"That's your best time by a full second," Wilkes yelled through the comms, and I nearly collapsed with relief.

The car slowed into the pit, the crew racing out to help Anders out. I watched him as he climbed from the car and yanked his helmet off, his eyes searching through the chaos to find mine. As soon as he was on his feet, he was racing toward me.

I ran out from the pit wall, and he caught me, lifting me off my feet and spinning me in a circle before he planted a kiss on my lips. We broke apart as Wilkes and McKinnon joined us.

"You're a damn machine." McKinnon thrust his hand out. "I shouldn't have believed the rumors. I can't believe I'm saying this, but I don't remember the last time I was this excited about an upcoming season."

"Thanks." Anders grinned and shook his hand.

"I was worried after you took this season off. It was understandable given the accident and everything," McKinnon added quickly, "but the investment is worth it."

"It's good to hear that." Wilkes gestured to the pit wall. "My men will show you some more of the data if you like."

"I don't need to see any more to tell you I'm still in," he said, "but the kid in me wants to see it."

He followed the engineer over to the monitors, and we all stared at each other for a minute before we collapsed into relieved laughter.

"We did it," Anders said, hugging me tightly.

"*You* did it," I corrected him.

"*We*." He shook his head. "You were right, boss. McKinnon doesn't determine my worth because this isn't just about me. It's about all of us. I couldn't do this without my crew." He met my eyes. "I couldn't do this without you. You were the missing piece of my team."

Wilkes cleared his throat, and we jumped apart. "Sorry,"

he said with a grin, "but I was starting to get worried you were going to mount her on the spot."

"Don't tempt me," Anders warned him.

"We have some stuff to discuss," Wilkes said. "Like how we keep you driving like that."

They shared a look that told me they needed to talk. I squeezed Anders' hand.

"I'll see you back at your house to celebrate."

He nodded as Wilkes began spewing technical information. I made it a few steps before he called out. "Hey, boss, just make sure rule number 5 is still in play when I get home."

I flashed him a wicked smile and headed out.

CHAPTER FORTY

ANDERS

The world looked different on the other side of that track time when Brex dropped me off a few hours later. I paused outside my front door and smiled. Lola's McLaren was parked in the drive. She was inside. Everything was right.

At least it would be. Just as soon as I handled one more matter.

The door was unlocked, and I couldn't resist the urge to call out, "Honey, I'm home."

Lola appeared, wearing a grin and a black silk dress that skirted a very fine line between underwear and apparel. She held up a bottle of champagne and smiled wider when she saw the pink roses I was carrying.

"I thought we should celebrate," she said.

I walked to her and hooked an arm around her waist, dragging her to me. "My thoughts exactly."

"Anders, you were incredible today." She stared up at me, love shining in her eyes, and I knew what I had to do.

"You're incredible every day." I kissed her softly and sighed. "There's something I need to talk to you about."

The smile fell from her face, but she pinned it back on quickly. "Before or after champagne?"

"Before." I'd been going over this in my head since I left the track. Hell, I'd been thinking about it while Wilkes went over the engineering report from the day. It couldn't wait any longer.

She swallowed. "You're scaring me."

"What?" I blinked, realizing I'd been caught in my own head for too long. "No, boss, don't be scared. It's a good thing. I think."

"You think?" she repeated. "Maybe I should open the champagne."

She twisted in my arms, but I tightened them around her. "Wilkes and I talked. Securing McKinnons was a start, but I'm going to need to perform like that all the time. He says I need to keep a clear head, stay away from all my family bullshit."

"Oh." Her voice was small. Looking down, I noticed her lower lip trembling slightly.

I was already fucking this up. "He's probably right," I continued before I lost my nerve. "Maybe today was a fluke."

"Maybe it was a miracle," she challenged me.

"Lola, racing has been my whole life," I explained to her. "It was all I ever wanted—"

"I get it. You don't have to spare my feelings."

I was really fucking this up.

She tried to pull away again, but I wouldn't let her go.

"Until you," I said, and she stopped fighting me. I laughed softly. "And now everything has changed."

"And you don't know what you want?" she guessed, her lips flattening into a thin line.

"I want you," I said incredulously. Clearly, I was going to have to work on my boyfriend skills. "That's why I'm quitting."

"Quitting?" Her eyebrows shot up. "I don't understand."

"Racing. I'm done." It felt good to have it off my chest. I hugged her.

She clung to me for a second before pulling back. "You can't quit racing. I won't let you."

"It's not a matter of letting me. If I have to make a choice, I choose you."

Lola studied my face for a moment before pushing onto her toes to kiss me.

"I choose you, too," she murmured, "but you aren't giving up racing."

"Has anyone ever told you that you're stubborn?" I asked her.

"I am the boss."

I couldn't help but smile at that. Letting her go, I took her hand and guided her toward the couch. I sat down and pulled her into my lap. "Wilkes needs to know my head is in the game, but if I'm in London, I can't make that type of commitment."

"Wait." She blinked rapidly. "You want to move to London?"

"That's where you are." I shrugged. There was a lot to

like about the city. I just had to get used to my overbearing brother, but I could handle him.

"You're not moving to London," she said firmly.

"So, you're moving here?" I pressed, already knowing the answer.

"Hell, no." Her laughter was far from soothing.

"Then, how are we going to make this work?"

Lola shifted until she was facing me directly. She took my face in her hands. "I love you, but that doesn't mean we have to have all the answers. We'll figure it out as we go."

"Not much of a plan," I grumbled. The truth was that I didn't want her to be in London while I was here. I wanted her where I could see her, kiss her, touch her.

"Actually, I do have a plan. Hear me out." She took a deep breath and launched into it. "I heard what Wilkes said before I left about keeping you driving like that, and I think he's right. You've worked too hard for this to just give it up, Anders."

"I'm not sure I can handle racing and dealing with the press and giving you unlimited orgasms," I admitted to her.

Her eyebrow arched. "Unlimited?"

"A veritable buffet," I promised. She wriggled a little on my lap, and I reached for her skirt. "Speaking of, is rule number 5..."

Lola smacked my hand. "Patience. I'm not done. I heard what you said last night, too."

"I said a lot of things last night."

"About wanting something of your own," she reminded me. "Something they couldn't dissect and judge."

"Yeah," I said darkly. I was pretty certain I didn't like where this was going.

"So, we keep us a secret." She pointed from her chest to mine.

I groaned. "Because that worked so well the first time."

"We were not on the same page," she reminded me. "And we were trying to fight our feelings. But what if we just let this be ours for a while—something that belongs only to us. We'll have to face the press and our families and all of that soon enough."

"Sounds like you are thinking pretty far into the future, boss."

She blushed and turned away. "Sorry."

"Don't be." I tilted her face back to mine. As far as I was concerned, every version of my future included her. "I just want to make sure we do this for the right reasons."

"And I want you to have your career. It's not like we won't see each other. I'm pretty sure I can convince everyone you desperately need me around to keep you in line."

"Thanks," I muttered.

"You did it to yourself," she teased before she lifted a shoulder. "And if we get caught, we come clean. But I don't want you on the track worrying about your brother or the media. I don't want you skipping practice to be with me in London. I'm not going anywhere. You love racing, and I love you, so you are not giving it up, Anders. And we deserve to get to know each other on our terms, not theirs. We just have to believe it will work," she tacked on nervously.

I stared at her for a moment as the weight of what she

was saying sank in. It wasn't a sacrifice. It was a gift. One we could give each other.

"Say something," she begged.

"I don't have to believe. *I know*. So before you offer me these terms for one year, I need to know something."

Her throat slid, but she nodded. "Anything."

"That I can spend the rest of my life loving you."

Her teeth sank into her lower lip, tears welling in her eyes. She swiped at them with annoyance, giggling. "That sounds like a pretty big commitment."

"I'm up for it," I vowed, knowing I meant it in my soul. "You?"

She nodded, completely lost for words. Emotion swelled inside me, and I seized her, claiming her mouth with a hard, unyielding kiss. I had never felt this way with anyone else, and I knew that I never would again. She was it. My forever. I'd gotten a win at the track today, but she was the real prize. Love had won.

Lola moaned softly as we broke apart, our lips still inches apart. Her eyes hooded with desire, her heat radiating against my body.

"I need you, Anders," she whispered, her fingers sliding down my chest.

I groaned, my hands digging into her hips so I could pull her even closer. "Me, too. Why do you think I drove so fast today? It wasn't a miracle. It was you."

"You mean rule number 5?" she giggled.

My mouth cruised along her jawline. "Just you," I told her, meaning it entirely, "but knowing you left your knickers at home definitely helped."

"I swear I'll never wear them when you're racing," she said in mock solemnity.

"That's my girl."

Her face lit up, and I knew then that she belonged to me as much as I belonged to her.

I leaned in and kissed her again, my hands sliding down to explore her bare ass. I cupped her cheeks and hauled her up so that she was straddling me.

"You're mine," I said roughly.

"And you're mine," she replied breathlessly.

I groaned and surged up, lifting her off the couch and carrying her toward the stairs. Slipping one hand lower, I brushed my fingers over her bare sex.

Lola gasped as I pressed my fingers against her wetness and bucked her hips against me like a command. I growled low in my throat at the sensation of her against my palm, her sex sliding wantonly as I teased her with my fingers.

"Don't stop," she begged, her fingers digging into my shoulders as I continued to stroke her.

I took the stairs two at a time, nearly losing patience and stopping at the top to fuck her on the floor. But there would be time for that later. Tonight I wanted her in my bed.

Reaching the bedroom, I kicked open the door and carried her to the bed. We pulled apart, our hands frantically pulling each other's clothes off. When she was naked, I dropped to my knees and spread hers apart.

"I've been thinking about this all day," I warned her.

Lola pushed onto her elbows, her eyes bright and needy as I leaned down and licked. Her breath hitched, her whole body going loose and tight at the same time. Burying my mouth into her, I watched as her eyes rolled back. Her moans filled the room as I explored her with my tongue. She writhed beneath me, her body tense and trembling with pleasure.

"Oh, God, Anders," she moaned, "don't stop."

I didn't intend to. I flicked my tongue over her clit, then sucked it gently between my lips. Her body arched off the bed, and she cried out my name, her hands twisting the sheets tightly. But I kept going until her whole body was shaking, relishing the taste of her climax. When she collapsed onto the mattress, I finally slowed.

I crawled up her body, letting my cock fall between her legs. She reached for it and wrapped her hand around it, stroking as I captured her nipple with my teeth and gently tugged.

"Harder," she demanded, and I smiled, happy to oblige.

Grabbing her hips, I flipped her onto her stomach and yanked her hips up. Lola moaned into the sheets as I positioned myself at her entrance.

"I love you," I whispered and plunged inside her with one powerful thrust.

Her back arched up, and I leaned forward, covering her body with mine. I wrapped her hair around my hand gently, guiding her body to match my pace until she was sobbing my name. I felt her clench around me, her climax prompting my own, and we came together.

She went limp beneath me, and I hauled her into my arms and collapsed onto the bed. We lay there in total silence. I counted her breaths, marveled at the rapid beat of her heart, and kissed her shoulder.

"Are you sure you don't want me to move to London?" I teased, nuzzling into her hair.

She twisted in my arms to face me. "Yes, but feel free to spend the rest of the night persuading me."

My fingers traced the lines of her back as I held her. My mind refused to quiet down. Now that I had her, I never wanted to lose her.

"Be honest with me. How do you feel about me racing?" I asked, adding, "I see how much it scares my mom. If it scares you..."

She took a deep breath and laid her head on my chest. "It does scare me," she admitted, her voice quiet, "but I still don't want you to give up racing. It's part of who you are. I don't want to change you."

"Says the woman who threw out half my clothes and replaced them with suits," I chuckled.

She tilted her head up and looked at me. "A decision I stand by. You look good in a suit. And a T-shirt." She trailed a finger down the length of my abs. "And nothing at all."

"That's doable."

She kissed my pec. "But I don't want you to think racing defines you. You're more than that. You're everything."

I stared down at her. Stared at the woman who saw me, who knew me, who dared to love me.

"I love you," I said, rolling her onto her back and settling between her legs. "Racing. Winning. None of it matters."

"Don't tell McKinnon," she teased. "I think winning is pretty important to him."

I laughed and nipped her lower lip. "I already won when I fell in love with you."

I captured her lips, drawing a breathy moan as my hands roamed her body. The soft curves of her breasts, the dip of her waist, the swell of her hips. I leaned and whispered in her ear, "We'll always be like this, Lola. No matter what happens. I am never giving you up again."

She shifted and let her legs fall open.

"Promise me," she whispered.

"I promise," I said fiercely, feeling the truth in my words as I filled her once again. Our lips met as our bodies began to move again, sealing our vow.

AUGUST

Your Highness: Track time slipped again.

Boss: You'll get it under control.

I might need some incentive.

A blowjob for every quarter second you knock off today's time this week?

You are an evil genius. I love you.

SEPTEMBER

> **Your Highness:** Did I ever tell you about the time I got a tattoo?

Boss: You don't have a tattoo. I would know.

> Would you? I haven't seen you in two weeks.

Anders, tell me you didn't get a tattoo.

> It's of your face, because I miss you.

God, I hope you are joking.

> You'll find out in a few days.

> You sure we can sneak around London?

It will be fun.

> There's gonna be paparazzi.

Guess we better not get caught.

OCTOBER

> Boss: How would you feel about a puppy?

I braced myself for his response. Next to me, the eight week-old chocolate lab that was still nameless nuzzled my hand.

> Your Highness: Did you get a puppy?

Of course he'd seen through that.

> I'm just asking how you would feel about a puppy.

> You got a puppy, didn't you?

He knew me so well. Sighing, I confessed.

> Madeline is not pleased.

> "The Bishops aren't dog people."

She had given me until the weekend to find him a new home or move onto the street with him.

> I don't know how you're still living there.

Well, that wasn't the suggestion I was hoping for. Three more dots appeared as he typed.

> So, I got a puppy?

I breathed a sigh of relief and patted the dog's head. "Daddy's in."

> You're going to love him.

NOVEMBER

> **Your Highness:** You ready for the bonfire?

Boss: I thought you were joking about that.

> I never joke about arson, boss.

We're really going to have a bonfire?

> I already have the wood.

I know you do.

> Dirty.

Wait, do you even celebrate Bonfire night? Or are you too American?

I'm not answering that.

> Burning effigies it is.

Every girl's dream date. See you in a few hours. Love you.

DECEMBER

> Your Highness: At the risk of sounding cheesy, all I want for Christmas is you.
>
> In nothing but a bow.
>
> Under my Christmas tree.
>
> Boss: That's doable.
>
> You're doable.
>
> On Christmas morning.
>
> Anders...
>
> I will reenact a scene from Love Actually daily until you say yes.
>
> ...I'll figure something out. Stand down.

Penny snuggled in my arms while Belle ran to the bathroom. I didn't have much experience with babies, but I could see what all the fuss was about.

Not that I wanted a baby. Maybe ever.

But she was cute, so small and pink and perfect. I grabbed my phone and took a quick selfie with her and sent it to Anders.

> Baby snuggles.

His response was swift.

> Uh-oh. You coming down with a case of baby fever, boss?

I rolled my eyes. Considering the man sent me at least fifteen pictures of Baxter a day, he was one to talk. That man loved our dog. On second thought, putting ideas into his head about babies might be a bad idea.

> A woman can hold a baby without falling victim to that ailment.
>
> Don't worry.

I added the last bit so he wouldn't think I was feeling him out on the whole baby thing. I was perfectly content to keep him all to myself.

> I mean, we could practice.
>
> Like right now.

I snorted and Penny stirred in my arms. Carefully, I rocked her back to sleep while responding.

> I'm in Sussex.
>
> I think you have baby fever.

I wouldn't put it past him. I'd seen him with the dog, after all.

> Come and find out.
>
> On second thought, I don't want you to drive in the dark.

Love swelled in my chest, and I found myself kissing Penny's soft forehead. Was this how it happened? One day you just realized you'd found your person, and then everything fell into place? Life? Babies? The future?

> You worry too much.

But I smiled as I sent it.

> I love you too much.

I brushed my fingers over Penny's fine, silvery baby hair. Practicing couldn't hurt, could it?

> Raincheck for this weekend?
>
> ...
>
> You're on, boss.

JANUARY

> **Your Highness:** You. Me. Scotland. This weekend.

> **Boss:** I could be convinced.

> Wasn't a question. Mum is taking Baxter. We are puppy-free.

> Who is being bossy now?

> I need you alone. Christmas was...

> Crazy?

> I can't believe your mom almost caught us.

> It might have killed her. But I still want to unwrap my present.

> You just want to tie me up.

> You're not wrong.

> Fuck, I love you.

I know.

FEBRUARY

> Your Highness: I was thinking about our arrangement.

Baxter flopped down on the couch and rested his head in my lap. I scratched his ears and waited for her to respond.

> Boss: ...ok

It was now or never. My fingers flew over the keys while Baxter watched with interest.

> Baxter is ready.

> Baxter is ready for what?

Of course she was going to make me spell it out. Like I hadn't been slowly trying to talk her into something a little more serious than weekends and texts only.

> For his mum to move in.

The season just started.

> Hey, I'm only telling you what Baxter told me.

Baxter perked up and let out a small yowl of protest over being dragged into this. Traitor. "You want this as much as I do."

He whimpered and laid back down.

Tell Baxter that the season just started.

> Baxter says my track times are better than ever.

Because I'm not distracting you.

> You do realize that I think about you pretty much every second of the day, right?

Same.

I just don't want to rush it.

> I'm tired of only getting you on the weekends. It's like a bad custody arrangement.

You have full custody of me.

> Hardly. If I did, I would tie you up every night.

Promise?

> Only one way to find out.

How long was Lola Bishop going to torture me?

MARCH

"Does he ever stop texting you?" Beatrice complained, taking a sip of chardonnay as my phone dinged. She was the only friend I'd confessed my secret relationship to. Mostly, because she'd caught me with my hand down my pants sexting him last fall.

"I think he knows when I'm with my mom," I said. Thankfully, she was in the loo. I snuck a peek at my phone, hoping it wasn't one of his dirtier texts.

> Your Highness: I cleared a spot in the garage for your McLaren. Baxter helped.

"You're blushing," Beatrice said

I showed her the text, and she rolled her eyes.

"He wants to marry you."

I did my best to ignore the thrill that shot through me at her assessment. "It's not a ring. It's a spot in the garage."

"Which is practically a proposal for a guy like him."

"It's too soon."

"You two already have a dog."

"Who has a dog?" My mother asked as she returned to her seat.

"Every person in America." I swiped the napkin from my lap and stood up. "I think I do need to use the facilities."

"I just went," Mom pouted.

"And I'm very proud of you." I slipped my phone into my pocket. "I'll be right back."

As soon as I was in the bathroom, I locked myself inside a stall. Lately, every one of his texts had sent my heart racing. Not that he was serious about any of it. Beatrice might think he was ready to propose, but I doubted it.

Even though he had cleared out half of his closet.

And a drawer in the bathroom.

And now a space in his garage.

> You didn't have to do that.

It took him a minute to respond.

> I wanted to. I want your car to feel at home.

> It does.

It wasn't like I could leave London, even if that's what he wanted.

Could I?

> Good, because I love your car.

> I love your garage.

APRIL

> Boss: Mom is getting suspicious. I better hang here this weekend.

Madeline Bishop probably had a tracking device on her daughter. I wasn't sure how we were going to make it through the next nine months without her finding out.

I flopped back on the bed and stared at the Dubai skyline. I'd asked Lola to come with me. I hated these long trips, hated seeing places without her. But she didn't want to risk it. Now I wasn't going to see her at all. I swallowed my disappointment and tapped reply.

> I'll probably be jet-lagged anyway.

> I would prefer you only see me as a high-performance machine.

> Noted.

> I'll be watching tomorrow, completely knickers-free.

Fuck, now I was thinking about her naked, which was honestly a constant problem. My dick hardened but before I could give in, there was a knock on the hotel door.

"You ready?" Wilkes shouted.

I groaned. Cock-blocker. "Give me a sec."

> You better be. Gotta run. Love you.

MAY

> Boss: I know I'm supposed to be in town this afternoon, but I forgot that I have a birthday party for Wills.

> Your Highness: Shit. I meant to remind you.

> Huh? How did you know?

> Clara sent an invite to Uncle Anders.

> Maybe I should get him a present?

> A racecar?

> Good thinking, boss.

I pocketed my phone and sighed. I needed to be across London in fifteen minutes. Thank God Belle had reminded me about the party. Lately, I'd been too preoccupied to remember simple things. Probably, because I was completely preoccupied with Anders.

He wasn't being shy about his hints. But he couldn't be ready to move in together.

Could he?

EPILOGUE

LOLA

There are birthday parties, and then there are royal birthday parties. A handful of tables dotted the lawn behind Buckingham, and it was clear that while the guest list was small, the event was lavish. Thanks in no small part to my mother's party-planning skills. Even the May weather was cooperating, and there wasn't a cloud in the sky.

"Lola." Belle rushed over to greet me. "You look gorgeous. Did you steal this from our closet?" she teased, twirling her finger.

I obliged her request, turning to give her a better view of my Diane von Fürstenberg summer dress. "I picked it up at Harrods the other day."

"I love how fluid it is." She touched the sleeve thoughtfully. "We need to bring this one in for our clients to borrow immediately."

"No shop talk," Smith interrupted, shifting a giggling Penny in his arms. "It's a party."

"Says the man who hired me to go to dinner with him,"

she said dryly. Belle blinked. "That didn't sound right." She looked at me. "I wasn't an escort."

"Just a very *personal* assistant," Smith added.

"Not helpful." She knocked his shoulder, looking at him with such obvious adoration I felt a twinge of jealousy. Soon that would be me, standing next to the love of my life. I just had to wait.

"I need to get this one a new nappy," he told her, and she sighed.

"Let me help." She shot me an apologetic smile and headed into the palace with him.

I hated feeling jealous of them, especially after the year they had endured. Belle deserved the happiness she now radiated. I just wished I could show off my own glow.

I walked over to the gift table to put down my present and smiled when I saw the collection of teddy bears assembled like a small guard. A shadow fell over me and I turned to say hello to whoever was joining me.

And froze.

"In my defense," Anders said, carrying a toddler-sized racecar with blue stripes down its sides, "I was invited."

"You're here." I didn't move, afraid he would vanish into smoke if I did.

"I'm here, boss. Mind if I set this down?"

"Y-yes. I mean, no," I fumbled, moving out of the way. My heart sped up as I drank him in. He was clean-shaven—a rarity—and he had on the blue suit we'd picked out last summer. His hair, which he'd let grow past his ears was tucked behind them now. Maybe it was the fact that I hadn't expected to see him *here*, but I couldn't tear my eyes from him.

When he turned, he shot me a smirk that told me he knew exactly how good he looked.

"I can't believe you came." I wasn't sure what was weirder: seeing my boyfriend at a family event or the fact that it was weird at all.

"Can I tell you a secret?" He glanced around us like he didn't want to be overheard. "I decided to come a few days ago. I already had the car bought. Wills is going to be a rebel like his uncle."

I snorted. "Alexander will love to hear that." I shook my head, trying to process what he was really telling me. "But we had plans for me to come to Silverstone."

"Yeah, which is why I felt like shit for forgetting to remind you about the party." He shoved his hands in his pockets, his eyes roving down me as he spoke. "Are you mad I'm here? I wasn't sure you would want me to come."

"Mad?" I blurted out. Surprised? Yes. Slightly turned on by the show of familial duty? Also yes. Okay, *very* turned on.

"Anderson!" Clara called, and we moved away from each other like we were kids getting caught with the cookie jar. "You came! I can't believe it." She leaned in to give him a hug. "We're so glad you're here."

Anders lifted his eye to a spot in the distance, and I knew he was looking for Alexander. To his credit, he simply said, "Of course, I came. We're...family."

Clara and I shared an incredulous look, quickly moving in for a hug before we made him uncomfortable.

"Did you talk him into this?" she whispered in my ear, and I felt a stab of panic. Had she figured it out?

"I had no idea." That much was true.

A shrill cry rose in the air and we pulled apart, Clara immediately switching to mom mode. "Elizabeth fell! I'll catch up with you later."

"Parenting seems like a lot of work," I told Anders when she left. Dashing off to change nappies and kiss boo-boos and plan parties.

"It doesn't look so bad to me," he murmured, his voice taking on a gruffness that sent my mind straight to the bedroom.

I raised an eyebrow, even though my center went molten. Seeing Anders here around his family was much hotter than I'd expected. "You know I think I left something inside."

"What a coincidence. I think I did, too." He winked at me.

We started back to the palace, stealing small touches as we walked. Each brush of his hand on my wrist, my shoulder, the small of my back stoked the flame growing inside me. I'd seen him last weekend, but it might as well have been an eternity. The same hunger blazed in his eyes. I couldn't look away.

Which was why I didn't see my mother coming.

"Where are you two headed?" she demanded, stepping in front of us.

"Anders needs the loo," I lied smoothly. "I told him I would show him the closest one."

"Yeah." He cleared his throat. "I forgot what a long drive

it is to London. I should have gone before I left, but, you know, I don't get up here much."

I resisted the urge to roll my eyes as he oversold the lie. I went to Silverstone more often than he came here, but he'd been in London at least once a month since we'd met. Not that my mother needed to know that.

"Hmmm." She didn't look like she was buying any of it. Her gaze remained on us like a hawk sensing weaker prey. "I'm sure he can find the facilities without assistance."

"It's a palace," I said, sidestepping her. "He could get lost. I don't want him to miss the party."

"He's been here before," she pointed out.

"Briefly," he said.

She drew a long-suffering breath and shrugged. "Don't take too long, you two."

"We'll be right back." I scurried away, Anders at my heels.

"Is it my imagination or does your mum know that we're going inside to—"

"Shhh!" I giggled. "Someone will hear you."

He leaned closer, his hand ghosting across the small of my back. "If I have my way, they'll all hear you in about two minutes."

I held my breath as we pushed open the large glass doors that opened into the Bow Room. As soon as we were inside, Anders pushed me against a large marble column, his mouth finding mine. I moaned into the kiss, desperate for more of him.

"I missed you," he growled, nipping at my lower lip. "I don't like being away from you."

"I missed you too," I panted, running my hands over his chest, feeling the hard muscles beneath his suit jacket. "But we should find somewhere more private."

"I can't wait any longer. I've been thinking about this all day, boss." Anders kissed down my neck, nipping at the sensitive skin just below my ear.

"What about your family?" I murmured, brushing my lips over the lingering stubble on his jaw.

"What about them?"

"I thought you came here to be with them."

He hitched my skirt up to my hips and pressed his leg between my thighs. I gasped as his fingers danced over the band of my garter belt.

"I did," he whispered. "This is very sexy." His hand moved up, finding the lace knickers I wore. He pushed them to the side and brushed his thumb across my sex.

"We can't." But I spread my legs wider anyway.

"Why not?" I could hear the smirk in his voice. "Afraid we'll get caught?"

My eyes closed as his mouth ghosted to my collarbone. He pushed a finger inside me, and I groaned, managing a single "Yes."

"Hear me out, boss." He drew back, still working that single finger in and out of me. "It will be worth it."

I lunged forward and kissed him, giving in completely to my need for him. He'd promised me nearly a year ago that it would always be like this between us, and he wasn't wrong. I wouldn't be able to think until he'd claimed me—until I felt him inside me.

His finger disappeared, and I let out a squeak of protest,

grinding my hips closer to him as he unfastened his belt. He unzipped his pants, and I shoved them down to his ankles. Anders laughed against my mouth and scooped me off my feet, bracing me against the marble.

"Is this what you need?" He angled the broad tip of his cock against me.

"Yes." God, yes. My nails dug into his shoulders as he filled me.

"I need you," he growled as he began to move, each thrust primal. Consuming. Demanding.

I clung to him as he moved, finding a rhythm that was all ours. It didn't matter that we were pushing our luck or that someone could walk in on us at any moment. Nothing mattered but the way he made me feel. With every stroke, I felt him claim me until the world around us faded away, leaving only us.

"Come for me, boss," he ordered in a low voice that sent me over the edge. He followed behind, spilling inside me over and over, until we were both spent.

"That was worth it." I smiled, still panting, as I pressed my forehead to his.

"And we didn't—"

A flurry of movement startled us, and Anders moved to shield me from our unexpected guest.

"Pardon me," the maid squeaked, scurrying off as we both held our breath.

"I spoke too soon." He shot me an apologetic grin that looked anything but sorry.

"Let me down." I kissed him. "Before someone else walks in. Like my mother."

"Now that would be a party," he teased, yanking up his pants and refastening them quickly.

I smoothed my dress, glad that I'd worn knickers today.

"How do I look?" I asked, running a hand over my hair.

"Well-fucked," he said with a look of purely masculine arrogance.

"Anders!"

He reached over and ran a finger under my lip, wiping away my smeared lipstick. "Perfect. You look perfect as always."

I took a step and discovered my legs were still wobbly. He caught me around the waist and held me steady.

"Do you think she'll say anything?" I asked him.

"Probably not," a drawling voice interrupted us, and we both turned to find Alexander standing near the door. His mouth twitched. "People around here are used to stumbling on that sort of thing."

"Oh shit." I clapped my hand over my mouth and tried to think of something to say—anything to say.

But Alexander strode forward and extended his hand to Anders. "Anderson. It's good to see you."

Anders stared at the outstretched hand for a moment.

"Don't worry. It's not a trick," Alexander told him. "I'm not planning to grab you and force a crown on your head."

Anders glanced at me, and I nodded encouragingly. He took his brother's hand. "I'm glad to be here."

"Well, that was painful," I said, breaking up the tension. I slapped Anders on the back. "Don't worry. It will get easier."

"It looks like it will have to." Alexander looked away, that almost grin still threatening to show itself. "If you two will excuse me, I need to find Norris." He started to walk away and then turned back to us. "And there's a closet hidden behind that wall panel, for future reference."

I dropped my head on Anders' shoulder as soon as he was gone. "Great. Now what do we do?"

"I have an idea," he said.

Before I could ask him what it was, he marched back toward the gardens. I followed him before he did anything crazy. Everyone but Alexander was outside, chatting and visiting. My sister and Belle, each with a baby on their hips, gossiped with Edward and his new boyfriend, Tomas. Elizabeth was twirling for my parents, and Brex and Georgia were in the corner talking to Smith.

"So, what's your plan?" I asked him, twisting my fingers together.

"Wait a sec."

A minute later, Alexander appeared alongside Norris.

"He'll say something to Clara," I warned him in a low voice.

Anders sighed. "I know. Looks like it's time to face the music, boss."

"Wait, what?"

But he was already grabbing my hand and dragging me closer to the others. "If I can have just a second," he called out.

"What are you doing?" I whispered furiously as they all turned to look at us.

"I wanted to let you all know that I'm madly in love with Lola, and we've been seeing each other secretly for months."

I closed my eyes and waited for their reaction, my hand clutching his to anchor me.

"Yes, son, we know," my dad said.

My eyes flew open, and I looked at him. Then I looked at all of them and discovered they were each wearing a knowing smile.

"We all knew." Clara shrugged, grinning widely.

"*All* of you?" I repeated weakly.

"Brex has a big mouth," Georgia said.

"Hey, I didn't say anything." He held up his hands defensively. "Except maybe to Georgia…for security reasons."

"I told Clara things were back on." Georgia didn't sound the least bit sorry.

"And I have eyes," Belle teased. "You don't get that kind of a glow from a face cream, love."

"Oh my God." I buried my head into his shoulder, but he began to laugh.

"Well, if we're making confessions, I have one of my own," Clara said loudly. She looked over at Alexander, who moved to her side and placed a hand around her waist. "We're having another baby."

"Of course you are," Edward yelled, moving to give her a hug.

The news did the trick. Everyone clustered around her to share their congratulations. I found my sister's eyes and gave her a grateful smile for the distraction.

Anders seemed to realize what she was doing as well because he pulled me close and leaned down to whisper in my ear. "We'll do a better job of eloping. They won't see it coming."

Eloping?

I drew back, my eyes searching his face for signs that he was joking, but all I found was love staring back at me. "Are you asking me to marry you? Here?"

"This is *our* family. *Our* future. It seemed like the right moment. What do you say, boss?" He slipped a hand into his pocket, and I forgot how to breathe. A moment later, he opened his palm to reveal a stunning emerald-cut diamond ring.

I looked from him to the ring and back again. "Are you sure you can handle me?"

"Lola Bishop." He grinned and slid the ring on my finger. "I've always known how to handle you."

ACKNOWLEDGMENTS

The last ten years with these characters have been a wild ride. They aren't fictional to me. They're family. They're friends. Writing the Royals has changed my life in so many ways, so I need to thank them first. (Yes, I am thanking fictional people). You've been there during dark times, given me joy, showed me light when I needed it most. I think you're even responsible for the third addition to our family. I was writing Alexander and Clara when my husband and I found ourselves expecting our youngest daughter.

My deepest gratitude belongs to my editor, Tamara Mataya for being on this journey since the very beginning. You make every book you touch better. Here's to new adventures together.

Thank you to Elise for late night strategy sessions, endless support, cheerleading, and picking me up when I thought I couldn't. I finally wrote you a funny Royals book (don't get used to it).

I am so blessed for the gift and friendship of Shelby Lynn. You showed up in my life at a time when I didn't even know how to ask for help, and you've never looked back. I'm so proud of the woman you're becoming and so grateful that we're on this journey together.

Big thanks to my tireless agent Louise Fury, who works

her ass off day and night. I'm so thankful that you're my agent but even more grateful that you're my friend.

To both The Bent Agency and The Fury Agency teams, thank you for keeping my shit together when I can't, answering endless questions, and being all around awesome.

To my publishing teams abroad who have brought Royals to the world, my endless thanks. Helping me share my words with readers has been the greatest gift I could have ever asked for.

Thanks to my author friends who have been there every step of the way, especially Audrey Carlan, Rebecca Yarros, Robyn Lucas, and Cora Seton. I admire you all more than you know.

Thank you to Becca Syme for coaching me through some of the craziest transitions of my life, for helping me find my own answers, and for becoming a true friend.

Thank you to Team G for getting those engines revved! And to the Loves for cheering on, supporting, and being generally awesome.

A huge thanks to the amazing crew of booktokkers and bookstagrammers that have welcomed Anders and the rest of these crazy royals into their homes and ereaders.

A special shout-out to all the incredible readers I have met over the last two years. You are my people! And to all my international readers, language barriers be damned, I adore your posts!

Sometimes I still can't believe this is book thirteen in The Royals Saga, especially since I almost never wrote a second. It's here because of my readers, because you love these characters and this world as much as I do. I've hinted this may be the last Royals book but I've learned never to say never. But this book is for you. Thank you for staying up at midnight to read, for showing up again and again for Alexander and his family, for believing in true love. Love won, in the end (which this may or may not be...I have to keep you guessing).

Thanks to my teens, who are starting to understand the kind of books I write and managing not to be too horrified, and thank you to Sophie, for showing me every day how a princess behaves (or doesn't).

And if this is the end, then I have to thank the man who has been there since the beginning, who has been there every day since. My own happily ever after, my Prince Charming, my forever, my always. I'm so grateful for the life we've built, for the support and love you show me every day. Thank you for lifting me up, for fighting for me, for being the other half of my soul. Thank you for our life and our family. Forever will never be long enough.

ABOUT THE AUTHOR

Geneva Lee is the *New York Times*, *USA Today*, and internationally bestselling author of over a thirty novels. Her bestselling Royals Saga has sold over three million copies worldwide. When she isn't traveling, she can usually be found writing, reading, or buying another pair of shoes.

Learn more about Geneva Lee at:
www.GenevaLee.com